RELIABLE IN LONDON
An Asian Thriller

by
Valerie Goldsilk
& Julian Stagg

The Reliable Man Series

Reliable in Bangkok
Reliable in Jakarta
Reliable in Hong Kong
Reliable in Da Nang
Reliable in New York
Reliable in London

The Inspector Scrimple Series

Classified as Crime
Dragon Breath
Perfect Killer
Fatal Action
Random Outcome
Yellow Hammer

Other Books by Valerie Goldsilk

The Oldest Sins
Negative Buoyancy
Sins of Our Sisters
Sins of Our Elders
White Bishop

About the Authors

Valerie Goldsilk is English and lived in Hong Kong for over thirty years. She is now retired but used to run her own business, travelling frequently around Asia working with factories. Her better half is a former Hong Kong police inspector.

Julian Stagg is a British investment banker who, after a thirty-year career as an adviser, entrepreneur and investor, can still be found plying his trade in the City of London.

Authors' Note

The events of this novel take place before and after the General Election in the UK in 1997 and in the months leading up to the handover of Hong Kong by the United Kingdom to the People's Republic of China. Inserting fictional characters into real historical events is an established literary device. It is not the authors' intention to imply that any of the events related in this novel actually took place or that the public figures with whom their characters fleetingly interact are anything other than fictional simulacra of their real-life counterparts, for which the authors ask forgiveness.

To Callum, you know who you are.

To Michael, who let me in on the secret of the lobby correspondents.

To Charles and Ilona, who know Devon and Hong Kong better than me.

To Darius, in fond memory of the 1997 FA Cup Final.

To the Plantmeister – most excellent copy editor.

To Simon, a brief cameo.

To Mark and memories of Tango Martini.

To Ange, who lives in Buffalo and is a good man.

To Christian – RIP

To Alison, Первая любовь

"In London you met sooner or later everybody you had ever known; you could lay your hand on any knowledge you wanted… Romance lay in wait for you at every street corner."

John Buchan, *Sing a Song of Sixpence*

"Evil indeed is the man who has not one woman to mourn him."

Sir Arthur Conan Doyle, *The Hound of the Baskervilles*

"No doubt there are fat or dumpy Chinese women in Hong Kong, but I never saw one."

Ian Fleming, *Thrilling Cities*

1

The clock was counting down. In less than ninety days this painted harlot, this incandescent harbour, this melting pot of East and West, this city I had grown to love and loathe in equal measure - Hong Kong - was going to be returned to China.

It was really none of my business, of course. My business was making money. But if it hadn't been for Hong Kong teaching me - when I was barely out of my teens - that money was everything, I would not have been lying on a cement floor looking through a telescopic sight at a fat American in a wrinkled suit.

Money gave you the freedom to determine your own destiny, and I never forgot that. I earned 888,888 Hong Kong dollars every time I pulled the trigger and ended someone's life. I was the Reliable Man. My reputation, as an assassin who delivered consistently when I accepted an assignment, brought me regular business all over Asia. With each professional kill, my bank accounts grew and my retirement day came closer. Because I'd told myself that when I hit a magic number, that would be it. I'd hang up my gun and my knife and leave the work to younger men.

It was almost 8 p.m. The air was humid and the sky was dark but the night was bright with neon. Hong Kong's bustling streets never stopped. Even at four in the morning taxis would be plying the streets, old ladies would be sweeping them, drunks would be staggering down them and sirens would be punctuating the night air. More than any other city in the world, Hong Kong never stopped. It was always buying and selling, wheeling and dealing, hustling to make another dollar. This city of 6.5 million souls made up twelve per cent of Britain's entire GDP and some lunatic in London had decided to hand it all over to the Chinese.

But that wasn't any of my business. I'd flow into town from Singapore to kill a man called Brent Kowalczyk who worked at the American embassy. I hadn't been told what his exact job was, simply that he was selling US passports without the approval of his bosses. Selling them by the truckload.

Looking at him through my Hensoldt scope I could see that the man was exceedingly pleased with himself. He was sitting by the Grand Hyatt swimming pool at a table with four other men and they were drinking beer. The pool was on the 11th floor rooftop that joined the Grand Hyatt to the Renaissance Hotel next to it. From where they were sitting, Kowalczyk and his companions had an excellent view of the harbour. It had been an even better view before they built the extension to the Exhibition Centre. It was supposed to be in the shape of a dove and site of the handover ceremony taking place at the end of June.

I was using a Heckler & Koch PSG1, a bracingly good sniper rifle that I'd first handled in the Royal Hong Kong Police's Special Duties Unit. I'd never used the PSG1 to kill anyone while I was in the Force but over the last few years I had used it many times to great effect. I owned four of them.

My perch was in the far corner of the refuge floor of Wan Chai Tower. This was technically the 16th floor, which separated the law courts from the offices. It was a strange empty space designed as shelter in case of fire. Reaching the refuge floor had been simple because I'd been provided with a key card for the lift. My target was 380 metres away, at a downward angle, and across Harbour Road which separated my building from the hotel.

The job had started a few days ago as I was lifting weights at the Boat Quay gym in Singapore. Larry Lim, my old buddy and principal factotum for Brigadier Wee, the Chief of Singapore's intelligence apparatus, had walked through the door and leant against the squat rack with a smirk on his face.

"Bet you I can do five more reps than you on that weight," he'd said conversationally. Larry was a few years younger than me. He was wearing a black polo shirt that was tautly stretched across his pecs and biceps. He knew his way around a gym, an assault course and a firing range.

I didn't say anything as I squeezed out the last two reps on the bench press, my arms shuddering. I dropped the bar into place and sat up.

"Always train to failure on the final rep," I said.

"Yeah, yeah. I've heard you say that a million times." He sat down on the empty bench opposite me. It was three in the afternoon so the gym wasn't busy.

"Along with progressive overload it's the most important principle of bodybuilding." I flexed my right bicep to make my point.

He flexed his right bicep to make his: "Don't teach your grandson to suck eggs."

"You cheeky little sod," I said affectionately.

"Finished your work-out?" he asked.

"No, I was going to do eight more sets on the incline press but I can tell I won't be able to concentrate if you keep making sarcastic comments."

He shrugged. "He wants to see you."

"Doesn't he use the telephone like normal people?"

"He's downstairs in 'Harry's Bar'."

"Is he now? Mixing with the great unwashed."

"Are you referring to the British and Australian expats who frequent 'Harry's Bar'?" Larry said with a winning smile.

"This time of the day," I glanced over at the big clock on the wall, "they'll all still be in their banks and law offices. Dirty foreigners."

"You said it, my *ang moh* friend, not me."

Twenty minutes later I was sitting at a corner table with Brigadier Wee. He had a tall glass of iced lemon tea in front of him and was wearing a white shirt, no jacket and the striped regimental tie I'd seen him wear before. I'd never got around to asking him what it was but suspected it was a Ghurka tie of some kind. It was green with red and black stripes.

"Do you know why nobody messes with us in Singapore?" Wee said, by way of greeting. His hands lay on the table on either side of his drink, his fierce eyes glared at me and there wasn't a single bead of perspiration on his bald, liver-spotted head.

I knew the answer to his question but assumed it was rhetorical and so shook my head politely. I had concluded a long time ago that the man deserved respect at all times.

"You remember SQ Flight 117?"

I nodded. The incident was only six years old and had made headlines because Singapore had been utterly efficient and ruthless.

"Four Pakistani terrorists hi-jacked one of our planes," Wee reminded me. "Larry was on the back-up assault team, weren't you?"

His man nodded gravely.

"Four dead Pakistani terrorists, hostages freed, no other casualties," the Brigadier said. "Nobody messes with Singapore because we strike first and we strike hard when we feel our country is at risk."

"I know that, sir." I smiled at myself. I'd tried to bite it off but it was so damn hard not to call him 'sir'.

"You, Bill, are part of my strike capability," he said.

"I gathered that."

"Hong Kong's transfer of sovereignty from Britain to China will unbalance the geo-political see-saw in South East Asia. It won't happen overnight. It will be a slow, barely noticeable process."

I said, "Nobody expects Beijing to send the tanks down Nathan Road and rename it Mao Tse Tung Drive on the first day after the handover."

"Some Americans in the State Department do think that. They don't understand that China takes a very long-term view of history. China is still smarting about losing the Opium Wars and having to give up the fifty treaty ports."

"That was 150 years ago," I said.

"My point exactly. They will take 30 years before they turn the screw on Hong Kong while nobody is looking."

"That's a long time in the future," I said. The waitress started to hover near us and I wanted a cold drink but the Brigadier waved her off as if she were a pesky insect.

Wee gave an irritable grunt. "That's what some fool in the Hong Kong Club said when they came up with the silly idea of leasing the New Territories for 99 years so they could have more Godown space. And now look at the mess it's caused. Nobody understood why Thatcher would give Hong Kong back. Go to war over six sheep in the Falklands but then quietly hand the jewel in Britain's economic crown to Beijing without even a proper negotiation." Wee shook his head in honest disgust. "One of our assets told us Deng Xiao Ping was speechless for two minutes when he was informed of this by the British Foreign Office."

I nodded to show I was still paying attention and waved at the waitress to come back so I could order a big, cold Coke. Brigadier Wee would come to his point presently, I was sure.

When the girl had gone, he said: "Singapore will benefit from all of this nonsense. We too will play a long game because we are also Chinese and we will make ourselves richer and more powerful while Hong Kong fades into oblivion."

That was about my assessment of the situation.

He went on: "There is a US embassy official who has been selling American passports to middle-class Hong-Kongers desperate to have a place to go after the handover. The rich got themselves sorted with passports years ago but now for 150,000 US dollars an ordinary accountant or bank manager can buy himself an escape route to the United States." Wee took a measured sip of his iced lemon tea and continued: "The British are too busy burning their records. The Hong Kong Police are turning a blind eye. The Americans don't know and, for reasons you don't need to understand, Singapore has decided to put an end to this trade."

I'd had a similar job a few years earlier in Pattaya where one of the Hong Kong Triads had set up an expert passport forger, only for him to be kidnapped by the German mafia who controlled that sleazy town. It had been a messy job. I was not planning to make the same mistakes.

I leant forward and lowered my voice. "Kill the corrupt American official?"

"Yes," Wee said.

"No visible links to Singapore?"

"Yes," Wee said, because, after all that was the only real reason they ever used me. Larry and his gang were all as good as me with a sniper rifle.

"You will pay me?"

"Yes," Wee confirmed.

Larry said, "100,000 Singapore dollars into your DBS bank account minus 40% that will go directly to your Central Provident Fund."

I gave him a dirty look. I thought it was a joke, but you never know with Singaporeans. I did have an official State pension like every other local, who had 40% of their income deducted to ensure that nobody was indigent in their old age.

"First Class on Singapore Airlines into Hong Kong," I made an effort at negotiating.

Brigadier Wee stared at me for longer than necessary, then nodded his assent.

2

The *Präzisionsschützengewehr PSG1* was developed for the German Special Forces after the Munich Olympics massacre. With the Hensoldt scope that I had fitted it was effective up to a range of six hundred metres. I was using a Brügger & Thomet silencer: the long tube slightly unbalanced the rifle, but it reduced the sound of a shot to that of a very loud fart. That made it easier for me to pack up my things and calmly walk away.

My black combat trousers had padding sewn into the knees and I favoured a little cushion which I placed under my left elbow. Every sniper has their little quirks. I'd been taught to shoot as a child by my father. He was an officer in the Coldstream Guards, so a Lee Enfield .303 was the first rifle that he handed me at the age of nine. They had been used in the Six Day War in the New Territories in 1899 and were still going strong during the Malay Emergency. Mine was a venerable old lady that kicked like a mule, which taught me even as a youngster how to screw the butt tightly into my shoulder.

All things considered I was confident that my target would not be enjoying any more beers after that evening. Kowalczyk's companions were a soft-looking Chinese man and two burly Westerners. The conversation was mostly between Kowalczyk and the Chinese man who was buttering up the fat American with all the skill of a eunuch from the Forbidden City. He was probably the contact who found the customers in desperate need of an overseas passport.

The other two men seemed out of place. They both wore dark jackets and navy-blue shirts with red ties. Hired muscle, I thought. They didn't laugh much and when they did there was no mirth in their eyes. That's how good my scope was, I could see right into their souls.

There was no rush to pull the trigger. They were sitting by the pool so the chance of anyone walking across my line of fire was zero and nobody was swimming in the water. They'd just ordered another round and so I spent a bit more time studying the two bodyguards.

Broad-shouldered and grim-faced, they had closely cropped blond hair and angular Nordic features that put me in mind of Nazi stormtroopers. They sat perfectly still while watching everything that went on at the other tables. Nothing would escape their attention. The larger of the two men held my attention for longer. He had a vicious scar that started by his left ear lobe and ran down across his chin ending just above his Adam's apple. It didn't look like a knife wound. It was probably an injury from grenade fragments. The man had been a soldier.

A quiet voice of reason told me that I should not only kill Kowalczyk but also these two men. The Brigadier's brief was deficient. Why would a corrupt American embassy official have two mercenaries as bodyguards and who was paying for them? Specialists in that business charged over $1,000 US dollars a day.

It was time to earn my wages. Ours not to reason why, as my father had always said when the army sent us to another base just as we had unpacked our boxes. If the Brigadier said Kowalczyk was the only target, then that's what he would be.

I closed my eyes for a few seconds, then reacquired the target and began my breathing routine. I slowed down my heart rate and focused all my attention on the scope and the trigger. I checked that the field of fire was clear.

I calmly squeezed the trigger. Ataraxia, my Bisley mentor had called it once. The state you want to be in when you fire that single, vital shot.

Kowalczyk's head disintegrated in a dark cloud and his body slumped sideways in the teak garden chair. I didn't wait for the reaction of his companions. They would be diving for cover, waiting for further shots and at the same time trying to determine from where the round had been fired. That would not be hard to work out. The clearest and most obvious line of fire was my building. The other buildings all had glass windows which could not be opened.

By not firing a second shot I gave them nothing to locate. Now I had to pack up without leaving a trace, make my way out of the building and escape across the footbridge into the bustling bar life of Wan Chai. It took two minutes to disassemble the rifle and pop it all into a ragged rucksack, the sort that would pigeonhole me as a backpacker.

I took the stairs up two floors then travelled down in a lift with two young Chinese office workers chatting to each other in Cantonese. They were heading home after work and too busy discussing football to pay me any attention. Hong Kong people regularly worked late. A few floors down, a girl in her twenties with the air of an accountant got in. She was carrying a heavy briefcase and stared at her feet. Then the lift doors opened in the lobby and we filed out. If my fellow-passengers were questioned by the police they might remember a bearded foreigner wearing an Australian bush hat, which was what the security cameras in the lift would show.

I didn't expect anyone to have reacted rapidly enough to have reached the lobby before me, but I was ready to start running if they had. The two bodyguards sitting with Brent Kowalczyk had upset my calculations. They could have quickly determined that the shooter was in Wan Chai Tower, but to get there would have had to race down from the 11th floor of the Grand Hyatt, dodge the heavy traffic on Harbour Road and run up the twenty stairs that led to the building's entrance. I'd timed it the previous day and it had taken me sixteen minutes. That was without running or attracting too much attention. Only nine minutes had elapsed as I exited from the other side of the building onto the plaza that led to Immigration Tower.

I planned to take an escalator up to the first floor then the covered walkway which ran across the four-lane Gloucester Road. I would then walk down the stairs to O'Brien Road. The Luk Kwok Hotel was a hundred metres from there. One of Larry's men would take the rucksack from me as we brushed past each other in the lobby.

I was halfway across the plaza when a booming voice, in what I thought was a South African accent, yelled out: "You, stop now." I should have ignored him and carried on walking, but I had to be sure he wasn't pointing a gun at my back. I risked a quick glance over my shoulder and our eyes locked.

3

The man with the scar was staring at me. I looked a likely suspect: a white male carrying a rucksack big enough to store a rifle. But there was no gun in his hand, and he was fifty metres away, so I ignored him. The other bodyguard appeared behind him and grabbed his shoulder as he pointed in the other direction.

I carried on walking at a steady, innocent pace. Weapons are very hard to obtain in Hong Kong and it was unlikely the two men were armed. But if they came running after me, I had a snub-nosed revolver in the side pocket of my rucksack.

I entered Immigration Tower and got on the escalator. This allowed me to look through the glass wall and back across the plaza. The man with the scar was not coming after me. At the top of the escalator, I exited on the mezzanine floor and crossed over to the footbridge. At eight in the evening the streets bustled with people going places. Walking casually and calmly, keeping my senses alert and trying not to draw any attention to myself, I left the crime scene further behind.

The Luk Kwok Hotel was the one Suzie Wong had frequented in the novel. It had since been rebuilt a few times and the lobby was all polished marble and burnished steel. As I paused by the concierge's desk and took off my rucksack to mop my sweaty brow, a young Indian man dressed in jeans and a loose linen shirt made eye contact with me. I nodded imperceptibly. He stood close to me, picked up the rucksack and walked out of the back entrance onto Jaffe Road.

I took a lift to the eighth floor. The door I knocked on was opened by a young Singaporean.

"Did all go well?" he asked, closing the door behind me.

"All good so far," I said and walked over to the big black bin-liner that was lying by the bed. I stripped off a pair of skin-coloured surgical gloves, followed by the rest of my clothes, and dropped them into the black bag.

"Take them and leave now," I said to the young fellow. His eyes showed excitement, but I didn't think it had anything to do with the fact that I was now buck naked. Larry had told me he was only a year out of his national service and this was his first operation in Hong Kong. As I walked into the bathroom, I heard the room door open and close as he left. The bag would be incinerated.

I scrubbed my body from head to toe with Lifebuoy carbolic soap with its intense old hospital aroma. They were still using the original formula in India which is where this one had come from. It was my favourite because it removed all traces of cordite from my skin and hair.

On the bed, was a complete new set of clothing. I dressed quickly, admiring my choice of a shocking pink Tommy Hilfiger polo shirt. When you switched disguises, you wanted to stand out from the crowd.

Ten minutes later I was sitting at the bar in Tango Martini, on the fourth floor of a building on Lockhart Road, the heart of the Wan Chai nightlife district. I'd arranged to meet a few former RHKP colleagues there to strengthen my alibi, but there was no sign of them yet. Probably still earning overtime, I figured. Ahead of the handover they were cracking down on minor crime to make their lives easier when the world and his wife turned up at the end of June to join in the festivities. It promised to be the diplomatic jolly to end all jollies and the RHKP weren't going to let whores, junkies and muggers spoil the party.

At the end of the bar, dressed in an elegantly tailored Zegna suit was Mark Hudson, the owner. He was there every evening auditing the quality of the martinis after he finished his day job running the Asian office of a big American corporation.

"How're you doing, Mark?" I said, nodding at him.

"I'm excellent. It's Bill, isn't it?" Like a good owner, he made an effort to remember names.

"Correct." I leaned over and shook his proffered hand. Mark was from New England. He was always perfectly dressed. Both ends of his shoelaces were the same length. His ties always perfectly matched the sharply ironed shirts he favoured, and his hair never had a strand out of place. He was the Hong Kong avatar of Cary Grant in '*North by Northwest*'.

"What have you got there?" I asked him, nodding towards his martini glass.

"Bombay Sapphire, two olives and three sprays of Noilly Prat," he explained.

"That's dry," I commented.

"Don't want to spoil the gin with too much vermouth." He held up a small device like a perfume container but filled with alcohol.

The Filipino barman, his ponytail touching his collar, asked me to name my pleasure.

"Six parts Finlandia Vodka to one of Cinzano Bianco. Stirred with a squeeze of lemon juice on top," I instructed the man. I wasn't sure if Mark would approve of my choice of sweet white vermouth, but it was the way I liked my martinis.

"Tough day in the office?" he asked.

"Just the usual bullshit," I said. "You need a drink to make sure your head won't explode."

"I find," he took a small sip from the V-shaped glass, then dabbed his lips, "that I need three martinis before I can face my conference calls in the evening."

"Your head office in the States?" I asked. He nodded.

"They're twelve hours behind us, so when they come to work they start by talking to us in Asia." He checked his watch, a slim, gold Patek Philippe with a leather strap. "Nine-thirty they'll be calling in and wanting to know whether our sales figures are right," he smiled and shrugged. "We can't help it if our Asian sales guys are so good that they're 40% higher than budget."

"That's the thing about a boss," I said, taking my first sip of the drink that had been placed on a small paper napkin in front of me. A shiver of pleasure ran down my back as it bit into my throat, "The man is never satisfied. That's why I stopped working for others and do my own thing now."

"And what is it you do, Bill?" he enquired, with polite interest.

"I'm a security consultant. Help companies get their policies and procedures in order. Used to be in the police here until about seven years ago."

"Will your old colleagues still have a job after the handover?" he asked.

"They all hope so, but who can tell for sure?" I said. "Are you staying in Hong Kong for the duration?"

He nodded and smiled, although there was a hint of sadness in his eyes. "Hong Kong is my home. I love it here. All my friends are here. I own this place and a restaurant in Central. Where would I go?"

"I'm sure Hong Kong will be fine," I said and took another sip. Tango Martini's atmosphere was as refined as its owner. It had low lights, comfortable sofas covered in fur and leather and in the corner, a dining area with eight tables. The place was full every night. I glanced around the rectangular room. The bar took up half of one wall. By now all except a few barstools were still vacant. At the far end was a cigar room which was reserved for smokers. Cigarettes were frowned upon.

"You've got a great place here," I said. "Are you making good money?"

He nodded and looked mildly sheepish. "A lot of money. More money than the day job."

"It's what the Chinese call riding a cow to buy a horse. Eventually you'll be able to tell your bosses in the States to take a running jump."

"Maybe," he said. I could tell that the idea of giving up his corporate job was not really enticing. He probably had a big expat flat, a Corporate Platinum Amex card, a maid who took care of all the ironing and no wife or kids to bend his ear if he came home in the early hours smelling of gin and vermouth.

As these thoughts passed through my head, my eyes focused on the table in the far corner of the dining room. A Chinese man was sitting, facing me. He was dressed soberly in a dark well-cut suit and was deep in conversation with a Westerner, judging by the colour of his neck and hair. The last time I'd seen the Chinese man had been the previous year in New York. His name was Hu Xianping and I knew from Larry Lim that he now headed up the Third Bureau of the Ministry of State Security.

Or to put it another way: he was Beijing's Chief Spy in Hong Kong.

4

"Mark," I said to the American, "Do you know who that is at the far corner table, having dinner with the Chinese fellow?"

He leaned forward and squinted, then said, "I don't know his name, I'm afraid. He's a regular though, a Brit like you. He's an engineer, I think. His office is somewhere in Wan Chai."

"He definitely looks familiar," I lied. "I must have bumped into him around town somewhere."

Mark gave a smile. "Sooner or later, everyone bumps into everyone in this town."

It seemed odd to say that about a city of six million people, but Hong Kong was like a village. We expats frequented a limited list of bars and restaurants, clustered in areas like Lan Kwai Fong, Soho, Causeway Bay, Wan Chai or Stanley. If you went out most nights - which wasn't uncommon - you'd keep on seeing familiar faces.

"In a few months' time there will be 50,000 fewer Brits around when all the civil servants pack up," I commented.

"Still leaves 50,000 Frenchmen and 40,000 Americans to drink in my bar," he said with a chuckle. He raised his finger at the Filipino barman then pointed at both of our drinks to indicate it was time for a re-fresh.

"How long have you been here?" I asked.

"I arrived in 1990. I was working for General Electric in Japan selling programmable logic controllers when I was head-hunted by Advanced Semi-Conductors to set up their new Asian operations. Started with a secretary and one engineer. Now I've got eight hundred people working for me." He shook his head as if he still couldn't understand what had happened and how fast companies grew in Hong Kong.

"Any concerns about the handover?" I asked.

"Should be great for business. My bosses are excited. China will be opening up even more." He aligned the martini glass carefully on the napkin in front of him. He seemed a man who enjoyed precision in all matters. "We've set up a Singapore office just in case. A little escape pod, if you like." A frown crossed his face. "Not my kind of town. A bit too strait-laced, so I hope we'll all be fine here after the handover and it will be onward and upward."

"I base myself in Singapore," I said. "It's not as boring as everyone makes out it is."

"I'll stick with Hong Kong. The Berlin Philharmonic is coming to town next week and then the Moscow Ballet is arriving with Swan Lake."

"You are a man of culture," I complimented him.

He shrugged. "There's too much *Sturm und Drang* in the world. We must enjoy the finer things in life in between chasing the mighty Dollar."

"Most of the men I know here spend all their time chasing skirt when they're not working."

He said with an appraising smile:

"*Purché porti la gonnella; voi sapete quel che fa.*"

I stared at him for a long minute, trying to remember where it came from.

"*Don Giovanni*, Leporello's famous Aria," I said eventually.

He nodded with approval. "An educated man."

"Just the sort of nonsense one remembers from a boarding school education." The answer had finally come via Mr. Parson's music class at prep school when I was ten or eleven. "'As long as she wears a skirt, you know what he will do'? That about sums up most of the rascals I know. Including myself."

The two men at the corner table were still deep in discussion and it niggled me.

"It's important to have a hobby and beautiful women are an art form in themselves," I said. "Some people simply work too hard and forget to stop and smell the roses." People like Hu Xianping, for one. I figured he would always be working on something to advance Chinese interests.

"We learn that from the Chinese," Mark replied. "They have such a single-minded focus on accumulating money." He gave a low laugh. "It took me years to truly understand them. I grew up around Boston where we think we're more cultured than other parts of the United States."

I told him I'd been in New York the previous year and had attended the Atlanta Olympics. It had been great fun, but I'd eventually started to miss Hong Kong and Singapore.

"I don't get back to the States more than once a year," he said. "Our head office is in Buffalo and who willingly visits that town? Half of the year it's under five foot of snow. Per capita it has the fattest people in the country."

That made me laugh. Then I noticed that Hu and his British friend had finished their meal and were standing up, getting ready to leave.

"Will you excuse me, Mark. I'll be back in ten minutes I just want to go and have a word with that fellow."

By now Hu and his companion - a corpulent man with florid features that spoke of an Anglo-Saxon heritage and a fondness for beer - were on their way to the door. I slid a credit card from my wallet and asked the Filipino barman to hold on to it until I returned.

By the time I got to the lift lobby the doors were closing on the two men, so I ran down the four flights of stairs and emerged into the ground floor lobby ahead of them. It was an old building and a tired lift. I stepped out onto Lockhart Road and turned my back, as if I was sending a text message on my mobile phone.

Hu and the British engineer shook hands and parted ways. I waited, still pretending to be busy with my Ericsson GH337. Hu walked off in the direction of Admiralty where his driver had probably parked up. The engineer walked towards where the MTR exit was located, crossing the junction of Luard Road and Lockhart Road diagonally, which took him past the 'Chilli Club', 'New Makati', the 'Old China Hand' and several of the girlie dancing bars. Outside the 'Waikiki

Club' the old mama-san tried to grab his arm and drag him in. He shook her off politely. I didn't have time to tail him onto the underground so I was just toying with the idea of calling out to him and pretending that we had met before - so I could get him to tell me his name - when he entered the lobby of the Gaylord Commercial Building.

It looked like he was going back to his office. I hovered for a moment and watched as he got into the lift, then entered the dingy lobby. An old security guard was sitting behind a tiny counter at the far end reading the *Apple Daily*.

I asked him in Cantonese if he knew which office the foreigner worked in. If a white man spoke Cantonese the locals knew he was a police officer. There was no need to flash a warrant card and in my time we never did. Hardly any other foreigners bothered to learn the language.

He cocked his head sideways and gave me a sly look. He didn't say anything, just went to the metal board that listed every company by floor. He tapped on the 22nd Floor and I could read the name: SatBox Communications.

"*Hai ying-gwok gung-si, Ah-sir*," the old *hong gan* informed me. It was an English company. I thanked him politely, told him to keep it between us and slipped him a red hundred dollar note.

Briskly I walked back the way I'd come. The same mama-san tried to grab my arm but I gave her a wide berth. Three middle-aged men in suits and loosened ties nearly bumped into me as they staggered out of the 'Old

China Hand', drunk already at this relatively early hour of the night.

I returned to 'Tango Martini' and slipped onto my vacant stool. My drink had been kept for me in the freezer and reappeared magically topped up. Mark was where I'd left him but leaning against the bar next to him was my old mucker Chop Suey.

"Where've you fucking been?" the Chinese man said with the thickest of Brummie accents. He'd been born in the New Territories but at the age of three his parents had emigrated to Solihull, so he'd grown up living and working in a Chinese takeaway, hence the rather cruel name we'd fostered on him on the first night of Police Training School. Although he could speak Cantonese he couldn't read or write it which always confused the constables and sergeants with whom he worked. He was now a Chief Inspector in G4, the Force's VIP Protection unit.

"Seeing a man about a dog," I said. "Do you know Mark Hudson, the owner?" I introduced them.

5

"So Sledge raids this love hotel, and there's a Yank sailor, a big black bloke, Chief Petty Officer or something. He's in bed with five buck-naked birds, with massive fake tits. But, they're not birds, are they?" Chop Suey said, pushing another shot glass of *Apfelkorn* across the table at me.

"Not birds," I repeated.

"The ugliest ladyboys you can imagine. You know the ones that hang around near the 'Beer Castle'."

I nodded. They came out after 2 a.m. and you had to duck around them as they hustled for business.

"So Sledge, always the gentleman, informs the Yank that prostitution is not illegal in Hong Kong but does he realise that they're actually geezers with their dangly bits still attached? The Yank blinks a bit and says thanks for the heads up but since he's paid for them already, he'll just flip them all over on their fronts while he does them from behind."

"Five ladyboys?" I repeated and put the empty shot-glass down on the table. "One more and he'd have a pool table."

"These sailors are out on the ships for six months without any booze or birds, you know. Must do their heads in," Chop Suey observed.

"They're usually pissed on two Budweiser Shandies," I said, nodding.

After 'Tango Martini' we'd taken a taxi up to Lan Kwai Fong and popped into 'Schnurrbart', a German bar which was a favourite watering hole for many coppers. One of our course-mates at Police Training School had died a week prior to our passing-out parade when he'd tried to climb up to his fourth-floor bedroom window. He'd been a great Germanophile - a former Captain in the Royal Tank Regiment - so we always thought of him when we drank here.

I held up my newly filled shot-glass of *Apfelkorn* and made the toast: "To Christian, wherever you are now."

My drinking companion was a lean, wiry lad who loved running. He and Christian had always led the pack on the Brick Hill Run which started with over 80 steep steps up a mountain behind the Wong Chuk Hang training school.

Chop Suey repeated: "To Christian," and we downed the sweet, sticky *Schnapps* in one. A Westerner with an easy smile stepped up to our table.

"What are you lads up to then?" he asked.

"We're reciting poetry here, what the fuck do you think we're doing?" Chop Suey snarled at him in a good-natured way.

The man everyone called Street Penis, pushed Chop Suey along on the bench and slid in next to him. "Jedburgh, how you doing?"

"Never better," I said. He was another inspector in the VIP protection team and the two of us were often mistaken for each other. He liked to point out that we were both equally tall, dark, broad-shouldered, long of leg and handsome of face.

"How come you're out and about?" I asked him.

"Been guarding Fat Pang for four days and I've got two off now," he said and helped himself to an empty glass which he topped up from our bottle. Fat Pang was our name for Chris Patten, the Governor of Hong Kong, a pompous English politician who had incensed the old men in Beijing by trying to bring democracy to Hong Kong at one minute to midnight. He wasn't a bad bloke, just a wordy windbag, from the wrong century and the wrong part of the world.

"What's he been up to?" I asked. Street Penis shrugged.

"Eating egg tarts and ranting on about universal suffrage."

"Insufferably misguided," I said. Not that I cared because, of course, it still wasn't any of my business.

"They didn't want him in Westminster," Street Penis said, "so they tried to send him as far away as possible. The Pitcairn Islands didn't want him either, so we got him in Hong Kong."

"He's nearly done his tour of duty," I said. "They'll probably make him a Lord and send him off to Brussels. That's another dead end posting."

We finished the bottle and bantered some more. The lads told stories from their work and I made up stories from mine. Then we walked around the corner to 'Club

1997' which was the trendiest disco in that part of town. It was usually full of investment bankers high on cocaine, dancing with billionaire's daughters back home from their posh boarding schools. Normally, indigent coppers struggled to get through the door but the burly, bodybuilding Gurkha who guarded the realm nodded at Chop Suey and waved us in. VIP protection made you a regular in these places.

Daft Punk's 'Around the World' greeted us as we pushed through the tightly packed crowd. It was a small venue with a dance floor in the middle and a railing that you could place your beer on and watch as the girlies grooved. The three of us found a gap and widened it with our shoulders, then Chop Suey went to get the refreshments.

It was too noisy to talk. This was a place for seeing and being seen. Before we left the German bar, Chop Suey had asked me if I was open to a business proposition.

"As long as it's legal," I said.

"Course it's fucking legal, you prick, I'm a police officer." I let that non sequitur go.

"Go on then. What is it?"

"You know who Sir Bernard Li is?" he asked me.

I shrugged. "Only what I read in the papers. Self-made Chinese entrepreneur who came to London when he was young, sold porcelain in Petticoat Lane Market and eventually got into Oxford. Wears brightly coloured glasses to make people remember him. Worth a few bob and these days is well connected with the future rulers in Beijing."

Chop Suey nodded. "That's the man. He's transformed Foreign & Exotic Retail into his own personal *Hong* so he can wind up Adrian Swire when they bump into each other at the bar in the Hong Kong Club."

"What's that got to do with me?"

"My uncle knows him from Zetland Hall," Chop Suey said. "You know, the Masonic Lodge up the road."

"Your uncle who owns noodle shops all over the territory and supplies the RHKP when they need a lot of noodles quickly on an operation?"

"Yeah," he admitted sheepishly.

"The sort of deal done over a drink in the Lodge?"

"No fucking comment," the Chief Inspector said rolling his eyes in an attempt at appearing embarrassed. "Anyway, Sir Bernard asked my uncle if I could recommend anyone who could do a bit of bodyguarding for him over the next few weeks. He needs to go to London and wants to look flash with a *gwai lo* butler hanging around him looking hard." Chop Suey gave me a big smile then. "So I thought of you."

"London? Starting when?"

"No idea. You'd have to meet and ask the man himself."

"He's a bit of a tosser, isn't he?"

"A huge fucking tosser who thinks the sun shines out of his arse and his shit stinks sweeter than the Queen's. Believes that just because he's been knighted for signing a big cheque to the Conservative party, he should get the best table in a restaurant."

"Three thousand US dollars a day," I said.

"Apparently he's got a horny daughter who goes to Cheltenham Ladies College or one of those nobby, posh, schools like you fucking went to."

"It's still three thousand bucks a day. I'll consider it seriously. Set me up."

The music in 'Club 1997' changed pace and Robbie Williams started telling us he wanted to be old before he died. The booze had started to hit the spot and I found myself staring fixedly at a girl who was dominating the centre of the dance floor.

She was petite, with shoulder-length black hair worn in a ponytail. She had a flawless oval-shaped face and a trim figure wrapped up in a tight little black dress that left her shoulders bare. Some fabric was creatively missing at the front of her dress, permitting me to see the forceful thrust of her breasts as she moved to the music. She was neither Chinese nor European, but that perfect blend of East and West, an exquisite Eurasian. The future of Hong Kong.

She was dancing with Leslie Cheung, the Canto-pop star and actor who was rumoured to be gay, so I quite fancied my chances, although I had a niggling suspicion that I was already too drunk to speak.

6

The Hong Kong Club was old money and had a rigid dress code to match. Fortunately, I'd packed a suit in my Samsonite. I usually did in case there was a job that required business attire. Chop Suey had woken me up with a call at 10 a.m. saying I was having lunch with Sir Bernard Li in a couple of hours. That gave me just enough time to get my act together. The hangover was painful, like being shouted at by my drill instructor for being improperly dressed on parade. But they always were these days. I was no longer in my twenties, when there was less blood in my alcohol stream.

I'd hit the wall at about 2 a.m., hopped into a taxi by myself and made it back to the Luk Kwok Hotel without throwing up over the backseat. I was in a different room, on a different floor, from the one I'd changed and showered in after shooting the American. It made sense for me to be in the same hotel since I could have been seen walking in and out of the lobby earlier taking the lifts.

My suit was the one I'd had made last year in New York by a famous Jewish tailor and it was still in great shape. It's all about the quality of the fabric and how many stitches per inch they have sewn into the seams. I hung it up in the bathroom and turned the shower to its highest temperature to fill the room with steam. Ten minutes of that would shake out all the creases and make the suit appear as if it had been recently ironed.

I selected a garish Hermès tie which would turn the heads of the old fellows at the Club. It looked like someone had cut out the middle of a Kandinsky painting and then made a tie from it.

New York was 12 hours behind, so it wasn't too late to make a phone call. I used an International Calling Card and my mobile. The hotel rates were extortionate, and this was a number I didn't want to appear on any bill.

He answered on the fourth ring. There was some mellow music in the background and the quality of his voice told me he'd been drinking.

"Who is this?" he demanded. My number would have been withheld and not many people had his.

"Starter for ten: "Scribble, scribble, scribble." Who used to say that?"

"Oh, it's you," Dominic Tweddle said.

"Answer the bloody secret question."

"Dr. Jenkins," he said. "Although the original comment was made by the Duke of Gloucester to Edward Gibbon," he added, showing off his Oxford education to register his annoyance.

"Correct and your next question is on famous Chinese spies: what was the name of the senior intelligence officer hanging around last year in New York?"

Tweddle gave an irritable grunt. Perhaps he was with a woman and in the middle of something more important. "Hu Xianping, as you very well know."

"And your final question: where do you think I saw him being incredibly pally with an employee of a British company called SatBox Communications?"

"Somewhere in Hong Kong?"

"You are a clever fellow," I said.

"I have a First Class honours degree from the best college in the best university in the world. I don't think that was ever in doubt." I assumed he was saying this for the benefit of the other person in his room, so I laughed and went on.

"I got the sense that Hu was grooming a new asset. The man is apparently English and an engineer but perhaps he likes the finer things in life and isn't earning as much as he feels he's worth."

"Umm, SatBox Communications?" he said at the other end of the line.

"Is that a name that's crossed your desk on a file?" I asked.

"I'm afraid it has. This is very interesting information."

"We aim to please," I said. Although Dominic ostensibly worked for a crusty old bank called Ashenden Delacroix, he had a secret life working for MI6, the Secret Intelligence Service. We'd known each other since we were in shorts at prep school and had caught up in New York after I'd attended the Atlanta Olympics.

"What are you doing in Hong Kong?" he asked.

"I'm about to have lunch with Sir Bernard Li in the Hong Kong Club. He's looking for a butler."

"You've finally found your level in domestic service. Can't they get decent staff nowadays with the handover coming up?"

"He wants a butler who knows how to handle a gun and has bulges in all the right places."

"Is that the only reason you're in Hong Kong?" Tweddle said with what may have been a smirk.

"Went out drinking with some of my old copper mates," I said cautiously.

He chuckled but the line wasn't clear, so it sounded more like a cough. "Nothing to do with a signal I read earlier this evening about a senior US embassy official being shot by a professional sniper as he sat by his swimming pool?"

"Shocking. Hong Kong just isn't safe any more. City's going to the dogs. Or is it the Chogs?"

"None of your colonial racist remarks. This is an open phone line and someone at the NSA might think you actually mean it. You know how literal Americans are."

"I've got to get on," I said. "Just thought you might like to know about Hu Xianping. If I take this job, I'll be in the UK for a few months. It would be good to meet up if you've any annual leave planned."

He laughed. "As a matter of fact, I may well be in London very soon. Date's not been confirmed for my new posting, but I'll be waving goodbye to the Big Apple soon."

"Good news. I'll let you know if I do end up in London and we'll get together."

I returned to my preparation. I spent ten minutes bringing my black Church's brogues up to a high polish.

By 12.30 p.m. my reflection in the full-length mirror on the back of the bathroom door looked pretty sharp. If I screwed up my eyes, I could barely see the bags under them.

The Hong Kong Club is the oldest such institution in the territory and all decisions of import relating to the Fragrant Harbour had been taken here since 1846. It represented the real power in the City as its members were government officials, judges, barristers, *taipans* and other captains of industry. To become a member you had to be proposed by two other members and then endure three or more social events where you were poked and prodded metaphorically by other members who would then approve or blackball your membership application. When you progressed to the next stage, the membership committee grilled you with intrusive questions about your wealth and probity. Only nine new members a year were admitted. It was very much dead men's shoes.

I arrived at ten minutes to one, gave my name to the concierge and sat on one of the sofas waiting for my host. Sir Bernard arrived five minutes later. He was wearing a Prince of Wales' check suit, a black tie spotted with white *fleur-de-lis* and bright red Prada glasses. His hair - which he wore longer than the current fashion - was entirely white.

"How do you do. I'm Bernard," he introduced himself and grasped my hand firmly, for a few moments longer than is customary. He seemed to be studying me intently. It was probably an affectation he'd learnt on a Dale Carnegie course.

"Have you been to the Club before?" he asked.

"Once or twice, Sir Bernard."

"Excellent grub here, you know." His accent could only be described as lower upper class. It wasn't quite the way the Queen enunciated but it had strong aspirations. He must have spent a lot of money on elocution classes before or after he went up to Oxford. We took the lift up several floors and turned left when we came out.

"I've got us a table in the Red Room," Sir Bernard said. The maître d' led us across the plush carpet towards a table by the windows.

"Do you know Brigadier Hammerbeck?" Sir Bernard said waving at a military-looking gentleman at the next table who was lunching with a man called Vickers who commanded the Force's Criminal Intelligence Bureau.

"Not personally, Sir Bernard," I said as my chair was pulled back for me and I sat down with my back to the other table. Vickers probably recognised my face but he blanked me as he was deep in conversation with the Brigadier, who was the Deputy Commander of British Forces in Hong Kong.

"Splendid, splendid," the Chinese tycoon said amiably gazing around the room and waving at a few more faces familiar to him. It really was that sort of a restaurant. "You see that lady over there. That's Carina Lau. Very famous actress. A dear friend of mine. Perhaps you know of her?"

"I've seen her on television," I said. The waiter handed me the menu.

Sir Bernard's expression showed he approved, although watching TVB soap operas was hardly the height of cultural achievement.

"When I was young, I never dreamt that I would become a member of such a club as this." He beamed at me. "That is the wonder of this city and of capitalism. If you work hard and you have a dream, everything is within your reach."

"I don't disagree, sir. Hong Kong has been a marvellous place for foreigners to live and work."

"Oh," he caught my mood, "it will continue to be a brilliant city after handover. Mark my words. It is the best thing that could happen to this town. Hong Kong is a vital cross-road on the new Silk Road."

"That is good to know," I commented. There was no intention on my part to be particularly obsequious, but I was trying to be punctiliously polite because I felt like a holiday in London and being paid three thousand US dollars a day to enjoy myself. It had taken me many years to learn this lesson: the less you said the more people liked you, because they filled in your conversational gaps with their own impressions.

"I have a copy of your reference letter from the Royal Hong Kong Police's Personnel Department," he said after the food and wine had been ordered. He unfolded a piece of A4 which he'd produced from an inside pocket.

"How clever of you, Sir Bernard."

"Connections are everything in life, Bill," he said with a supercilious nod. "Let me read it to you: 'During his eight years of service Mr. Jedburgh served in Uniform Branch as well as the Special Duties Unit and VIP

Protection. He showed that he could handle administration but proved less than enthusiastic about the more routine aspects of police work. In his last year in the Force he appeared to lose interest in his job." Sir Bernard paused and gave me the hard stare that must have sent his employees running for cover. "What happened, Jedburgh? Why did you lose interest?"

I gave him a smile. "I won't bore you with the details but sometimes in life we realise it is time to move on and find new challenges."

He nodded slowly for a while then said, "That's a good answer."

"I wanted to work for myself. I thought I was good enough to do my own thing. And it's worked out so far. I've been able to put food on the table."

"You're not married?"

"No."

"Are you gay?"

"Not to my knowledge."

"I don't mind if you are gay. I'm a man of the world. Tolerance is so important these days."

"I could provide references from girls who will attest to the fact that I am heterosexual."

"That won't be necessary," he said, oblivious to the sarcasm. He took out another sheet. "I have a document here from a Superintendent Callum Forrester that says you are an excellent shot with the Glock 17."

"That's nice of Callum to say that. He's pretty shit-hot with a Glock himself."

"And you shot at Bisley when we you were in the Army?" Sir Bernard continued his interrogation.

"That's correct."

"You won the Conan Doyle cup."

"You are well informed, sir."

"And that is a finely cut suit. You have taste. Is that a Willie Cheng?"

"No, it's a Mr. Alan. 'Think Yiddish, dress British' is the firm's motto in Manhattan."

The first course arrived. I had chosen the escargots because I'm very fond of slimy snails in garlic. Sir Bernard had chosen a bottle of crisp Sancerre that went perfectly with the dish. He watched me as I used the pincers to hold the shell, applied the tiny fork to extract its contents assiduously and then mopped up it all up with a gobbet of my baguette. My table manners seemed to be up to his standards, judging by the expression on his face by the time we were on the Armagnac. The dining room had emptied by this stage as it was nearly 3.30 p.m.

"I have a daughter," Sir Bernard finally came to the point. "She's terribly wild and I can't control her. I need a man of character who can watch her and make sure she doesn't get herself or our family name into trouble."

I smiled. "If you wish to hire me, I will do my best. It sounds like a minder's job."

"If that is what you wish to call it."

"I'm not very fussy about nomenclature. Minder-factotum-troubleshooter-bodyguard-dance-partner."

"You won't be expected to dance with her. Just make sure she doesn't consort with unsavoury characters or get involved with crooks or blaggards."

I nodded. "I can do that."

"I am working on a vital business deal that will change the face of my company. I cannot have my daughter cause me any embarrassment. That is why I want her close at hand and on a tight leash. Are you willing to be the man holding the leash?"

"I've had some experience in that department, Sir Bernard," I said, thinking of the 'Eden Club' in Bangkok on Soi 6. "It sounds like an interesting challenge."

7

I was flying Cathay Pacific from Kai Tak into LHR. There was no chance of running into my old sparring partner Jane Tan, who worked for SQ, but two stewardesses I vaguely recognised smiled frostily at me as I sat in Business doing my prep work for the assignment. Were they smiling at me because we'd slept together or because they knew my reputation? I couldn't quite be sure.

I had an empty seat beside me, ruining my lascivious plan to use the journey to get to know Sir Bernard's daughter. I had been pleasantly surprised when I turned up at the check-in to discover it was the same Eurasian beauty I had seen in 'Club 1997', as stunning as I remembered. This time Leslie Cheung was nowhere to be seen. Farewell to his concubine then.

"Melissa," Sir Bernard said peremptorily, "this is Jedburgh. I have employed him to keep an eye on you and your antics."

"Hi," I said, trying to sound avuncular. I put out my hand, but she studiously ignored it.

"You can call me Missie," she said. "That's what people who know me call me." She looked daggers at her father.

"We named her Missie at Wolditz," an English girl standing beside her said as she took my hand and shook it. "It's a joke. A book by Arthur Ransome. '*Swallows and Amazons*'."

She was attractive, if slightly chubby, with curly strawberry-blonde hair that cascaded down to her shoulders. She had a naughty smile that played all the way into the corners of her mouth.

"I'm Lola Beaulieu," she said. "Or at least that's my pen name. I write rather saucy chick-lit and they thought that would sell better than Lizzie Brown. Missie and I were at boarding school together and she invited me out to Hong Kong for a few weeks."

"An exotic pseudonym seems to be a pre-requisite for writing that sort of stuff. I hope there's lashings of sex in your books?"

She was still young enough to blush.

"Absolutely," she looked seriously into my eyes and batted her long eyelashes at me. "I'm engaged in a lot of research to get it right."

Missie giggled.

"He's ancient," she laughed. "He probably hasn't had sex for years. Don't tease him."

Missie and Lola were a couple of seats ahead of me in the business class cabin, still talking nineteen to the dozen and replenishing their vodka and tonics regularly from the bar. Sir Bernard was in glorious isolation up ahead of us in first class.

I was watching a Jackie Chan movie on the video on demand system out of the corner of my eye. I'd see it in Singapore in Cantonese. Then it had been entitled

'*Police Story 4*', but now it seemed to be called '*First Strike*' and was dubbed into English with a new soundtrack. I missed the mix of different languages – without them the film felt sub-Schwarzenegger and it suffered from the uneven production values common to many Hong Kong movies. I let its inane plot about Ukrainian terrorists and Australian Triad families run in the background as I worked.

I had a copy of *Asiamoney* on the pull-out table in front of me with a cover article 'Where next for Foreign & Exotic?' complete with a flattering picture of Sir Bernard Li. I also had the latest issue of *HK Magazine* with numerous pictures of Missie partying.

More useful was the file that Chop Suey had given me when I visited him at the Police Training School in Wong Chuk Hang before I left.

"This takes me back," I said, as we met on the pistol range. "What's the idea?" He was clutching a clipboard and had a pair of ear defenders around his neck.

"Another favour for Sir Bernard," he said. "He wanted me to reinstate you in G4, but I told him that was impossible, so I've done the next best thing."

He fished in the inside pocket of his jacket with his free hand and pulled out a sheet of RHKP Letterhead which he opened out on the clipboard to show me.

'To whom it may concern. Retired Senior Inspector William Jedburgh is acting as a close protection officer on the instructions of His Excellency the Governor of Hong Kong and is hereby authorised to carry the following firearm – Glock 17 Serial No. JH162NHF'

Beneath were his signature and alongside it the loopy curls and strange knifelike 'P' of Fat Pang's. Attached to the bottom was a laminated version of my former police ID photograph.

"You'll need to take this to the Met firearms team when you get to London and have it counter-stamped," he said. "The contact details are inside."

He put the letter back in the envelope but when I held my hand out to take it, he made no effort to give it to me.

"Not so fast, Deadeye Dick," he said. "I'm under instructions to check if you remember how to use it first."

"Good point," I replied, trying not to sound sarcastic. "Where is the safety catch again? I can't quite put my finger on it."

"Ha ha, very fucking funny. I'll mark you down five points for that comment."

"I used a P228 in the States on the close protection gig I did for the Singaporeans, but I do love the Glock."

The weapon was on the table in front of him. The armourer must have parted with one under duress because this was an early Second Gen – about five or six years old. It looked like it had had a hard life. But when I picked it up it was well-oiled with as smooth an action as I would have expected from a properly maintained police weapon.

There was a target downrange – the RHKP used NATO-style Fig. 11 targets, but, perhaps in the belief that you would be hard pressed to find charging Russian soldiers when policing Wan Chai, they had made the faces look North Korean. I clicked the magazine in place and took up the classic firing stance I had been taught on that very range. At that distance, with a bit of thought, I could have put the entire magazine through the same hole. But I didn't want my buddy from G4 to know just how useful I was these days with a pistol. When I wasn't working, I spent a lot of time at the Pattaya Range in the basement of the 'Tiffany's Ladyboy Cabaret'.

"How many do you want?"

"At least ten please, Bill," he said. "You might want to put these on."

He handed me a pair of ear defenders and put his own pair over his ears.

The Glocks are Austrian engineering at its very best. Some thought this model was called a 17 because its magazine contained that number of rounds, but in fact it was their 17th patent. I admired its cut down shape, its use of composites to keep it light and the integral safety catch on the trigger. Point and shoot. Which is exactly what I did. I put a careful ring of eight shots around the target's nose then dropped down to put two through its centre mass.

Chop Suey pushed the button that brought the target towards us.

"Well it wouldn't fucking well do for G4," he said - exactly as I had hoped. "On the other hand, it's more than good enough for where you're going. Good luck, and please try not to kill anyone unless they really deserve it."

He handed over the letter and clapped me on the back.

"Thanks," I said. "I won't let you or the noodle shops down."

For now the Glock was safely stowed in the hold, and I was turning the pages on his other present to me. It was a fascinating story. Bernard Li had come to London as a teenager, not speaking a word of English beyond the Kowloon street argot he'd been brought up with. With that strong Asian drive to succeed - which I recognised from most of the Hong Kong natives I knew - plus a scholarship from the Swire family, for whom his grandfather had worked, he had studied hard and won a place to read law at Worcester College, Oxford. During the vacation, however, he had continued to flog porcelain in Petticoat Lane and had founded his first boutique - 'Kowloon Junk' – at the age of 23. He went back and forth between Britain and China and was known as the 'Asian Terence Conran'. In 1982, during the economic slump that followed the introduction of Thatcherism, he had pounced on a tiny listed company, Foreign & Exotic Retail, founded in 1893 and completely ignored by investors. What he had spotted was that they owned a small piece of City real estate in Cheapside, once a jewellery shop, that fifteen years later formed part of a large office block after Sir Bernard sold it for seven times the cost of acquiring F&E. An acquisition spree then transformed the group into a major player in housewares, textiles and clothing. Now it was rumoured to be moving into consumer electronics. 'China has clothed Western bodies for many years,' Sir Bernard proclaimed. 'In the 21st Century we will clothe their brains.'

He was a playboy, a self-proclaimed polymath and a ruthless businessman. He had married a beautiful model and Melissa – Missie – was the product. Although he was now divorced from her mother, Sir Bernard had retained custody and as a Catholic convert had sent Missie to a convent boarding school near London.

On the screen in front of me a pretty young Chinese actress was smiling sweetly at Jackie Chan, who was beating up a phalanx of baddies with an aluminium stepladder and a couple of paper dragons. He was starting to look his age. He was about ten years older than me. I'd met him once and found him charming, although his cold eyes told me that there was much more to him than the image he liked to present.

I thought about what Missie had said. Was I really getting too old? I was in my mid-thirties. I liked to think there was plenty of fight left in me. I could still kick as high as Jackie did and my style was more lethal than the entertaining mix of styles he employed in the movies.

The pictures of Missie in HK Magazine showed she appeared to have learned little in her young life, other than how to party hard. I didn't see her in the company of many people my age. Instead she was photographed next to the *jeunesse dorée* of Hong Kong. I recognised most of the locations and quite a few of the incidental characters on display, but while she always smiled, it was an inscrutable look that I couldn't read. If I was going to get close to her, I would have to find a way in that I couldn't spot at present.

As the plane descended into Heathrow, I contemplated this return to the old country. I didn't particularly like Britain. It was fine in small doses, but its weather, its ugly, manly women and dull nightlife soon had me yearning to return to the vibrancy of the Orient. But a few weeks on a well-paying gig wasn't a major hardship.

After we came through security and I had reclaimed my Glock, Lola headed towards the underground, but not before she had stuck her tongue in my ear, scribbled her telephone number inside one of her books and thrust it into my pocket. She was clearly serious about her research. I fondled her buttocks experimentally as a farewell, but I really didn't get much of a kick from English women, even the younger nubile ones.

I travelled into London in the front of Sir Bernard's Bentley Brooklands. He and Missie shared the rear, but it was clear from the body language that they were estranged. Missie could not have positioned herself further away from her father if she'd tried.

From the front of the Bentley I watched her surreptitiously in the vanity mirror. She was quite beautiful. Her English mother had bequeathed her well-developed breasts and long legs. Her Chinese father had provided flawless skin and lustrous long black hair which she wore in a ponytail. She was lithe and I could see well defined muscles beneath her tee which hinted at sportiness. I thought she was a bit older than I had originally thought – maybe 23 or 24. In a Western family she would already have left home and be making her own way. Here it was the usual combination of Chinese duty and billionaire lifestyle that kept the apron strings in place.

When we reached Sir Bernard's home in Upper Brook Street I was escorted to the highest floor in the house, in what had once been the servants' quarters. I fell asleep looking at the sky above London, trying to make sense of why I was here. Something was wrong. Sir Bernard didn't really need a trained operative as a housemate and Missie seemed to be in no more danger than any other spoilt brat of a billionaire's kid. No, I had been put in play for something else. I was annoyed with myself that I couldn't work out why.

8

I was breakfasting by myself in Upper Brook Street when I heard a beeping sound in my pocket. I had surfaced from a deep well of sleep to discover that the townhouse was silent. I wandered through tastefully appointed but sterile rooms, admiring the modern British and traditional Chinese art that filled them. Finally I located the breakfast room. An almost motionless butler stood in front of a steaming buffet. He explained that Sir Bernard had already left for his office and that Missie rarely surfaced before midday. It was already late afternoon according to my body-clock, but I had slept well and a large black coffee and a kipper with scrambled eggs set me up for the day ahead.

My latest toy was a pager. When Sabeer, my ever-helpful and discreet tech man in India had FireMailed me to see if it might be of interest to me, I had been surprised.

"Aren't pagers old hat?" I had emailed back.

"Ordinarily yes," he replied. "But this is a bleeding edge two-way pager."

Sabeer was right, but what really made it clever was the work my Indian buddy had done to make it usable all across Asia and now in England. It was a RIM-900 'inter@active pager', made by a small Canadian company called Research In Motion. It looked a bit like a pillbox but when you flipped up the clamshell top it revealed a small keyboard and an even tinier screen. I had it linked up to a very confidential answering service in Singapore that could relay messages to me on the move and Sabeer had promised me in time that I would even be able to send and receive FireMail messages like the Nokia Communicators that were starting to appear. For now I contented myself with typing short messages which my helpful service could relay to the recipients the old fashioned way, via a phone call.

The screen displayed an 0171 telephone number – I still couldn't get used to the fact that the code for London was no longer 01 – and a message that said: 'Call Me, Dom'.

I had a Motorola StarTAC in my pocket, which Sir Bernard had given me the previous evening: 'So we can keep in touch.' The nine-digit number was spelled out on black Dymo tape attached to the back. I debated whether to ring Dominic from the cell phone but thought better of it. I wouldn't put it past Sir Bernard to monitor my calls. I wandered out and found a red phone box on Grosvenor Square, close to the ugliest building in Mayfair, the US embassy. The call was answered on the third ring.

"Tweddle."

"No secretary to direct my call, Dom? Everything OK?"

"Since you ask, I'm borrowing this office and my new PA will be based in Jardine House.

"The house of a thousand arseholes?" I assumed he meant the one in Hong Kong. It had fifty-two storeys of narrow porthole windows, hence its local nickname. "That's appropriate."

"Behave," he said. "I thought you'd be pleased."

"I'm delighted we're going to be able to drink together more often. But I'm still not certain what the place will be like post-handover. How come you're over here?"

"Partly briefings ahead of my new deployment, partly the conversation we had the other day. I came in on the redeye from New York. Can we get together?"

"Will I have to take the tube?" I asked.

"I doubt it, I'm in our Mayfair office in Brook Street."

"Which I'm guessing may be somehow attached to Upper Brook Street, home to Sir Bernard Li?"

"We're just opposite Claridges. But why don't we meet in my club? It's the Savile and it's halfway between us.

The Savile was more or less deserted. It was a typical wood-panelled oasis of calm, designed for people who might equally choose to ignore each other or engage in random conversation. We found a seat in the empty bar where we could talk without being overheard. Caricatures of famous authors kept an eye on us from a distance. Dominic explained that the Savile drew a lot of its membership from artists and writers.

He looked as deceptively fatuous as ever. He was in a City chalk-stripe suit but his shirt looked ruffled and his maroon cashmere jumper had congealed egg on it. With his unruly fair hair and round tortoise-shell glasses he looked uncannily like an owl. A waiter had brought him a Bloody Mary, without comment as to the time of day.

I settled for a black coffee with a shot of brandy since I was also between time zones, as it were.

"I didn't expect to see you so soon," I said. "How long have you known you were coming to Hong Kong?"

"I put in for it before I saw you last year in Manhattan," he said. "I didn't want to say anything, because knowing the way that the Firm works, I could just have easily ended up in Helsinki."

"At least you would have known your way around on skis," I said. "Didn't you grow up in Austria?"

"Switzerland, and only during the school holidays."

"I can only water ski." I said. "The frozen stuff is for using in cocktails."

I wasn't sure where our conversation was going, and Dominic didn't seem keen to start it. I was worried he had done a deal with the Brigadier to trade me. I liked working for the SID and I considered Singapore my home now, but I had mixed views about the British Government. Nor did I know what that might do for my personal friendship with Dominic and I began to regret not having a second shot of brandy in my coffee.

"You've set a cat amongst the pigeons, you know," he said finally. "You've also ended up here at the right time to be of assistance."

"I'm already employed by Sir Bernard Li," I said. "I hope you haven't forgotten our discussion that I don't work for SIS?"

"Of course not. We don't want you in any official capacity, but I need you to help out our old mate Johnny Aston unofficially."

I had first met Johnny Aston the previous year in New York. He worked for Burcott & Co, the City investment bank.

"Johnny will be here in a minute," Dominic continued. "He's delighted you're in London. I dread to think what you got up to with him in Oxfordshire."

"Let's just say," I said enigmatically, "that no birds were harmed, but quite a few were plucked."

Johnny was a larger-than-life character. He was as dedicated to the hedonistic lifestyle as me and I was looking forward to seeing him again.

"Jedburgh!" he said, bounding into the bar a few minutes later. "Too late for the shooting season, but we could still make the Grand National on Saturday. I've got a monkey on Go Ballistic, the favourite, at 12-1."

"Sorry, Johnny, working," I said. "I've got to go to Devon with my client to see her mother apparently. How's tricks?"

"Tricks are, well...," he searched for the right word, "...tricky. The government is screwed, New Labour are going to win the election and us City types may all be coming to join you in Singapore."

"Will it really be that bad?" I asked. "I don't do politics but Blair seems to be a decent enough chap. Knows which end of a spoon to hold. Not like Kinnock or Michael Foot."

"Let's hope you're right," he said. "He's certainly trying to sound more Tory than the Tories at the moment. Anyway, John Major is finished. When the Murdoch press has written you off then you are up the creek without a paddle."

The waiter came over and he ordered a gin and tonic. My resolve cracked and I joined him. We sat in silence until they arrived. To be honest, my body clock was so confused we could have been back in the Royal Hong Kong Yacht Club having a sundowner.

"Dom seems to think I might be able to help you out," I said.

"Yeah," Johnny drawled. "He tells me you're working for Sir Bernard Li. The White Tiger." I nodded. "I think he might be about to bid for one of my clients."

"I'm not being paid to advise on a takeover," I said. "I'm baby-sitting his daughter."

"Sly dog," he said, digging his elbow in my ribs. "I've seen pictures of her in the wife's *Daily Mail*." He leaned back in his chair. "That's good, because you won't be conflicted if we need your help."

I felt the walls of the venerable Mayfair club close in around me. I didn't like where this was going. I might not warm to Sir Bernard Li, but I didn't want to make an enemy of him either.

"Have you heard of the Red Fox?" Dominic asked.

"A Russian?"

"A British MP," he said. "Giles Guedella."

"Sorry," I said. "I've been in Asia a long time now."

"Giles is my client," Johnny said. "He made his fortune in electronics and I floated his business on the stock market a few years ago. Then the bugger went on a trade mission to Russia with Mrs. T and came back gagging to become an MP. Before we knew it, he's won a seat back from Labour and he's everyone's darling."

He lit a cigarette and the reflection of the match flared against the shiny dark frames of his glasses. He took a deep draught before he continued: "Can't last. It never does. He's too flamboyant, too different. He wears his bright red hair in a ponytail. Looks like a fox's brush. That's how he got his nickname. *The Sun* gave it to him. They love him. Especially when he refuses to toe the line on Europe."

"Guedella is a genuinely clever entrepreneur," Dominic picked up the conversation, "but he's bored of his business. He knows that there's going to be a clear-out at the top of the Conservative Party when they lose. He reckons he might get one of the top jobs. Personally, I doubt it, but if enough of the front-runners lose their seats then who knows? He's desperate to sell his business to fund his political career and there's a strong rumour that Foreign & Exotic is interested in buying."

"And that matters because?" I asked.

"It matters," he said, "because Guedella's company is the UK's leading player in satellite communications after Inmarsat."

"Satellites? That's a bit Flash Gordon, even for you Dom."

"That's where you're wrong," he said. "It's very much at the heart of big business now. The ITU – the International Telecommunications Union - is one of the oldest regulators in the world. It was set up in the 19th Century to police radio frequencies and a few years ago it decided to allocate radio spectrum for satellite telephony. Imagine a fleet of satellites whizzing over your head allowing you to speak to people when they're in the middle of nowhere – Siberia, the Falklands, or remote islands in the South China Sea. Guedella has one of the franchises. More importantly, his boffins have come up with a new encryption system for the handsets which GCHQ is trialling. At the present time they reckon that even the NSA would struggle to crack it."

"I can understand why any secret agency worth its salt would be interested in a system that could allow its operatives to communicate covertly from anywhere in the world," I said. "But I still don't see why selling it from one British company to another would be a problem. I thought Sir Bernard was a member of the Establishment?"

"Ordinarily," Dominic said, "it wouldn't raise an eyebrow. However, things are about to change. Today, Sir Bernard is a loyal British subject, but come the first of July he will generate over two thirds of his profits in the Special Administrative Region of Hong Kong and in mainland China. He will have new lords and masters to impress, who would be extremely pleased to discover what SIS's operatives are saying to each other."

I thought about this. I had seen the way that my Chinese former colleagues in the RHKP had started to change their tune over the past few years. They were all working out what they would need to do to get on with the new regime. Why should retailers be any different?

At last my brain started to assemble the jigsaw. I realised why Dominic had hustled over to London on the redeye and why Sir Bernard might want to have a trained professional like me on hand. Maybe, he wasn't worried about Missie, but about his own position.

"Guedella's company," I said. "It wouldn't be called SatBox Communications by any chance?"

9

I found Missie in the morning room in Upper Brook Street when I returned. She was dressed as a skater girl in baggy combat trousers and her top of the range Vans were propped up on the arm of a white leather couch. She was reading that week's edition of *Hello*, presumably to see whether the news of her arrival in London had reached the society columns yet.

The day's newspapers were ranged on a side table. The *Daily Mail* led with a story knocking the government. An investigation had finally begun into some cash-for-questions scandal. There was a picture of Giles Guedella on the front page of *The Times* under the headline 'Renegade MP criticizes Government's trade policy'. He was pictured outside the Houses of Parliament wearing a check shirt and a blue Guernsey sweater. He was smiling broadly, his slightly coarse red hair pulled behind his prominent ears – I couldn't make out the ponytail that Johnny Aston had referred to but presumed it was swinging somewhere off to the rear. I liked the look of him, certainly compared to the identikit British politicians I had guarded in Hong Kong. They had come out on their 'fact finding missions' in their fancy suits, but it hadn't taken them long to end up drunk in Wan

Chai bars buying expensive drinks for Thai hookers. Unless, that is, they had brought their mistresses with them on state-funded shagging and shopping trips.

The Guardian featured a large picture of a grinning Tony Blair, the Labour leader, above a report of his latest trip to Merseyside during which he had been mobbed by voters and had criticized John Major for focusing on traffic cones rather than crime statistics. 'Tough on crime, Tough on the causes of crime,' seemed to be one of Blair's slogans. I wondered if the Reliable Man needed one. 'Reassuringly Expensive,' like the beer perhaps?

I couldn't face any more politics. I picked up a copy of *Country Life* and plonked myself down in an armchair opposite Missie. She continued to ignore me, so I occupied myself looking at adverts for country houses. I'd enjoyed my trip to Ashurst Manor, Johnny's pile in Oxfordshire. I had enough money to buy my own 'sporting estate' now, but I wasn't sure I had the inclination to fund the army of gamekeepers, stable girls and housekeepers it took to do the thing properly. My simple life by a beach in Thailand, with the sea for company, seemed infinitely preferable.

I hunched forward in the chair tapping Missie's leg with the rolled-up magazine to get her attention.

"It's time we talked," I said. She looked at me insolently.

"Why? I didn't ask for you to be here. What is there to talk about?"

"We don't have to be friends," I said, "but I have a job to do and it will be a lot easier if we find a way of coexisting. Your father," - she grimaced at my mentioning him - "wants me to keep an eye on you. I don't care what you do, or who you see or sleep with, but I'm paid to keep you safe."

"So stupid, and embarrassing," she muttered. "I can take care of myself."

"We all think that," I said. "But the truth is that the modern world is a dangerous place, especially when you're related to someone who is extremely wealthy."

"I've had bodyguards before."

"Think of me more as an educated minder. I'll be discreet and I won't try to cramp your style, but if things start to go south I will be there for you. I'll be like a slightly annoying uncle."

"My uncle – not a real uncle but my father's best friend from university – tried to rape me when I was sixteen. I stuck a fruit knife in his thigh. I can defend myself."

I was impressed. Maybe I had this kid wrong. There was a fire and a self-possession about her.

"If you can, that's great, but none of us have eyes in the back of our heads. Do you carry Mace?"

"I don't need to spray stuff in men's eyes – I can knee them in the groin."

I fished a small can out of my pocket and threw it at her. She dropped the magazine and caught it deftly. She had good reflexes.

"Hope for the best," I said, as she examined it, "plan for the worst."

"Have you killed anyone?" she asked suddenly, looking at me curiously through intelligent dark eyes.

"The worst," I said, "happens far more often than you would imagine."

I wasn't expecting the worst that evening. I had dressed for a night of upper-class clubbing, in a lightweight Paul & Shark sweater and Henri Lloyd chinos. The key to successful minding is not to look out of place. Missie had gone full Spice Girl for the evening. She had on a tight crop top and Adidas jogging bottoms and her neatly tanned and sculpted midriff was sporting a thin waist-chain. In deference to the British spring, she had a white merino cardigan covering her shoulders, but I could see tiny goosebumps forming on her exposed waist. I shivered as well. Neither of us was acclimatised to the London weather. It had been 22 degrees Celsius in Hong Kong.

We started in the 'Coburg Bar' at the Connaught. I think she had been drinking before we started, because she was already weaving a bit as we went in. She met a couple of girlfriends in the bar, upper-class airheads trying to dress like Princess Diana. I stayed at a respectful distance drinking Perrier water and reading a Robert B. Parker novel I'd brought with me to pass the time. It was going to be a long couple of weeks. Eventually she wandered over to me.

"Come on, minder," she said, giggling and slurring her words. She had already filled her body up to the red line with alcohol. "We're going to 'Pamela's'."

"Are your friends coming with you?"

"They're going to 'Tramp', but I want to go to 'Pamela's'." She stamped a pretty, Airwalk-clad, foot.

We walked down past the Connaught towards Berkeley Square. 'Pamela's' seemed an odd choice for a young Eurasian girl, as had the 'Coburg Bar', but as the hired help I didn't get a vote. The club had been around since the 1970s. It was generally full of trust fund hoorays and older celebrities who liked the sedate décor and treated it like an extra drawing room. I had imagined that Missie would have been more likely to head to a superclub like 'Ministry of Sound'.

We presented ourselves at the door and she was greeted as an old friend by the security guy. We all have places that make us feel comfortable. I took it as a sign she wanted to demonstrate to me that she was in safe territory.

"Is Leighton around?" she asked. The doorman was a wiry individual in a black bomber jacket. He was ex-military. He looked me up and down and tried to appear inscrutable.

"Don't mind him Terry," she said. "He's some paid goon that my father has got trailing after me."

"Evening Mr. Jedburgh," Terry said, shaking my hand. "Will Mr. McAlistair be joining you both this evening?"

"He's safely in Thailand, counting his wife's millions, hacking away at his next thriller," I said. "I'll let him know you were asking after him next time we speak." Terry was an afficionado of McAlistair's literary work.

Missie hadn't expected that. Terry turned back to her and touched her lightly on the arm.

"Leighton's in the bar, Miss. He came in by himself." He smiled as we moved into the club and turned to greet the couple behind us.

"You've been here before," she said.

"A few times. My friend Julian is a member."

"My father bought a membership for me too. He used to party here when he was younger. He danced with my mother here."

"I'm supposed to drive you down to Devon to see her tomorrow."

She started to answer but was distracted when her handbag started beeping. It was tiny and pink and carried high under her left shoulder on a thin strap. She pulled out a Nokia phone and read a message on the screen. I was forgotten as she smiled to herself and tapped a reply out on it. I wandered over to the bar and ordered a Campari and soda. I was damned if I was going to drink Perrier all night.

Missie finished texting, put the phone back in the handbag and rushed past me to embrace a tall black guy at the other end of the bar. I guessed this was Leighton. I watched them and winced as the bitters-with-iron-filings taste of the Campari hit the back of my throat. Leighton was tall and powerfully built with a long stallion-like face. A sprinter maybe, or a footballer, or maybe just a well-heeled drug dealer up from Brixton on an away fixture. Missie had finished pawing him and was now dragging him onto the dance floor like an over-eager puppy in need of walkies.

"She's the daughter of Sir Bernard Li, you know." The accent was so neutral it had to belong to a foreigner. I turned to find a Chinese face beside me. It was attached to a long leggy body wearing a well-tailored pantsuit paired with a V-neck silk blouse that was surprisingly well filled. Another Eurasian, but from different bloodstock to Missie. Scandinavian perhaps? Her symmetrical features were framed by wavy shoulder-length hair that seemed to shimmer under the flashing disco lights. She had large oval eyes which were sparkling back at me like a cat's and she was licking her lips as she drank some exotic syrupy cocktail through a straw.

"Mei Ting," she said. "I write for the *Svenska Dagbladet.*"

"Society pages?"

"Business correspondent."

"Bill Jedburgh. I dabble in financial consulting. I've a good head for figures, usually." This one had high maintenance written all over it.

"I'm writing a profile of Sir Bernard Li," she said. "I was told he comes here sometimes. I was hoping for an introduction."

"I understand he's tucked up in bed. If you give me a card, I can see that he gets it. I work for him."

Her eyes brightened and I realised she must only have been using a fraction of her charm on me before, because my cheeks started to flush.

"I'll give you two," she said, inviting me to journey deeper into her gaze, "so you can keep one yourself." She produced two stiff rectangular boards from a silver card case and wrote on the back of one before handing them to me with a small pulse of pressure on my palm.

"It was nice meeting you, Bill," she purred. Then she turned her back and walked away, leaving me lusting for more. I turned the card over. She had written down her private number and had underlined the word 'private' twice.

I sipped on my drink while I indulged in an erotic reverie. When I recovered my senses, it took me a couple of minutes to realise that I could no longer see Missie on the dance floor. A quick scout round the club led to the realisation that the little minx had given me the slip. She obviously wanted Leighton's company all to herself without Nursie telling her it was time to go back to her own bed. I'd served with enough black soldiers in the Army to know that their reputation for generous endowment was well-deserved.

I rushed back to the door and spoke to Terry.

"Did Missie come past you with Leighton?" I asked.

"Yeah, she was with Leighton. They went that way." He pointed north, back up towards Davies Street.

"Shit, they could have gone anywhere. First night on the job and I've lost her."

"Losing your touch then." I was so angry with myself it took me a moment to realise Terry was smiling. "Leighton always parks his Beemer round the back in Hays Mews," he said. "Turn first left then left again. It's a blue Seven Series."

"Thanks, Terry," I said, and thrust a tenner into his grateful fist.

I took off after them, turning the corner into Hill Street and then zigzagging sharp left past drunken couples spilling out of a pub called the 'Coach & Horses'. I slowed my pace, because I could see Leighton and Missie ahead of me silhouetted by a streetlamp. They were walking along holding hands, but Missie was pulling away from him and now he had hold of her wrist and was forcing her towards him. It looked like he was getting too fresh too quickly for Missie's liking. I increased my pace. Leighton had pulled Missie towards him and she was struggling in his arms. She was in danger of getting something she hadn't voted for. I saw her try to turn to throw him. She obviously had some basic martial arts training, but he was far too big for her to get any purchase. Plus, she was blind drunk.

"Oi!" I yelled, in approved cockney geezer fashion, "the Lady's not interested."

He turned towards me and raised himself up to his full height. He was still clutching Missie, holding her under the arms and pulling her off the ground as she wriggled to get free. She had the look of a toddler being stopped from slapping a much older brother.

"Fuck off home," he said, with the arrogance of a big man who was used to getting his way. "Not your fight."

"It very much is my fight," I said, and moved towards him. I couldn't make a frontal assault because he was using Missie as a human shield. But we were effectively in a back alley and there was a metal dumpster, overflowing with rubbish, beside a wooden garage door to my left. It was on large rubber castors so I spun it out into the roadway with my left hand and, as it gathered momentum, I pushed it towards him, running behind as fast as I could. With about five yards to go, I launched it and stood back. The road was part-cobbled and it careered off on a diagonal towards Leighton and his car. He jumped out of the way, taking Missie with him, but the dumpster kept going and clattered against the bonnet.

There was an ugly, metallic scraping sound and then its motion was diverted back out into the road by the wing mirror which snapped off and fell to the ground in a lazy arc.

"You bastard," Leighton snarled. Hell hath no fury like that when you come between a black man and his motor. He flung Missie aside and she fell backwards onto the cobbles.

He was angry now, and he thought he could take me. Exactly the kind of situation that *Wing Chun* kung fu is designed for. They say all martial arts are about using the energy of your opponent against them, and the more mad, unfocused energy your opponent has, the more it hurts them.

He was off balance before he reached me. My shoulder throw made him even more so. My knee winded him. And a vicious kick in the jaw - that owed more to the playing fields of my boarding school than the elegant moves my *Sifu* taught me in Hong Kong – put him down and out.

I made sure Missie was OK and sat her behind me to recover her breath well out of his way. Then I bent down beside him and put my knee on his cheek. I had a vicious little Mikov flick-knife, a Czech cold-war veteran that I routinely kept on me for occasions like this. I casually inserted the point into his nostril.

"Leighton, Leighton," I said. "You need to learn when 'No,' means 'No'. Now I could mark you externally with this, but I'd prefer not to. You're a fine-looking man and I'm sure that the women wouldn't find you quite as attractive afterwards. Just stick to the ones that are willing in future." He wore the look of a man who knew when he was comprehensively beaten now, so I continued: "Just nod your head to indicate that you're going to leave Missie alone from now on, and then we can all go home and get on with our lives."

He glared at me, then slowly and painfully nodded his head – my knee on his cheek wasn't making it easy.

"And I think an apology is in order."

"Sorry," he gasped it up reluctantly.

I helped Missie up and held her hand as we walked back up towards Berkeley Square. She clutched me tight for support. She was flushed, and the events of the night seemed to have shaken her sober.

"I'm such an idiot, Bill," she said. "Thank you."

10

"I've told Daddy that we're taking the E-type," Missie announced as she swept into breakfast the following day. "After last night, I think you've earned it."

I was eating granola, reading the *Shooting Times* and trying to decide whether I would prefer a pair of Boss side-by-sides or Beretta EELLs. Johnny Aston swore by his Boss, but he was an old school, hand-made, traditional kind of pirate, whereas the over-and-under Italians were precision-made and yet still beautiful.

With that decision taken, I moved on to consider the Jaguar. If it were my own money, my Beretta logic would have led me to purchase instead an early Porsche 911, or a Ferrari GT 250, but it wasn't my money and who wouldn't jump at the chance to drive one of the sexiest cars ever made?

I was both delighted and disappointed to discover, when I visited the garage in the mews behind the house, that Daddy's E-Type was a Series 2. Disappointed because it had the six-cylinder 4.2 litre engine rather than the completely over the top six-litre V12 of the Series 3. Pleased, because the Series 2 displayed, in my opinion, the most beautiful lines of all the E-types and we had a fighting chance of making it to Devon on a single tank of petrol.

I hadn't been to Devon since I was a subaltern, when I had travelled down in a Mini with a dodgy carburettor to visit my girlfriend at her parents' house. I took a quick look at the map and decided that only one route would do in an open-top sports car:

"We're not taking the M4," I said.

"Whatever," Missie replied.

I took the A3 out of London and within an hour, after a brief blast along the motorway, we found ourselves on the A303. The engine alternately growled and purred beneath the long bonnet and Missie sank back into the leather seat alongside me and idly rested her right hand on my left thigh. I manoeuvred the transmission deftly up and down through the gears as we ate up the hills between Winchester and our destination, overtaking where I could the slower wagons and cars. It was a slightly awkward driving position, with the gearstick too far back behind my elbow, but the surge of power when I changed down and gunned the accelerator, kicked us beyond Stonehenge and onwards toward the West Country.

Missie was asleep – still recovering from the after-effects of the previous night – when we surged up the A38 over Haldon Hill and turned off beside Exeter racecourse. I filled the tank up at the petrol station opposite and nudged her awake to navigate the narrow country lanes. We took our lives into our hands, almost able to touch the hedgerows on both sides of the Jaguar, as we swept down past the Belvedere and steered a zigzag course across the Teign Valley that eventually led us to a low A-frame wattle-and-daub manor house on the edge of Dartmoor.

"Don't judge my mother too harshly," Missie said as we pulled up outside, touching my arm. "She's still living in the Sixties."

In the Sixties, Missie's mother, The Honourable Catriona Mountfleming, must have been one of the most beautiful women in Britain, because thirty years later she was still stunning. Her features reflected, I imagined, a life etched in sex and drugs and rock and roll – she had apparently dated two of the Rolling Stones at the same time – but the miles on the odometer only made her look more alluring. She appeared at the door, framed in the glow from the entrance hall behind her, wearing a kaftan that might have been purchased from the Maharishi Yogi. She air-kissed her daughter, whose own beauty was temporarily eclipsed, and turned to me with a smile that could have launched a thousand E-types.

"Come in Bill. I've made a light supper for us. Tony is painting in his studio," she said, breathlessly. "When he's like this we can't disturb him."

We ate a simple meal at a long oak table in the kitchen. She sat, whether artlessly or by design, in front of a full-size picture of herself by Lucien Freud, which showed her reclining naked on a chaise longue.

"You've grown," she said to Missie as we moved on to cheese and biscuits and a third or fourth glass of rustic red wine.

"I'm the same height as the last time you saw me, Mummy," Missie replied.

"Really," she said. "You must have shrunk in my memory. How old are you now?"

"Twenty-five," Missie said, hurt that she couldn't remember. Her mother was quiet for a moment.

"By the time I was your age I had slept with Michael Caine, Sean Connery and Omar Sharif," she said finally.

"And I have kept my dignity," Missie replied.

At the end of the meal, after a mug of herbal tea, Catriona dismissed me:

"Thank you, Mr. Jedburgh. Now, I need to speak with my daughter alone."

But first she showed me across a courtyard to an upstairs room in an old brick outbuilding, decorated with portraits of my hostess from the pages of Vogue and Tatler. Next door was a wooden barn from which electric light escaped into the darkness of a Dartmoor evening. I peeked in through a gap in the barn doors and saw a man in a carmine-red dressing gown and wellington boots, throwing paint at an easel. He could not have been a day under eighty and yet he was wiry and energetic, stalking up and down his studio like an animal predator. If there was a meaning to the image on the canvas, I could not divine it.

"My husband, Anthony, paints until all hours," she said. "I hope he doesn't disturb you." She laid her hand on my forearm as she said it.

I folded my clothes neatly on the chair beside the bed – a habit learned in childhood and impossible to unlearn – and lay back on it. I picked up the Robert Parker novel, but was unable to focus properly on the words. I tried to count the beams but couldn't get past seven. The wind rose in gusts over the moor outside and whistled through holes in the roof. My imagination conjured huge spectral hounds and victims dragged into the Great Grimpen Mire. Eventually the nightmare visions subsided and I drifted off into a deep sleep.

I woke later, unsure of the time, as the smell of jasmine drifted over me and I felt a gentle hand shaking my arm. I looked up to see Catriona Mountfleming floating above me. She put her fingers to her lips and the kaftan fell to the ground, revealing a pair of breasts still upright and thrusting. She knelt beside me, felt beneath the covers and grasped my manhood in her hand, which responded lazily to her touch. She bent her head to mine and kissed my cheek.

"Embrace it," she instructed.

Before I could suggest otherwise, she had thrown the bedclothes aside and was straddled on top of me, knees pressing into my sides, her strong, lithe, body ranging up and down over a compliant victim. I couldn't help myself, grasping her around the waist and moving my body to meet her until I came in a shudder deep inside her. An anguished moan started from low within her body and finally emerged in a rush of released tension.

She lay down beside me, pulled the covers over us both, and we embraced. I dozed again.

I was woken for a second time by the sputter of a match and the smell of sulphur and tobacco. The tip of a cigarette glowed beside me and smoke cascaded in waves from her pursed lips. When she saw that I was awake she proffered it to me.

"A filthy habit," she said.

"I gave it up a couple of years ago," I said, taking a drag nevertheless. It coated my mouth in a sticky menthol taste. "I smoke cigars after a good dinner."

She snuggled into the nook of my armpit and ran the fingers of her left hand through my chest hair.

"Thank you," she said.

"Did I have a choice?"

"Think of it as an after-dinner mint. Sweet, indulgent and too insignificant to be remembered the following day."

"Would Tony think that?" I asked, imagining the man I had seen through a gap in the barn door hard at work with his oil-paints.

"We have an open marriage," she said, dragging deep on the cigarette and seeding the gloom above us with menthol clouds.

"Did you sleep with other men when you were married to Sir Bernard?" I asked, curious to learn more about my employer.

"Not intentionally," she said. "But when you move as the spirit dictates, things happen as they will."

I rolled over onto my front and propped myself up on my elbows, nuzzling my cheek against her breast.

"Bernard was a force of nature," she continued. I caught an electric flash of the younger Catriona as she delved into her memories. "I was on a photo-shoot in the South of France with David Bailey. This sleek, phallic, powerboat was roaring up and down behind us. The pilot didn't seem to care if he mowed down swimmers, pleasure boats or yachts. But he avoided them all. I found the man's arrogance intoxicating."

"Missie seems to struggle with him as a father," I observed.

"He can be a brutal man," she said. "I would not knowingly have made an enemy of him if he hadn't lifted his hand to me."

"Is he a good businessman?"

"I have no idea what that means." She stubbed the cigarette out on the floor and encouraged me to enter her again. I found myself responding despite myself. Here, in the Devon gloaming, she was like some elemental goddess and I was powerless to resist.

As we lay gasping for breath afterwards, she resumed her commentary on Sir Bernard:

"I had a lover, a kind man. We met on the set of a movie. Bernard was working all hours, building his business. Gordon was there for me when I needed him. One night he drove home from the studio and, if the police report is to be believed, drove straight into a tree. I know that Bernard had him killed."

"That's quite an allegation."

"Years later, and quite by accident, I slept with the man who cut his brake pipes. He confessed to me while I pleasured him that Bernard had paid him a thousand pounds."

I lay quiet beside her. I literally didn't know what to say. Some minutes later she got up, refastened her kaftan about herself and silently left the room.

When I awoke, sunlight filled the room and Missie was standing over me, dressed in a white T-shirt and jeans.

"It's lunchtime, minder," she said. "We both missed breakfast and I'm hungry."

11

Outside in the stackyard, once I had dressed, we found Anthony Wolf-Madden, Missie's stepfather, wearing a pair of faded blue overalls and cleaning paintbrushes under a standpipe tap. He permitted Missie to kiss him on the cheek while he was fussing over the tools of his trade.

"Bill and I are going for lunch, Tony," she said. "I thought we might drive up to the 'Rock Inn'."

"If you see Ivor Swann up there," he said, colouring in rage like a thunderstorm from a clear sky, "tell him I will whip his hide if his dogs get into our field again. Worse than foxes they are. I'll shoot the next one I see."

He swung his arms, pointing the brushes like he was sighting a shotgun, taking an imaginary potshot at an innocent pigeon flying overhead. Then calmly resumed his cleaning.

"Did he mean what he said?" I asked, as we walked to the E-type.

"He supposedly had a terrible temper as a young man," she said. "Mummy told me they were once banned from a drinking den in Soho called 'The Colony Club' after he started throwing metal ashtrays at the owner. The man's offence was saying that Francis Bacon was a better painter. I asked him once if the story was true and he said: 'Now the old fraud is dead, I'm definitely the better painter'."

We motored up on to the top of the moor and drove past small herds of the famous ponies. It had rained overnight, leaving the kind of sharp, clear spring day I remembered from army exercises on Salisbury Plain. As we reached the top of the hill The Teign Valley was spread below us, but I couldn't make out the Torbay coast beyond because of a haze in the distance.

The 'Rock Inn' was in a village below a granite outcrop called Haytor, which presumably gave the pub its name. It was mid-afternoon and we parked in a public car park on the moor and walked back down the slope towards the village. The E-type looked incongruous beside a couple of Land Rovers and a yellow Fiat Punto held together by binder twine. One of the Land Rovers had a "Re-elect Giles Guedella" poster taped to the outside. A cheerful smiling redhead beamed out from the photograph. Someone had added a thin pencil moustache to it. Someone else had traced the outline of a cock and balls in the dirt on the tailgate and written 'lick me cleen'. It was amusing to see that British educational standards hadn't improved much since I was last in the country.

"Is he the local MP?" I asked Missie.

"Yes," she said. "Mummy hates him. She's a Liberal Democrat. Would screw Paddy Ashdown in a heartbeat."

I didn't recognise the name but assumed Ashdown was the leading rock star in liberal politics. "Does Guedella know your father?" I said, seeing an opening.

"Daddy knows all the Tories. Hasn't forgiven them for getting rid of Mrs. Thatcher. He worshipped her. But he likes Giles, I think he sees him as a kindred spirit."

"And you?"

"I just can't see his ponytail without laughing. He looks like a carthorse."

Haytor Rock was deserted, apart from a solitary rambler sitting at the top of the cliffs. He was eating his lunch and observing the view through a pair of binoculars. He had a flat cap on his head but there was something vaguely familiar about the way he held himself. Maybe he was ex-army, or maybe I had just spent enough time in similar positions over the years and recognised a kindred spirit.

When we entered the Rock Inn, the first person we saw, minus an inked-in moustache, was Giles Guedella. He had just finished lunch with a small balding man who either had several days' stubble or a very pronounced five o'clock shadow. Guedella was paying at the bar while his lunch companion was buttoning up a Burberry trench coat and putting on a Harris tweed hat that made him look like Inspector Clouseau.

Guedella smiled when he saw her: "Missie Li, how is Sir Bernard?"

"As boring as ever Giles. He has packed me off to see Mummy. This is my…" she decided to choose her words carefully, "…friend, Bill."

Guedella looked me up and down, trying to work out if we were an item. Missie realised and burst out laughing.

"Not that sort of a friend, silly. He works for my father."

Both the men seemed to take an interest at that and I saw a glance pass between them.

"Missie is being disingenuous," I said. "I'm a security consultant. I used to be in the Royal Hong Kong Police. Sir Bernard has asked me to keep a protective eye on Missie. I haven't been in the UK for a while and it seemed a nice excuse for a change of scenery."

"Hong Kong, eh?" Guedella said. "What's your view on the handover?"

"Honestly, sir," I said, "I don't understand why we are throwing away the most vibrant part of the British economy. If it was the French they would have stuck a couple of Hong Kong MPs in the House of Commons and told the Chinese to go screw themselves."

"Couldn't agree more," he said. "I've got operations there myself. Sold a lot of kit to TVB and RTHK over the years."

"I've moved to Singapore now," I said. "I think it's a safer bet."

"Yes, TCS are a customer of mine as well. I like the people there. I don't suppose you've met a man called Larry Lim in the Government Procurement Office?" he asked casually.

"Can't say I have," I lied.

"Came to see me in my offices. Told me the Government wanted to bug its own ministers as part of an anti-corruption drive. We have the kit these days to do that, you know."

"It sounds fascinating," I said, genuinely intrigued and grabbing what felt like an opportunity. "I'd be interested to see what you've got, given my profession. I do a bit of work for some large American corporations." That wasn't entirely true – the CEO of a pharmaceutical company had hired me to stop his mistress blackmailing him – but I thought it might make Guedella keen to show me his kit.

"Well come down to the factory after lunch. Missie knows how to find us."

He stood up: "I'll leave you to have your lunch before they stop serving. Come on, Abe, if we leave now I can just get you to the station in time to catch the Paddington train."

"In that lousy Land Rover we'll be lucky to make the night sleeper," his companion grumbled in an American accent as they ducked out of the bar.

"Will it be boring for you if we go to see SatBox?" I asked as we looked at the menu and I sipped on a pint of Reel Ale, the excellent local bitter. Missie had a small white wine in front of her.

"He didn't say what his company was called," Missie said. I was starting to understand she was sharp as a whip.

"I do read the business section of the newspapers occasionally," I said, "not just the sports pages. I'm on first name terms with the Business Correspondent of the *Svenska Dagsbladet*, I'll have you know."

"Mei Ting? I'd be careful if I were you. I hear she eats poor saps like you for breakfast," she said. "The morning after."

"Sounds like you read the business sections as well."

"If your inheritance was linked to the stock market, you might too," she observed accurately. "I've spoken to Mei Ting at 'Pamela's' in the past. I got the impression she was stalking Daddy. I don't like her. Call it women's intuition."

"Or jealousy?"

"Why do all you men think with your dicks?" she said. "It never ends well."

"Are you worried that you'll end up with a stepmother who is young enough to be your sister?"

She snorted: "My father has a mistress. She's foreign, and exotic and he's been in bed with her since 1982." And she left it at that.

We walked back to the car after an excellent pub lunch. Both Land Rovers were gone and Haytor Rock was deserted. I let Missie drive the E-type as she knew the way. She might have looked tiny in its bucket seat, but she drove the powerful machine well and in about thirty minutes we were pulling up outside a low complex of factory buildings on the edge of the A38 in a place called Heathfield.

After negotiating a gatehouse and security barrier - the site was protected by a fenced perimeter topped by razor wire – we pulled up beside Guedella's Land Rover, which was parked in front of a two-storey Victorian office building. It was faced in brick and tile and seemed out of place beside the modern buildings around it.

An attractive blonde girl showed us up to Guedella's corner office, with a view in the distance of Haytor above us on the moor. On the other side was a picture of the Wailing Wall in Jerusalem.

"My great-grandfather painted that," he said, when he saw me admiring it. "He worked with Moses Montefiore building the Mazkeret Moshe community in Jerusalem."

"How do you come to be based in Devon?"

"My mother's family. It's funny, you know. *The Sun* christened me the Red Fox, but they may not have realised her maiden name was Fox. They were bankers in Newton Abbot. Owned the fireplace business that used to occupy this site until it went bust. This was the office block. Everything else was knocked down."

He sat back in this chair and sipped tea from a large ceramic mug with 'RE-ELECT THE RED FOX' on the side.

"How did you get started?" I asked.

"I was a television reporter," he said warming to the task of expounding his personal history. It was the favourite topic of most self-made men. "Local news in Bristol but I was always fascinated by the equipment side of the business, so I started a company supplying kit to television stations. When direct broadcast by satellite began, we chose the right side of the battle. My partner wanted to develop D-MAC kit for BSB. It was technologically more satisfying, but I knew Rupert Murdoch and Sky had the better and cheaper business plan. So we developed an analogue set-top box instead and the profits from that enabled us to float."

He pointed to a lucite block on the desk in which a toy rocket was embedded. I recognised the Burcotts and SatBox logos on it.

"The really clever decision though," he said, "came later. When BSB merged with Sky and we bought their D-MAC IP."

I think he sensed I didn't understand a word of what he was saying, so he searched in his head for a way to dumb it down for me, then started again:

"BSB played by the rules. The Government wanted a high definition digital system that used a new unproven technology called D-MAC and forced BSB to use it to get a licence, so they were late and over budget. Rupert Murdoch saw an opportunity to launch a system using the same analogue system as your television at home on commercial satellites and ended up with a cheaper product that launched thirteen months before BSB and ate its lunch."

"Clever man," I said.

"A cheat," Missie countered languidly from the corner of the room where she was lounging sideways in a leather armchair.

"Why not compromise on him being a clever cheat," Guedella said. "But it became a very profitable one from SatBox's perspective. The real jewel for us, however, was D-MAC. We modified it for use on BSB's old satellites and ended up with a high quality, encrypted, system that corporate customers loved. They could communicate around the world without their competitors listening in. From there it was an easy decision to develop it for use on our own low earth orbit satellite system."

"I'm assuming corporations pay top dollar for that privacy?"

"Absolutely," he said. "And not just corporations. Even our own government is interested in purchasing it."

"And the Chinese or the Russians? How would you feel about them using it?"

Guedella's face darkened, just for a second, then recovered its equanimity.

"We're capitalists," he said. "If HMG tell us we can sell it in a market, we sell it. But I have to say," he continued, "I'm a patriot. I used to work in Moscow. Did some favours for our lads in MI6. I'm not allowed to go back, even after the fall of Communism."

"And of course, you're an MP now."

"Well, given the way the polls are going, I might not be for much longer."

"I'd have thought this was a pretty safe seat?"

"Safe?" Guedella laughed. "This is Lib Dem territory down here. I got in last time because the vote was split. I may not be so lucky this time round. On top of everything else we have the Referendum Party down here, but luckily my anti-EU stance means they've agreed not to stand."

"What will you do if you lose?"

"I doubt I'd stand again, but I'm not intending to lose. The last five years have been pretty toxic, but I reckon the Conservative Party that emerges afterwards might be a bit of a happier ship. Anyway," he said, looking at the clock above the fireplace, "you didn't come here to talk politics, you came to see round the factory. I'll get Charlie to take you round while I entertain Missie here. We both play Mah Jong."

There was a rap on the door and I was introduced to Charles Westaway, Guedella's Operations Director. He was a bluff ex-marine with a bushy moustache and an infectious love of manufacturing.

"Do I show him Q Block, Giles?" he asked as we were getting ready to leave. Guedella thought for a moment.

"I have signed the Official Secrets Act," I said, "if that helps. I was in the army as well as the police."

"OK then Charlie, but not too close," he said finally. We left Guedella and Missie to the sound of rattling tiles and headed over to the factory.

I had to suit up in paper overalls, shoe covers and a hair net before being allowed into the main production area, which was a clean environment. I occasionally dressed like this in my own profession when I didn't want to leave trace forensic evidence.

"The room is under positive pressure," Charlie explained. "That helps to keep it dust-free. We make some of our own specialist chips here and contamination is a real problem. If they end up in space and malfunction, we are totally screwed."

I'd been round a few factories in Asia in my time – I occasionally undertook more conventional security consultancy – and this looked as efficient as any factory I had seen. There was the usual contrast between the highly automated robot sections, populated only with a few supervisors carrying clipboards, and the manual assembly and packing lines which still consisted of troupes of largely female workers soldering together components or putting the finished articles into cardboard boxes. The only difference here was they were chattering to each other in a Devonian burr rather than Chinese or Vietnamese.

We came out of the factory and headed over to the 'Lucius Fox Building' – apparently named after Guedella's great-grandfather - and colloquially known to the employees as 'Q Block'.

"So I'm guessing this is where you keep the prototypes of the laser death cannons," I said.

"Not quite so exciting," Charlie replied. "But we do have an Intel Paragon XP/S in the basement, which until recently was the fastest supercomputer in the world."

"That's a lot of computing power, I'm guessing."

"Absolutely. And we've used it to design and operate some amazing products. The key problem in satellite communications is how you do it so that it's fast and reliable. Motorola have gone for a system in which all the satellites communicate with each other in space, like a mesh. Giles thinks that's barmy because an equipment failure up there could render the system useless. We are relying on ground stations – and we already have them all round the globe – and really fast and high-quality encryption. That way we can keep the moving parts in the satellites to a minimum."

He showed me round, proudly, but there were only so many people looking at computer screens you could take. Mission control, with a large map of the satellites in orbit, was interesting, but Charlie had to admit it was using simulated data because the first satellite launch was still a couple of months off.

By the time we got back to Guedella's office, Missie was smiling broadly. Guedella admitted he had been comprehensively beaten and he was handing over a £50 note. That girl was a bit of a dark horse.

"Thank you for having me shown around, sir," I said, shaking his hand. "It has been highly educational."

"I'm glad you think so," he said. "I've enjoyed meeting you. Perhaps we'll see each other again in London. It's always a pleasure to spend time with Missie."

"Give your father my love," he said, hugging her.

Missie drove the E-type back to the house, so I could think.

If I'd been driving, I might have missed it. Parked a hundred yards away, facing the entrance to SatBox, was the same Land Rover I had seen in the car park at Haytor. Or at least I could swear it was the same, except for the fact its number plate was different. Well, I supposed in a county like Devon, there must be a lot of Land Rovers. I turned to look into it as we went past. The man in the passenger seat averted his face. But not before I had registered a distinctive scar on his neck.

12

I was summoned to see Sir Bernard when we got back from Devon the following morning. He had a large office on the first floor of the house in Upper Brook Street. He sat behind an enormous white maple desk, in front of a large Luis Chan painting of a cityscape that bore no direct relationship to Hong Kong but instantly evoked it for anyone who was in touch with its soul. He was elegantly clad in a Prince of Wales check suit and a flamboyant Hermès tie.

"How was Devon?" he asked curtly. "How was my… …ex-wife?"

"She seems to be living a rural idyll with her painter."

"I expect she tried to seduce you," he said coldly. "She tries that with most men."

Given what Catriona Mountfleming had told me about her ex-husband's murderous side, I didn't reply.

"I understand there was some trouble before you left. Outside Pamela's."

"You're well-informed."

"I should have heard it from you."

"Security consultants are like priests. It was nothing I couldn't handle and I judged it to have no wider import."

He slammed his right palm down hard on the desk. "That is not for you to decide, Jedburgh," he said, raising his voice. "There are matters in play here that you do not understand."

"If there are things I need to know, sir, then I cannot protect your daughter, or," I said pointedly, "you, if you won't take me into your confidence."

The boiling milk subsided as quickly as it had risen and Sir Bernard was once again the inscrutable oriental.

"You have a point. Maybe things will be a little clearer after this afternoon," he said. "I have decided to appoint Melissa to the board of Foreign & Exotic. I am fed up with her refusal to do anything other than shop and party. You will escort her and ensure she is at the board meeting no later than 2.30 p.m."

I was dismissed. I went in search of Missie to deliver Sir Bernard's ultimatum. I couldn't find her downstairs so I wandered back up a couple of flights and knocked on her bedroom door, which was ajar.

"Who is it?"

"Bill," I said, "I've just spoken to your father."

"You'd better come in," she said.

I don't know what I had expected of her bedroom. A cascade of pink chiffon perhaps, or a goth den with painted black walls. What I saw surprised me. It was a large room with double windows facing on to Upper Brook Street. It was painted a neutral grey, very stylishly, and had exposed, sanded floorboards. There was an austere four-foot double bed against one wall with a cast-iron bedstead, its simplicity relieved only by highly-polished brass bedknobs in each corner. A yoga mat was laid out in front of it and in between the windows was an IKEA desk on which an Apple Macintosh had pride of place. One side-wall was taken up with bookshelves. I glanced at the titles. They ranged from well-thumbed paperbacks of classic novels like Dickens and Trollope, probably a relic of her schooldays, to weighty economics tomes. I had read this woman all wrong. She wasn't an airhead at all. What was going on?

Missie was curled up in pyjamas in a comfy armchair, reading what looked like a set of accounts. She had showered since our return and her hair was damp. The contours of her firm breasts nestled beneath the stiff sea-island cotton, twin nipple peaks just visible through the cloth.

"Does your father ever come in here?" I asked, curiously.

"He doesn't deign to speak to me alone," she said. I couldn't understand precisely the rift between these two proud people. Perhaps he didn't wish to be reminded of the wife who had betrayed him. Perhaps she resented him because he had chosen Foreign & Exotic over a normal family life. Either way, this estrangement diminished them both.

"He plans to appoint you to the board of Foreign & Exotic," I said, simply. "We have to be in Canary Wharf by 2.30 p.m."

I saw a range of emotions sweep over her face. Excitement, then reflection, then anger.

"He doesn't want to appoint me. He wants to control me," she said. "This is another of his tricks. I won't have it."

"You don't have an option," I said. "If I have to put you over my shoulder and carry you to the Bentley I will."

"It would probably turn you on," she said viciously. Then she smiled. "It might even turn me on." She stood up suddenly and padded over towards me. She slipped her hands around my waist and arched herself upwards on tip-toes to whisper in my ear. I could smell her perfume, and beneath it her animal musk.

"OK, Mister Minder," she whispered, "but for you, not him." Then she kissed me lightly on the cheek, and I was dismissed.

The Missie Li that presented herself, exactly on time, at the Bentley bore no relationship to the woman who had kissed me on the cheek. Her hair was up in a beehive and she was wearing a thigh length pink lamé dress with a halter-top and white platform shoes. She was holding an Adidas gym bag in her hand which she passed to the driver to put in the boot. She refused to talk to me on the journey. She was reading one of Lola Beaulieu's novels – it had a lurid lavender cover and was entitled 'Puff'. I couldn't even imagine what it would be about, or why anyone would want to read it.

The offices of Kowloon Junk were in Covent Garden, above their flagship store, but the corporate headquarters of Foreign and Exotic were in Canary Wharf, the tallest building in London. They occupied the 48th floor –

another financial coup for Sir Bernard, as he had bought the lease when the original builders had filed for bankruptcy and was paying a fraction of its real worth. From the window of the F&E reception area I could see the City of London spread across the horizon and just make out the black upright of the Nat West Tower below me in the far distance.

I remembered this area when it had been empty and derelict. I used to come out to the East End with my mates as a teenager to a couple of stripper pubs where we would drink too much and stick pound notes in a pint glass when the girl came round afterwards, after smearing our ties and glasses in her juice. Now the only juice you'd find around here would be wheatgrass, I figured.

As I took in the manicured squares and building sites below with the River Thames alongside, snaking its way through the middle of London like an electric cable, a man I vaguely recognised came through the door from the elevator bank. He was tall and rangy, wearing a suit that had been made for him, but had seen better days. His neck was slightly too long for his body, and he looked uncannily like a heron, especially as what remained of his thinning white hair had been combed backwards behind his ears and needed a trim. He gave me a look that said he too thought we had met before.

"I know you," he said. "I'm afraid as I get older, my wits desert me." It was the slight Irish lilt lurking behind his upper-class received pronunciation that triggered my memory.

"You're Thomas Field," I said. "The Earl of Newbridge. My name is Bill Jedburgh. I used to date your daughter."

"My daughter?" he asked, still confused. "Which one? I have three you know."

"It was me, dad," a voice behind me said. "Hello Bill." I shut my eyes and counted to five before opening them again.

"Hello, Flick," I said. "I wasn't expecting to meet you again."

I turned to face the woman behind the voice. She was older now, as was I, but still had the slightly bloodless features and straight blonde hair that I had once found devastatingly attractive. She was wearing a blue Alice band and a formal white blouse over a plaid skirt in what might have been the Newbridge tartan, except that I knew the Irish didn't go in for such things. She had on brown leather flats, which meant our eyes were on the same level. She still reminded me of a horse.

Flick smiled at me nervously. We had been together most of the time I was at Sandhurst and in the army, but it hadn't ended well. She was the reason I had run away to Hong Kong. We had been coming back from a horse trial in Gloucestershire and it had finally dawned that she loved her thoroughbred stallion more than me. There was no denying that Starlord was better hung, but as Flick's idea of a good time in bed was a box of chocolates and a face mask, perhaps she hadn't noticed that.

My friend McAlastair had recently applied for a job as a Probationary Inspector in the RHKP and been boring me silly about how Hong Kong was a land of milk, honey and wall-to-wall Asian totty. There and then, I decided to apply. I asked Flick to stop the horsebox and got out to hitch-hike back to barracks. A month later I was on a plane to Kai Tak and the rest was history. We hadn't spoken since, but I had received a care package several months later, without a note, containing a few items I had left in her flat.

When she spoke, all that seemed to be in the past: "Bill, it's lovely to see you again," she said. "I realise now I wasn't very nice to you. I was definitely immature. I don't think I accepted the fact that I was an adult until I turned thirty."

"I don't think I knew what I wanted then either," I said. "I'm sorry if I hurt you. I don't think I was cut out for marriage or monogamy." No need to tell her about the hundreds of one-night-stands and paid-for dalliances since leaving her. "What about you, are you married?"

"No," she said, wistfully. "But I have hopes. Perhaps we can grab a drink afterwards and I can tell you about him." She reached out and touched my arm. There was no electric spark for either of us, I could tell. Maybe we could somehow be friends, for old time's sake.

"I'd like that," I said. "I'm working for Sir Bernard as a consultant, staying at his house."

"Then 'Snap!'" she said, and I heard that slightly nasal bray in the back of her throat that had irritated me throughout our relationship. "He's my client too. I'm in City PR. That's why I'm here. Dad is the chairman of Foreign & Exotic – aren't you, Dad?" she said turning towards him and slightly raising her voice. He looked at her absent-mindedly.

"Felicity, dear girl, I think they're calling for us to come in. The board meeting is about to start."

13

There were seats for eight people formally arranged around the board room table, with half a dozen chairs by the window for hangers-on such as Flick and I. Thomas Field took his seat at the head of the table with Sir Bernard on his right. Missie sat down as far from him as was physically possible. The other directors were the usual mix of executives in cheap M&S suits and a couple of non-executive grandees in the Savile Row variety. There were no women at the table except for Missie.

The Earl of Newbridge cleared his throat.

"Shall we begin then? I'd like to welcome Melissa Li to the meeting and I believe Sir Bernard wishes to introduce this first item on the agenda."

"The time has come for change," Sir Bernard began quietly. "Melissa will be the next generation of Li to be involved with Foreign & Exotic. She is old enough now to start her apprenticeship."

It was clear this board was his creature. There was no voice raised against the proposal despite the strange spectacle of a Chinese Emma Bunton wannabe resting her platform boots on the table. She'd decided to taunt him. When he proposed her appointment to the Board, all the directors raised their right hands in agreement, even though if I could see her knickers, then so could half the room.

Things went from bad to worse. As the agenda was proposed by Newbridge and her father spoke, she raised her voice, interrupted him and stared pointedly out of the window. Finally she put on a pair of Walkman headphones and started singing 'I'm a Barbie Girl, in a Barbie world' at the top of her voice until eventually her father cracked. He stormed round to her side of the table and slapped her hard on the cheek. Her singing stopped and the Walkman flew from her lap pulling the headphones with it and landed with a crash on the floor.

"Take her home," he said to me. "I have had enough." His face was beetroot red.

She was whimpering. He had hit her with such force that the pins in her beehive had sprung loose and hair was cascading down her back. I gathered her up and carried her out of the door. The bovine board continued to ignore the drama unfolding around them. The last thing I heard as I ushered her out was Thomas Field saying: "And now we turn to Project Hatstand. I'd like to remind you that this is highly confidential as it is subject to the Takeover Code. Our brokers have got an update for us..."

And then I was beyond the doorway.

I sat in the back of the car with Missie. "Take us home," I said to the driver, but she countermanded me: "Take me to Wembley instead, Baker," she said. She knew his name. I hadn't even introduced myself or asked him what it was.

Eventually, after crawling round the North Circular, we pulled up outside a church hall somewhere between the foot of the M1 and Wembley Stadium. She retrieved the holdall from the boot and ran in. I stayed for a minute to talk to the driver.

"Sorry, I should have introduced myself properly. I'm Bill."

"Ray," he said. "And it's Baxter, not Baker. She always gets that wrong." That made me feel better.

"Do you bring her here often?"

"Three or four times a week, when she's in London," he said.

"What do you reckon she does here?"

He shrugged. "I dunno," he said. "She always brings a gym bag. I figured Dancercize?"

What I actually found when I entered the building was a group of mainly Chinese pensioners and a Tai Chi lesson in progress. At the front of the class, leading it, was Missie. She was good. Tai Chi was the acme of internal kung fu. It promoted inner calm and clarity. That Missie was a practitioner helped me make sense of the real woman I had started to discern behind the façade she presented to her father. I stood at the back, resisting the temptation to take part.

There are two main styles of kung fu and thousands of different forms. External, or 'hard', kung fu was practised in the North and internal, or 'soft', kung fu was prevalent in the South of China. My own preferred style,

Wing Chun, sat more or less between the two: soft in philosophy, hard in action.

When the class was over and the last of her students had dispersed, Missie strode over to me, swigging out of a plastic water bottle. She had swapped the pink lamé for loose gym clothes and looked much better for it.

"What's the story, here?" I asked.

"This is where the Li family's history is centred," she said. "Not in Canary Wharf. Did you know that the Li style of *Tai Chi Chu'an* dates back to the 10th Century? It's the most authentic British form of kung fu too, practised here since the 1930s." She scoffed. "If you asked my father about it he wouldn't have a clue."

"Do you want to talk about it over a drink?"

"Wouldn't you rather spar?" she said. "I know you must be a practitioner. What do you favour?"

"*Wing Chun*," I said. "What's the Li family style?"

"*Feng Shou*," she said. "You don't stand a chance. Did you know that Wing Chun was a woman?"

"I may have heard that story," I said.

"Then let's see if you can beat me."

She was still glowing from the class she had taught and completely warmed up, whereas I was stiff from sitting in cars and meetings and still wearing my suit. Missie gave a little giggle as I stripped down to my undershirt and boxers, but I wasn't going to rip a suit while taking her down a peg or two. In my line of work I had to be fit. I had spent hundreds of hours in class practising with my *Sifu* in Hong Kong, but Feng Shou was new to me. I had heard of the Li forms of kung fu and the story of the fourteen year-old Chinese orphan who had learned it from a sailor in Hyde Park in the 1930s and popularized it in the UK. But as I hadn't taken up martial arts until I arrived in Hong Kong, her style was new to me. We circled each other waiting for one of us to make a move, but eventually my testosterone kicked in and I attacked more aggressively. That was a mistake. Her simple, relaxed, style completely bamboozled me. *Feng Shou* was almost entirely defensive and extremely feminine, but occasionally her hands would hit out with tremendous force. Then while I was off-balance she would move in to throw me. It was like violent foreplay. After half an hour of being alternately pummelled and aroused by this fierce, composed, young woman, I accepted I was defeated and stayed down.

"Now we need a drink," I said, breathing hard. Let's go and check whether the Bentley still has its hubcaps."

I asked Ray to drop us on the Edgware Road. I didn't want to risk going back directly to Upper Brook Street in case Sir Bernard confronted her. We chose a Lebanese restaurant called Maroush. I had an urge for barbecued meat and red wine, while Missie stuck to baba ganoush and tabouleh salad with jasmine tea.

"You need to level with me," I said. "You are one of the brightest, most squared away, young women I've met in a long time and yet you've convinced your father that you are a trustafarian airhead. What's going on?"

She dipped a radish in tahini, popped it in her mouth and crunched it.

"If I tell you, you must say nothing to my father," she said.

"Scout's honour," I promised. "And I really was one."

"Be serious," she said, punching my shoulder affectionately. "I am, and I'm starting to trust you."

She took a sip of green liquid from the glass mug and told her story. It had started as a joke. When he split with her mother, Sir Bernard had become a remote and distant father. She had been sent to a Catholic convent near Croydon where she had applied herself diligently and had got top marks. She had subsequently discovered that Sir Bernard had never even bothered to read her school reports, so she had adopted the persona of a spoilt brat in revenge. After a few years it had become the secret identity behind which the serious SuperMissie hid herself.

"I've been doing an MBA at the Judge Institute in Cambridge under an assumed name for the last year and a half," she said. "Daddy hasn't even noticed."

"He has appointed you to the board of Foreign and Exotic," I observed.

"But as a punishment, not because I would make an excellent director," she said. "I am training to be the CEO when he dies. When he realises that, that's when I will be happy."

"It's a bit fucked up," I said. "But I do understand. I just think it's hilarious that he's paying me to defend a woman who doesn't need it." I adopted a mock American accent: "I'm surrendering my badge and my gun."

"No," she said, looking at me seriously through those dark, electric, eyes. "That's where you're wrong. I could have been raped by Leighton and you saved me."

"You're welcome," I said, finishing the bottle of red wine and signalling for another. It was a bottle of '89

Chateau Musar and every bit as good as a second growth Claret at a quarter of the price. "But all you proved was that it's not just men who think with their sexual organs. Plus you were drunk."

"Stay," she said. "I like having you around. Plus, I may have exaggerated to Lizzie how ancient you were. You're quite cute."

"Talking of Lizzie," I said, "what is it people see in her books? You seemed to be enjoying one earlier. Was that part of the secret identity thing?"

"Well, of course I read business books," she said. "But there's precious few examples in them of confident, independent young women succeeding in a man's world. Unless I want to be Anita Roddick or Laura Ashley."

"Who are they?" I asked.

"I rest my case. The women in Lizzie's books are exactly the kind of person I want to be. Smart, sassy and bedded frequently."

"And what kind of company would Foreign and Exotic be if you were the CEO?"

"It wouldn't be wasting its time acquiring satellite companies," she said. I filed that thought away. Clearly not much got past Missie and it was the first definitive indication that Dom and Johnny were right. "If it was left to me," she continued, "we would be opening new boutiques and backing the best British designers. Tony Blair is going to transform people's view of Britain. We are tired of being grey and boring, like John Major. We want to be cool again."

That seemed like a good idea. I thought of my friend Dago, the Anglo-Spanish shoemaker whom I had met in

New York. He and his friend Jimmy Choo would certainly agree.

"You could start your own business," I suggested. "I know a few people."

"That takes money," she said. "And mine's in trust for another two years. But when it does mature, you just wait and see."

I had to admit that, if she did, I'd be prepared to stake a modest proportion of the Reliable Man's pension plan on her succeeding.

14

Sir Bernard's manservant brought me an art deco rotary-dial phone on a long cord. I was reading about the Grand National in the morning papers. It had been delayed for a couple of days because of an IRA bomb threat. When it finally went ahead Johnny Aston's nailed-on favourite had burst a blood vessel and been pulled up. His 'monkey' – five hundred quid – had gone the way of all horseflesh. A 14-1 outsider had won the race. I took that as a good omen, I was usually coming up unnoticed on the rails.

"Miss Field, for you," he said.

"Flick," I said with genuine pleasure, "you tracked me down. Sorry I had to leave early because of the… …unpleasantness. Isn't that what you PR types call it?"

"Well, thank God that hasn't got out," she said. "The City pages are bloody enough as it is. We're spinning Melissa as the new face of F&E but all the tabloids are doing is running pictures of her blind drunk in 'Tramp'."

"I think she will prove them wrong," I said. "Give her some time."

"Well, she hasn't got long." Flick was serious. "The share price is off five per cent this morning. The City forgives a lot, but not when it hits them in the pocket.

Anyway," she continued, brightening, "That wasn't why I rang. I wondered if you were busy for lunch. I have a favour to ask."

"I don't think Missie is planning to go anywhere today. Nursing a hangover. I'm sure I can get away. I'm intrigued."

"It's not for me," she said. "It's for my boyfriend. I told him about you and he's asked if you would meet his boss. He wants you to brief him about Hong Kong."

"As long as he's paying for lunch. But I'm not sure what I can tell him he can't read in the papers?"

"Thanks. Come over and I'll brief you first," she said. "I've booked a restaurant nearby to meet him at."

"Are you still at your father's place in Islington?"

"With property prices as high as they are? Absolutely."

I left a scribbled note for Missie and jumped in a cab, which gave me some thinking time. I had tried to explain to Missie the previous day that her antics would do more harm than good. Flick's comments reinforced that. When we had returned to the house there was no sign of Sir Bernard. He had gone out for dinner and I hit the sack before he returned. Despite his behaviour I think he really loved Missie, he just wasn't emotionally equipped to manage her.

A lot had happened in the last week and I still couldn't fit it all together. Jedburgh's Law of Synchronicity said that things only looked like coincidences when you didn't have the script, and there were far too many coincidences at the moment for my liking. The most disturbing question was why the man with the scar had reappeared on the other side of the world.

I needed a tactical discussion with Dominic Tweddle. This was like a complicated bridge hand and he was the only man I was willing to show my cards to at the moment. Sir Bernard might be a pompous ass, but I had no real reason to betray him or his company's interests. Even if I did find Giles Guedella more engaging, Sir Bernard was the man paying me.

It was a dilemma common to all assassins. Whenever your victim found out you were paid to kill them, they tried to buy you off with more money. That was one reason I never got too close to my targets. Four hundred metres was a safe distance on the whole. But my rule was clear. You don't change horses in mid-race. Why then was I prepared to do it for Dom? That was the answer in itself: because it was Dom. I had known him for so long, and trusted his judgement so implicitly, that I was prepared to contemplate the idea.

Islington and the word 'gentrification' were designed to go hand in hand. Run-down Georgian houses in pretty squares were gradually being converted back from bedsits into the smart townhouses that merchant bankers, lawyers and management consultants needed as they started their families.

Newbridge House occupied a centre position in one of the squares south of the Essex Road. It had seen better days, a bit like its owner. Unlike Upper Brook Street, the only interior design applied had been that each of its chatelaines had added something they liked – generally pale watercolours, china figurines or embroidered fireguards - which sat alongside stuffed animal heads or pictures of dogs playing cards that were more to the taste of their aristocratic husbands.

Flick took me up to the second floor which she had taken over as her private space. Her living room looked over the rear of the house. It was a typical cross-section of London back gardens: some containing pretty flowers, kids' toys and drying clothes, some full of brambles, and buddleia, and abandoned washing machines.

She poured me a cup of tea into delicate Royal Doulton china. She had discarded her City uniform and was wearing a striped sailor top and cream pedal pushers teamed with navy blue slingbacks. Flick was somebody's idea of a perfect girlfriend, just not mine any more.

"So who is this guy you want me to meet?" I asked. "A City grandee worried about his Asian stock portfolio?"

"Not exactly," she said. "Jeff, that's my boyfriend, is in politics. Dad doesn't approve because he's New Labour. He's not in London at the moment because he's campaigning in the Midlands. He's fighting a safe seat in Cannock."

"I didn't know you were interested in politics," I said.

"Tony Blair is wonderful," she gushed. "He lives not far from here and I sometimes see Cherie, his wife, at receptions. She's quite a serious human rights barrister. The Tories have no idea how real people live. I've seen enough of them with their fingers in the till in the City to know that we need to get rid of their sleaze once and for all. Things really will get better once New Labour is in power."

"Well, that doesn't seem too far away now, does it?" I said. "The election is on the first of May, right?"

"And that was precisely Jeff's point when I spoke to him last night. The Hong Kong handover is the first big foreign policy event that they will have to deal with. When I explained who you were, he thought it would make sense for Robin to meet you and it just so happens he's down from Edinburgh today for a meeting of the Shadow Cabinet."

"Robin?" I said. "You'll have to help me out here: I live on the other side of the world now and I'm not up to speed with all the personalities. Missie was talking about Paddy Ashdown the other day and I only worked out from reading the paper this morning that he's the leader of the Lib Dems. When did they stop being just plain Liberals?"

She looked at me like I was an idiot. "Robin Cook," she said. "He's the Shadow Foreign Secretary."

I smiled politely and shrugged.

'Granita' was a Scandinavian's idea of what an Italian restaurant might look like if they had never been to Italy – all light wood and stainless steel. It was long and thin and had a plate glass window overlooking the street which said 'this is where someone comes to be looked at'.

We were offered a glass of Champagne when we sat down and as we clinked glasses, I quipped: "Here's to Champagne Socialism". Flick looked horrified.

"Don't say that in front of Robin," she hissed. "He's a proper socialist. Used to be into nuclear disarmament and stuff like that. He and Gordon Brown, the Shadow Chancellor, are always having arguments about nationalisation."

We were on our second glass when the man finally arrived. It wasn't a startling observation that he looked like a ginger gnome. He had that self-important bustle of the short man that I recognised from time spent guarding politicians and assassinating Thai businessmen.

He arrived with a red-headed woman whom he introduced as his secretary, Gaynor. They looked a little bit too close for just that, but she brought out a notepad and pencil to take notes of the conversation. We sat quietly like a pair of double-dating couples until we had chosen from the menu. Then he started interrogating me over a starter of mussels with lemongrass and coconut liquor and a glass of pinot grigio.

"I'm pleased to be able to speak with you," he said. "I've had briefings from the Foreign Office, but we politicians rarely get a chance to meet people whose view isn't filtered through the prism of diplomacy." He was quiet and measured with a surprisingly refined accent. This was no Clydeside welder.

"The pleasure is mine, sir..." I started to say, but he waved his hand.

"For God's sake man, call me Robin," he said. "I'm not some army officer and even if I am a Right Honourable Privy Councillor that doesn't make me any different from you." For a man who didn't want to make a fuss of it, he seemed keen for me to know that he was one.

"I want to preface my questions," he continued, "by saying that I think that colonies are an anachronism. We were absolutely right to give Hong Kong back to China."

"If Hong Kong is an anachronism," I said, "It's been a very profitable one for Britain. In my opinion we should never have let it go."

"Is that not a little jingoistic?" he asked sharply.

"Anything but," I said. "My view is based on economics as well as fairness to the people I used to police. When the British took over Hong Kong Island the population was 7,500. What Hong Kong has become today is entirely down to the qualities of its six and a half million people and the way that the British have let it develop under our system of justice. The anachronism was not giving the people of Hong Kong self-determination earlier, as we did the Dominions. I think that was a form of racism."

He considered my words, chewing carefully before replying.

"You are probably right about the racism. But in any case, even if I did agree with you that we should have kept Hong Kong, which I do not, it is too late to do anything now."

"On that, Robin," I said, "we both agree."

"I have two main questions for you," he said.

"I can try and answer them, as honestly as I can," I replied. "But if it is a technical question, I may struggle to answer. I am an interested layman at best."

"Don't worry, they are fairly broad," he said. "The first is: do you think we can trust the Chinese to adhere to their treaty obligations?"

I disguised my snort quite well by pretending that the Champagne had gone down the wrong way.

"We can always trust them to do exactly what is in their best interests," I said.

"And will that be contrary to British interests and those of the inhabitants of Hong Kong?" he asked, which was a sensible follow-up question.

"In the short term, not necessarily," I said. "I reckon they've got a taste for pretending to be capitalists. The changes will be under the surface. They need the West to trade with them and Hong Kong is the country-within-a-country that gets them around trade embargos and gives them access to world financial markets. For now, keeping the mainland and Hong Kong separate is a small price to pay. Whether that will be the case in twenty years is another matter. Over the fifty years of the treaty you are likely to see an increasingly controlling approach replace the current laissez-faire environment. And it's that which makes Hong Kong simply the most brilliant business city in the world."

I took another sip from my glass and continued: "The Chinese view is that Hong Kong will be part of China the morning after the handover. They will happily leave all the structures and systems in place until they feel it is to their advantage to do something different. They will not care one single jot about what Britain or the rest of the world says or feels."

"We cannot expect a Communist country to act like a democracy," he said. "However, New Labour is about using globalization as a force for good. We need good relations with the Chinese."

"Then be prepared not to criticise them in public. They don't like other countries telling them how to do things. Always try and see everything through their prism of four thousand years of civilisation. In their eyes we remain unutterable barbarians."

"I may have to criticise them if I am trying to develop an ethical foreign policy," he said. "Are the Chinese ethical?"

This time I couldn't hold back my snort.

"They wouldn't know what that means," I said. "Pragmatic is your best word for the Chinese. They use Marxist ideology as a cover for national socialism."

Perhaps that was a new notion to him. I didn't mean strutting Aryans. But being Chinese was a matter of racial superiority. Nobody could become Chinese through being born in the country or acquiring a passport. And even if your family had lived in a foreign country for five generations, you never ceased being Chinese, first and foremost. Singapore was a good example of how that worked.

He said: "So we cannot rely on them to negotiate with us in good faith?"

"With respect," I said, "I don't think any country really does that. I doubt your Mr. Blair will be any different."

"I think you will be proved wrong," he said. "At least while I am Foreign Secretary."

"I certainly hope so, for the sake of Hong Kong and Asia," I said. "But you are going to need a lot of luck."

"What do you think of him?" Flick asked as we walked away from Granita. She was clutching my arm, but only to use me as a windbreak from the wind gusting along the pavement on Upper Street. We had left Robin Cook and his secretary to 'go through some things' before getting back on the campaign trail. One of those things, I noticed, included gently massaging his inner thigh.

"As politicians go, which is not a high bar," I said, "he was serious and sensible and I felt he was interested in what I said. Also, I don't think he would send us stupidly to war with any country, which is a plus."

"You men always think in terms of battle."

"That's because life is one. In my case I quite like to avoid them. The world is a dangerous enough place when it's at peace."

"Jeff doesn't think like that," she said. "He's a gentle loving soul. It's funny, we lived quite close and I never met him for years. When I did I felt like I knew him instantly."

"That must be a wonderful feeling," I said, genuinely. "I can't say it has ever happened to me. Maybe my career choices have made me too suspicious of people and their motives."

"Well I hope you like Jeff when you meet him," she said. "He's hopeful of winning the seat, and then we can afford to marry."

"Is your father really that hard up?" I asked.

"You remember Pendragon Hall, don't you?"

I remembered a cold, austere, mansion just off the A38 near Chudleigh with an expanse of peeling plasterwork and mildewed furniture.

"There was a dragon's breath that whistled down into your room from the hole in the roof," I said. "Is that still not fixed?"

"We moved out of the East Wing 'for repairs' about five years ago and I don't think anything has been done since. Dad says it's simpler to heat the house if we just live in the West Wing."

By that stage, we had arrived back at the Earl's Islington home which was a relative oasis of dryness and warmth. I was surprised when, passing the library doorway, I heard him in conversation with Giles Guedella. I went in and Flick drifted after me.

"Jedburgh," Guedella said, "you get everywhere."

"Old friend of the family," I said. He looked at the Earl, who nodded vaguely. They had a bottle of Jameson whiskey open in front of them.

"Hello, Giles," Flick said, coldly. "We've been having lunch with Robin Cook."

"Ah, the dark side. Is Jeff with you or is he still hopping around Cannock Chase, scrabbling for votes?"

"He's diligently canvassing his constituency," she said. "Unlike you."

"I'll be back down there tomorrow," Guedella said. "I'm just covering off some business with your father."

"I see," she said. "In that case, Bill and I will head around the corner for a drink." At which we abruptly retraced our steps. I wanted to stay, because I suspected this business was connected with Sir Bernard Li and I would have liked to know what he and the Earl were talking about, but if you arrive with a lady, you have to leave with her, as my Mother used to say.

Flick didn't say a word until she had a large white wine in front of her in the King's Head.

"Bloody Giles," she said eventually. "I can't believe I ever went out with him." Poor Flick. If Guedella and I were examples of her choices in men, I dreaded to think what the current iteration would be like.

"Always a nightmare when two exes collide," I said. "I only met him for the first time yesterday. He seemed quite nice."

"He's a fascist. I didn't realise until I met Jeff. Also, he was barely interested in sex. Jeff is an animal in bed." She giggled. "I suppose if you have Wolf in your surname that might be the case."

Jedburgh's Law of Synchronicity was in action again. Given the way the coincidences were racking up, I shouldn't have been surprised to learn that Flick's boyfriend was Jeffrey Wolf-Madden, son of the famous painter and so technically Missie Li's stepbrother.

15

My chance for a heart-to-heart with Dominic Tweddle came more quickly than I expected. My RIM 9000 pager beeped before breakfast and he picked up my call from the phone box in Grosvenor Square at the second ring.

"I'd like you to come up to Balliol with me," he said after we exchanged pleasantries. "I'm having lunch with my old tutor. He's an expert on cryptography. I thought we could stay over with Johnny Aston afterwards and take stock of where we are."

"Excellent idea," I said. "I know just the motor for me to borrow."

Saturday morning found us on the M40 in the E-type heading to Oxford. Missie had told her father she was at a friend's. She was actually teaching back-to-back Tai Chi classes for Chinese pensioners in Wembley and then finishing a dissertation on privatisation for her Cambridge MBA. She had promised me she wasn't going clubbing and I told her that if I found out she'd disobeyed me then we would be having a serious fight. She'd cocked her head, thought about it for a moment, and walked off with a mysterious smile on her face.

"You realise we're being tailed?" Dominic said, as we were passing through the Chiltern Gap.

"Red Toyota Land Cruiser," I said. "Five cars back. Does that happen frequently to you?"

"I'm getting more senior in the Firm," he said. "I suppose I should take it as a compliment."

"Unless it's me they're after," I said.

"If you were that important," he said, "I'd be concerned." Which I might be, I thought, because I couldn't get the man with the scar out of my head. Although Oxford's spires seemed a world away from a routine hit for the Brigadier in Hong Kong.

I'd missed out on university to go straight into the Army. Dominic had gone on from our boarding school to a top Oxford college, emerged with a first in Politics, Philosophy and Economics and eventually gone into the City, or so I had thought until I had hooked up with him in Manhattan the previous year.

"Tell me about Edgar Sharp," I asked.

"A brilliant mathematical mind," he said. "I didn't understand half of our tutorials. I put it down to the amount of Hook Norton bitter I was consuming at the time but I realise now he's one of those men who are simply on another intellectual planet."

"Why is he called 'Diamond'?"

"Allegedly he likes to keep his wealth in diamonds. Doesn't trust the banking system or what he refers to as 'fiat' currencies. That's any form of paper money whose value is fixed by governments."

"I take a similar view myself," I said. My portfolio also contained quite a few girls' best friends, including the remarkably rare Red Teardrop, a 5.11 carat cranberry coloured triangular brilliant that I had acquired recently.

"Maybe your old tutor could recommend a good diamond dealer to me. Mine left the business."

"Retired?"

"He had a run-in with the Buaya cartel."

Dominic and I had tangled with the cartel, and its then boss the Queen Bitch from Bataan, Lavender Daai, on our last co-operation together in New York.

I parked near the Ashmolean and we walked over to Balliol, which might have been near the top of the tree academically, but was pretty close to the bottom in terms of architecture. We had a couple of pints in the Buttery with Sharp then he took us for lunch in the SCR dining room below the Hall. He was definitely not what I had expected in an Oxford don. He was spiky-haired and of indeterminate age, his face etched in laughter lines. Dominic had explained on the journey up that he supplemented his relatively small salary, as a Lecturer in maths & economics, with professional gambling. That is, until he was warned off from Crockfords, allegedly for counting cards and was then blacklisted by the other British casinos.

"Rubbish," he said when I asked him about it. "You only need an advanced understanding of probability to beat the system. Counting cards would be a waste of memory and effort."

He was dressed in a green velvet jacket with a yellow woollen cardigan and a bow-tie whose random black and white design resolved on closer inspection into a series of ones and zeros. He looked like he might be auditioning for the role of Doctor Who.

"Edgar is the reason I joined SIS," Dominic said. "He's one of our 'talent-spotters'."

"Which is stretching the concept a little," he said, "given how little of it you demonstrated in my economics tutorials."

"It didn't harm my ultimate degree class," Dominic said tartly.

"No, but it might have spared you a viva," Sharp replied. "That's the oral exam they give you if they're unsure you're worth a first," he explained to me. Dominic looked miffed and I filed away, for future use, the knowledge that he was not academically infallible.

"It's actually maths rather than economics we wanted your advice on, Edgar," he said. "What can you tell us about encrypted satellite communications?"

"How long have you got?" he asked. "And I'm presuming you don't want me to bore you silly with the Chinese remainder theorem. It would help if you gave me a bit more context."

"How valuable would it be if you could crack uncrackable codes?"

"You can't," he said. "At least not the code part. You can crack the people or their computers. A rubber truncheon or a keystroke logger is how you do it. Which I'm guessing is where you, Bill, or you, Dominic come in." I didn't like the speed with which he had identified me as a blunt instrument, but it came with the territory. You don't get to be a Balliol don without majoring in effortless superiority.

"Have you come across PGP?" he asked.

"Sounds like a drug," I said

"It stands for Pretty Good Privacy and it's better than drugs, because it does work. It's about five years old and it has revolutionised cryptography."

"I've heard of this," Dominic said. "It was invented by some CND protester, who wanted to hide his emails from people like me."

"Spoken like a true member of the Establishment, Dom," he said. "The guy in question was American, but you're in the right ballpark. What he worked out was that you could have what he calls a 'web of trust' – which doesn't include the Government and people like you. It relies on interlocking public and private keys belonging to the sender and recipient. The public keys are used by the sender and recipient, but only their private keys allow you to encrypt or decrypt the message."

"So as long as no-one knows what both the private keys are it's completely screened from prying eyes? And each side only ever has their own private key?"

Sharp nodded in approval.

"It's like a safe deposit box where two of you each have separate keys but neither of you have both," I said.

"Exactly, and because you trust the other person, or the other person was introduced to you by someone you trust, you are happy to work together. Decentralised, or distributed, networks are going to be the future of the internet. Some people think they might even be capable of validating currencies that aren't issued by governments. Which will be pretty useful for anarchists, terrorists and criminals."

"Sounds interesting," I said, thinking that the Reliable Man needed to have a chat with his friendly Indian tech guy about it when he got back to Singapore. "But presumably it is equally useful for the good guys as well?"

"Absolutely," he said. "Anyone who needs to have complete security can use it. For now it's not available for voice traffic, but if it were…"

"And presumably if the assumption is that it can't be hacked, people will be incredibly indiscreet when they use it?" Dominic was just as interested as I was.

"It will be like eavesdropping on a man in bed with his mistress. He'll have more than his pants down, he'll be right royally screwed."

As we wandered back to the car after lunch, through the ugliest courtyard in Oxford, I took stock at what we'd learned. If Dominic was right and Sir Bernard intended to hand over SatBox's technology to the Chinese, then the havoc they could wreak with it would be unimaginable. If, say, the Brigadier got his way and the Singapore Government used it to eavesdrop on Ministers then the Chinese would literally hear everything that they said.

What I couldn't understand was why Guedella would sell if he knew that was a possibility. He was a patriot. Surely a simple call from one of his contacts in SIS would kill the transaction stone dead?

It didn't take us long to drive down to Johnny Aston's country estate, or to spot that the red Land Cruiser was still in discreet pursuit.

Ashurst Manor was a nice-looking Jacobean pile near Burford, which was a picture-perfect village that served as the gateway to the Cotswolds. It was the sort of place they might film a murder mystery series for American television.

We found Johnny on the front lawn, which he had converted into a makeshift driving range for the afternoon.

"Pick up a driver," he said. "See that pin over there?" The pin in question was a Jeroboam of Krug. "Nearest to it with the next five balls gets to take it home with him."

The Krug wasn't going anywhere except back into Johnny Aston's cellar. He was already zeroed in, and although I managed a creditable runner-up, within about five feet of his best ball, it turned out that Dominic's First from Balliol didn't translate into any sort of golfing excellence.

Johnny's wife Lucy had met him when she was responsible for arranging conference accommodation for Burcotts – I gathered they road-tested quite a lot of hotel mattresses together before the first Mrs. Aston disappeared into the sunset. She was pleasantly attractive and a good hostess. She first served up two small blonde children in pyjamas, for Johnny to dutifully kiss goodnight, then a game casserole and an excellent Burgundy – A 1988 Volnay Tête de Cuvée - for the adults. We made small talk until it was time for Johnny to abandon her to the telly and drag us into the library for a council of war over a decanter of vintage Hine.

"I heard the Board of F&E talking about the Takeover Code, Johnny," I said. "Can you explain what that is?"

"In a nutshell," he said, "it is all Siggy Warburg's fault. "If the old genius hadn't been quite such a good corporate raider we would never have needed rules on what constituted 'control' of a public company."

"It means," chipped in Dominic, "that if you want to acquire more than 29.9 per cent of a listed company's shares, you have to make a bid for the lot. Unless that is, you already own more than that when it floated. If half or more of the other shareholders don't accept your offer, it fails."

"Our Giles," said Johnny, "has forty percent of SatBox, so they effectively need his blessing and the Board's recommendation to proceed."

"Which might explain why I saw him having a drink with Thomas Field yesterday?" I asked.

"Absolutely," he said. "I'm sure Tom is much more congenial to deal with than Sir Bernard Li, and much easier to explain away than meeting the White Tiger. Wasn't he screwing Field's daughter?"

"Not any more," I said. "Or so she has informed me."

"Flick is an old flame of Bill's," Dominic explained.

"Really?" Johnny leered. "Wouldn't have said she was your type."

"Nor would I, now," I said. "It was before I passed through the bamboo curtain. What happens next?"

"I've been giving it some thought," Dominic said. "I reckon nothing is likely to happen before the election. The market is pretty jittery at the moment…"

"You can say that again," said Johnny.

"…plus, Guedella may still need an income if he loses his seat."

"He was definitely worried about that when I spoke to him," I said.

"And so he should be," Johnny said. "We commission independent polling and the Conservatives are heading for a disastrous defeat. A couple of cabinet ministers are in real trouble."

I said: "I met a bloke called Robin Cook yesterday."

"My next boss," Dominic commented, sounding mildly concerned. Of course, SIS notionally reported in to the Foreign Secretary. I'd briefed him on my lunch with the idealistic Scotsman on the drive up.

"Must be tough one day working for the Conservatives and the next day waking up and working for Labour," I said.

"It's pretty simple," he said, trying to sound pragmatic. "Whoever you vote for, the Government gets in."

16

I woke up early to the unfamiliar sounds and smells of the English countryside: cattle mooing, birds singing and fresh manure in the air. I showered in nearly-cold water – Johnny had bought classic English plumbing to go with his classic English manor house – and decided I needed a country stroll to clear my head. It was still heavy with the after-effects of Cuban cigars and expensive brandy.

Johnny had gone full-on gentleman farmer. Wandering through the farm buildings around the back of the house, I found a Massey Ferguson tractor surrounded by every conceivable agricultural gadget and a stable block where a stocky teenage girl was mucking out a hunter and a couple of ponies. Eventually I found myself in a large field that stretched as far as the country lane on which stood the pillars, topped with stone lions, which marked the formal entrance to the Manor. The lush green grass, with rolling Cotswold hills as a backdrop, made it an idyllic vista. That is until I spotted the roof of a red Land Cruiser visible above the hedge line.

I crossed the field and took a closer look, protected from sight by the hedgerow. There was a rusty five bar gate leading from the field into the lane and I could make out two men in the front seat of the Toyota. They looked

Chinese and one of them was reading a newspaper. Their attention was focused on the main gate of the Manor, so they missed me completely. It looked like a standard tail job. They weren't even bothering to hide the fact.

I went back to the house, feeling annoyed. I didn't like being disrespected. In my absence the rest of the house had surfaced and were sitting at a large oak table in the kitchen tucking into a full English breakfast. Lucy had the two kids dressed and was heading out with them to church and Sunday school followed by a visit to her parents, who apparently lived in the next village. Johnny was still in his dressing-gown and was reading the *News of the World* which was urging its readers to give New Labour a chance in the forthcoming election.

I nicked a sausage from Dominic's plate and dipped it in brown sauce before biting the end off. Nothing cured a hangover as thoroughly as a greasy fry-up.

"Get your own," he said, deep in the *Sunday Times* Business Section.

"I intend to," I replied and went in search of a plate. I had spotted a towbar on the back of the Toyota and a plan was forming in my head. I refined it as I scoffed down fried eggs, bacon, mushrooms, black pudding and beans with a couple of rounds of buttered toast. When the churchgoers had departed, I outlined my idea to the lads.

"We need to be careful," Dominic said, "I want to make a call first to my control room. If it's a Chinese embassy car then it will be off-limits, even if it doesn't have diplomatic plates. With the handover coming up HMG is scared stiff of any incidents between ourselves and the PRC. Shouldn't take long, Control keep a pretty up-to-date list of the index numbers."

It took him thirty minutes, in which time Johnny had showered and changed into a Tattersall shirt, Barbour jacket and moleskin trousers and was busying himself with his Boss shotguns.

"No visible connection to the embassy," Dominic said when he returned. "Rented to a shell company called NR Transport with an address in Folkestone. Still, be careful."

"I'll try my best," I said.

"And don't be rougher than you have to be."

"Yes Mum," I said. "The whole point is to find out what they are up to, which requires them being able to talk at the end of it."

"And for God's sake," Johnny said, "don't upset the neighbours."

"Which is one of the reasons for you taking potshots at clay pigeons while I'm doing it," I said patiently. "It distracts the watchers and covers up the sound of what I plan to do." Not that Johnny had any neighbours closer than a mile away, or that I intended to use my Glock, but it paid to be careful.

I was bored. Diplomatic niceties and business strategy frustrated me. I sensed a welcome opportunity for some targeted violence.

Half an hour later, Johnny and Dominic were out on the far side of the drive with a farmhand who was launching clays into the air to cries of 'pull' and the crack of shotgun cartridges. It was good to see that Dominic was better with a shotgun than at golf. I had the bag of clubs beside me in the tractor cab and was doing my best imitation of a diligent farmer driving to and fro and up and down the field. An observer who knew anything would wonder why I wasn't pulling a plough or harrow, but I didn't reckon either of the Chinese guys had attended the Royal Agricultural College. Eventually I was positioned beside the five bar gate and about to commence the riskiest part of my plan.

I lowered the tractor's rear supports, which anchored it firmly to the ground, and jumped out. There was a heavy-duty winch on the front and I used its electric motor to pay out several yards of cable. When I was ready, I signalled to Dominic from behind the hedge and he and Johnny moved onto the side of the drive closest to the Toyota, ostensibly to give themselves a harder target to hit, but in reality to distract the occupants. I waited until the clay pigeon shoot restarted before edging out behind the Land Cruiser and attaching the cable to the towbar on the back of the vehicle with a double loop. I was out of the direct line of sight from the side mirrors, but if the driver had looked in the rear-view mirror at the wrong time he would have seen me crawling along the centre of the road with the cable in my hand. Thankfully he didn't and I made it back to the gate unseen. Just as I engaged the winch and the cable went taut, I saw Dominic shatter a clay that would have been a fantastic high pheasant. There was a whine as the motor bit and then the Toyota was moving backwards towards the tractor, gathering speed as it went.

My actions had exactly the effect I had intended: two exhausted watchers, stiff from sitting in the front seats all night, suddenly found their vehicle being dragged backwards without understanding why. They did exactly what I would have done and opened the front doors to jump out. Which was when I hit the driver on his legs with a sand wedge. They buckled as the metal hit his kneecap in an explosion of pain. As he sank to his knees I jabbed the other end of the golf club into his solar plexus and winded him for good measure.

The shock of seeing me emerge from the gateway and hit his partner, distracted the other man. He stopped and started to fumble inside his jacket for what I presumed was a pistol. Before he could find it however, the passenger door, which was still open and continuing to move, hit him hard on the upper body and he fell awkwardly to the ground. As the giant SUV rolled on backwards and out of the way, I stepped forward into the space vacated by it and drove the club into the side of his face in a perfect golf shot. His head jerked backwards and forwards absorbing the impact of my stroke before he lost consciousness. A small pool of blood trickled from his ear.

By that stage I had turned back to the other man, who was sitting up on the tarmac holding his knee and yelling loudly in pain. I put my arm around his neck and choked the consciousness from him. Then I ran back to the tractor winch and turned it off. It had taken less than five minutes to disable them both. I was a little out of breath, but the adrenalin rush felt good.

The side of the Toyota was scraped where the winch had pulled it against a concrete fence post and the passenger door needed a shoulder heave to close it, but the big Land Cruiser was otherwise unscathed. The same couldn't be said for its former occupants. Dominic and Johnny had come running. Dom had put the man I had clobbered in the ear into a recovery position and I used some rope I found in the tractor cab to truss up the other guy so that he wouldn't be able to move when he recovered consciousness. By the time I had done that, Dom had turned the other man on his back and was trying to deliver CPR. After a few minutes he gave up. Johnny looked shocked. I doubt he saw many dead bodies in the countryside other than foxes and game birds.

"What did I say about not being too rough?" Dominic said angrily.

"It was a lucky hit."

"Not for him," he said grimly. "You don't know your own strength. I'd better call it in. We have a clean-up team that can deal with this sort of thing. Let's just hope they weren't Chinese agents."

"I doubt it," I said. Dominic had ripped open his shirt to deliver CPR and I was looking at the dead man's chest. It bore a large tattoo of a snarling tiger with a Fairbairn Sykes commando knife down the middle. "That's the emblem of the Grup Gerak Khas – the Malaysian SAS."

I paid the farmhand fifty quid to buy his silence and kept Johnny Aston company in the drawing room at the Manor with a bottle of 20 year-old Macallan, while Dominic dealt with the team of Security Service sweepers. They had arrived within the hour with a police low-loader to remove the SUV and an unmarked black van to take a body bag and the now-conscious live suspect back to London for interrogation.

"Don't get me wrong, Bill," he said. "I realised that you did this stuff for a living. But I never saw a dead body like that before. To date," he said ruefully, "I've only ever made a financial killing."

"I take full responsibility for this one, Johnny," I said. "Not going to lose any sleep over him though. You saw his body - it was covered in scars and he'd had his fingerprints removed. I reckon this guy had done plenty of his own wetwork."

That made him feel a bit better, I think, but when Dominic returned, having despatched the clean-up team back to London, it was clear we needed to make our farewells and leave.

Dominic looked like thunder as we took our bags to the E-type and slung them in the boot.

"I'll drive," he said curtly. I didn't argue. As the Jaguar roared away from the Manor he gave it to me with both barrels.

"That was a complete fuck-up," he said. "Have you any idea how much paperwork I have to complete to get rid of a dead body over here? Not to mention the fact that I now owe the heavy mob at Five a favour, which will come back to haunt me. And on top of it all," he said, giving a poor old dear in a Morris Minor a completely undeserved blast of his horn for not letting the E-type get past her quickly enough, "I'm going to have to open a proper file for you back at the Firm, which I was trying to avoid."

"Not my finest hour," I said, diplomatically. And I was sorry. I hadn't meant to kill the guy, and nine times out of ten I wouldn't have. But in the heat of an operation you can't always pull your punches.

"Well at least we found this," he said, pulling a sheaf of papers out of his pocket and handing them to me.

It was a copy of the top sheets of my P-File. It had come from the fax machine at one of the larger Hong Kong police stations, no doubt supplied by some bent Station Sergeant. With it was a photograph, taken with a telephoto lens, of me walking into the SatBox offices in Devon with Missie.

"I take it back," he said. "They were after you. And I think things are about to become worse. Especially," he said glancing in his rearview mirror, "because of what's happening now."

"And what is happening now?" I asked.

"One of those Chinese embassy cars whose numbers I dutifully memorised," he said, "has taken over the tail."

17

Sir Bernard Li had summoned me all the way to his office in Covent Garden this time. It was on Monmouth Street and, as Ray had already driven him over there in the Bentley, I braved the Central line from Marble Arch to Tottenham Court Road. It was as filthy and packed as I remembered. London really was creaking at the seams. Years of under-investment were taking their toll and the rewards of nearly two decades of Conservative government didn't seem to have trickled down visibly to ordinary Londoners. No wonder Tony Blair's optimistic message that 'things can only get better' was resonating with voters.

Sir Bernard's PA, Miss Maxwell, showed me into his office. Although a different shape, it was almost identical in décor to the one in Upper Brook Street. Another Luis Chan painting, this time of Kowloon, hung on the wall behind him. He was reading a report bound in a blue cover and barely looked up to greet me.

"How's Missie?" he asked, his head still in the report.

"No bother," I said. "Her appointment to the board has increased the number of paparazzi following her, so I have convinced her to stay in most nights. I smuggle her out to bars to visit a few friends when I can do it unobtrusively. She's going a little stir crazy, but otherwise is fine." I didn't mention that I was also escorting her to her Tai Chi classes, which were helping to keep her sane and toned. I had taken part in a few and I had to say they had improved my inner calm. The incident at Aston Manor had affected me more than I expected, especially as it had caused a temporary chill in my friendship with Dominic, who had been carpeted by his boss for failing to restrain me.

"Excellent," he said. "I appreciate what you have done, Jedburgh." He took off his glasses, polished them with a soft cloth and sighed. "But I have made a mistake."

"What do you mean, sir?" I asked. Sir Bernard didn't strike me as a man who was used to admitting to being wrong.

"It was foolish to think I could change her. Missie was not ready to be a director of my company, especially as it is Listed on the Stock Exchange. I have letters here from the major institutional shareholders. They are not happy. I think I must ask her to resign." He looked like a man forced to throw his toddler to a pack of circling wolves in order to get clear while they fought over the carcass.

This was serious. I knew if Missie was made to resign it would be very difficult for her to rejoin the board subsequently. She might not have liked the motive for her appointment, but if she wanted to be CEO in due course it was important that she remained a director. What I wasn't at liberty to tell Sir Bernard, however, was that she had deliberately pretended to be an airhead to disguise from him just how serious a businesswoman she really was.

"I think that would be a mistake, sir," I said.

"You're an expert in business now are you, Jedburgh? You think I should appoint you to the board as well?" I didn't like Sir Bernard's tone. I wouldn't have had much compunction in killing him if I'd been commissioned to do so before he hired me. Now I just sucked it up.

"I am a qualified financial consultant," I said. "Not in your league, but most of my clients think my advice is helpful. I am more concerned for your reputation." He stopped reading the report. Like most successful men, he cared about that. "This will be taken by the City as a sign of weakness. Your reputation is based on being a single-minded entrepreneur and you are the largest shareholder. I don't think you can afford to let the institutions forget it."

He seemed to be considering my argument, so I continued: "You need to find something to occupy Missie and fill her time up. Do you not have a small business within F&E she could run?"

"I hadn't thought of that," he said. "Maybe I *should* offer you a board position, Jedburgh. You are more perceptive than I gave you credit for." He thought a bit more. "I have been contemplating re-launching my casual fashion chain - 'China Crisis' - for a while now. It is aimed at young girls, perhaps Missie would enjoy that?" I knew she would. I had listened to a rant from her the previous evening about how appalling the clothing lines and store layouts were.

"I think that would be an excellent idea, sir," I said. "But only if you make some time to spend with her as a mentor. I think that would make sound business sense and benefit you both."

"An excellent idea of mine, then, so it is settled," he said. "And we will be able to get some good PR coverage. I must ring Miss Field and ask her to organise something. Anyway, it was not the only thing I wanted to discuss. I have an appointment at the Chinese embassy and I want you to come with me."

"Sir?"

"You know how they are. They will appreciate the idea of a *gwai lo* working for a high-ranking Chinese. And the fact I take a bodyguard will enhance my status. I don't know the official I am meeting very well, so I need every edge I can get."

"Then I'd be delighted to escort you, sir," I said, while inwardly debating whether I was putting my head in a noose after the events of the previous weekend. "You do realise I won't be able to enter the embassy armed?"

"I'm there to do business with the man, not kill him," Sir Bernard said, apparently without irony.

The Bentley took us past Centre Point and over Tottenham Court Road towards Oxford Circus. We turned right up Regent Street towards the BBC and pulled up in Portland Place outside the Chinese embassy. It looked like it had been there since the reign of George III, but Dominic had explained to me that they had pulled it down and rebuilt it in the early 1980s. There were so many electronic counter-measures at play inside, that apparently you could get no mobile signal within 500 feet of the building. If Dominic were with me, he would have cautioned me against entering, but I also knew that I operated best as a pinball, ricocheting around the table at random, lighting up jackpot plays.

The embassy was a large red brick and stone building with classical pilasters rising up to a mansard roof. Inside, it resembled an Asian potentate's idea of a 1970s five-star hotel, although I had to admit the walls were decorated with some fine examples of Chinese art down the ages. We were escorted through large inlaid wooden doors into a meeting room decorated with elaborately over-patterned wallpaper and carpet. The clash of styles told you everything you needed to know about modern China. The most dominant contents of the room were the wide red armchairs that allowed every important Communist official to sit in suitable grandeur during meetings. Sir Bernard sat down in one immediately and looked right at home. I decided to stand respectfully with my back to the wall, keeping my eye on the exit. Not that I'd stand much chance of fighting my way out if they chose to restrain me.

About five minutes later, our host arrived. He may have tried to maintain his inscrutability, but I would swear that the blood drained from Hu Xianping when he saw me standing behind Sir Bernard. Although I had last seen him from a distance in Hong Kong at 'Tango Martini', the last time the Head of the Third Bureau of the Ministry of State Security and I had been this close, I was being held at gunpoint by Lavender Daai and facing imminent execution. He put his face down to Sir

Bernard's ear and spoke quietly. Sir Bernard nodded then turned to me:

"Please return to the car and wait for me there." I couldn't get out of the building quickly enough. Ray was parked in one of the traffic bays in the middle of Portland Place, which was a wide thoroughfare that led up to Regent's Park. He was having a smoke, leaning on the bonnet of the Bentley and we shot the breeze for half an hour until Sir Bernard re-appeared. He was a Chelsea fan, and he wanted to talk about the forthcoming FA Cup Final, a victory in which might compensate them for their lousy league form. The semi-final had been a clinical victory against Wimbledon made all the sweeter by taking place at the Highbury ground of their bitter north London rivals, Arsenal.

When Sir Bernard did reappear, the conversation was short and not very sweet.

"I have decided to dispense with your services," he said. "I will employ a Chinese bodyguard to protect Missie. In a few weeks' time Hong Kong will be part of China and it will be more…" he had the good grace to look mildly embarrassed "…appropriate going forward."

"I completely understand your decision, sir," I said. No point in fighting it, and it resolved my dilemma. After the shock of finding out he was in cahoots with Hu Xianping I was now clear which camp I was in. Missie didn't need me to protect her, and my parting gift to her was a proper role within Foreign & Exotic. Not a bad outcome.

"I will pay you a month's notice and a business ticket home," said Sir Bernard.

"That's very kind," I said sycophantically. Money was money. "I will make alternative arrangements for accommodation and come round this afternoon to collect my things."

I left him by the car and walked down Portland Place towards the Langham Hotel. Dominic's office wasn't far away. We needed to regroup.

His offices were almost opposite the front door of Claridges. An ancient brass plate proclaimed: 'Ashenden Delacroix & Co, Bankers, Est. 1585'. It carried the burnish from several centuries of devoted polishing.

I found myself in a wood-panelled banking hall. A uniformed messenger was standing at a desk by the door. I explained I had come to see Mr. Tweddle and he took my name. He looked at a screen on his desk and said quietly:

"I believe you are carrying a firearm, Sir?" I showed him my carry permit.

"We'll need to look after it for the duration of your visit, sir," he said. "I'd be grateful if you would place it in here." There was a metal contraption like a night safe to his right. He pulled open the drawer and I placed the Glock 17 inside.

"Nice weapon," he said. "But I still prefer the Browning High Power." He was almost certainly ex-SAS, then. I'd come across his sort when I was attached to 14 Intelligence, the 'Det', in Northern Ireland.

I was unannounced, so I sat for about half an hour waiting for Dominic to appear. I watched a strange tide of visitors as it ebbed and flowed between the entrance and a bank counter to the right of the door. It carried along all kinds of people, to most of whom the messenger at the door nodded in recognition: City gents, East End wide boys, Arabs and Nigerians in their traditional national dress and a pretty redhead dressed in motorcycle leathers who left carrying a large pouch into which I had seen the cashier pour bundles of £50 notes. I watched her trim leather-clad bottom depart and realised I needed to have sex. Being semi-raped by Missie's mother had created an itch I needed to scratch.

Which led me to think about Missie herself. I had been *in loco parentis* while I was guarding her, but now I had been fired I could think about her in a different and much more exciting way. It wasn't just her body that was appealing, but her whole mindset. It was different to most of the Asian women I had slept with. The nearest to her in appeal was Jane Tan, but where Jane was severe and efficient as well as beautiful, Missie exhibited a serene calm that came from being both highly intelligent and emotionally and physically centred. Over the past week we had talked regularly about everything from business to Chinese philosophy. I wasn't an expert on anything other than guns and motorbikes, but I read a lot and was a good listener. She was something special and I realised I was slightly smitten.

"Mr. Jedburgh, our Mr. Tweddle is ready for you now." The messenger interrupted a reverie in which I was wrestling with Missie on a judo mat and developing a few unorthodox holds on parts of her inner body. He showed me down into a meeting room in the basement where Dominic greeted me warmly. He wasn't alone.

18

Dominic introduced his colleague as Darren Mace, a short, round-faced, Londoner in his twenties who was already starting to lose his hair.

"We employ a lot of bright people around here," Dom said with a self-deprecating smile. "Darren is one of them, so I don't have to be. What did you read at Birmingham, Darren? Economics and engineering?"

"Chemistry," he said. "Frankly I joined SIS because I thought I'd spend more time blowing things up, rather than looking at spreadsheets."

"You need to be in the private sector for that," I said.

"Don't knock spreadsheets," Dominic said. "You've a natural aptitude for financial analysis. We'll make a fund manager of you yet."

"Which is presumably why I've got a folder in my hand full of pictures of mercenaries?"

"Who hopefully won't grow old enough to collect the pensions you could be managing for them," I said lightly.

"Let's start with this one," Dominic said, taking the folder from Darren and putting down a picture on the table. It was the Asian man I had killed at Ashurst Manor.

"We don't have a name yet," Darren said, "but he's definitely ex-GGK. Here he is with someone you might recognise?"

The photograph had been taken over ten years previously. My victim looked younger, barely out of his teens, and considerably more alive. But the man standing at the side of his squad, wearing a sand-coloured beret and the uniform of a Major in the Malaysian Army, I had last seen in a Land Rover in Devon.

"He's missing a scar on his throat," I said. "It's an improvement."

"He picked that up a few years later. In Sarawak," Mace continued. "His name is Rip Van Ryjn. He was an instructor at PULPAK."

"Their Special Forces training school," I said.

"That's right. He taught long range reconnaissance, behind-the-lines operations and psyops. All subjects he learnt during his time with 1 Recce Commando in South Africa, then the Selous Scouts in Zimbabwe. Rhodesia as it then was."

"They were hard men, and good at what they did," I said. "I worked with two of them in SDU." The Special Duties Unit of the Royal Hong Kong Police got the toughest, dirtiest jobs. Sometimes we needed people who could disappear for weeks in a grim Tuen Mun housing estate and come back, metaphorically, with a couple of ears on a string necklace. "How did he get the scar?"

"He was an observer on an operation that the Malaysians were running against Chinese communist insurgents," Dominic said. "A mortar shell exploded beside his position. He was invalided out and became a gun-for-hire. We believe he has recruited dozens of former GGK troopers to work for him across the Far East."

"So no lover of the PRC," I said. "He's unlikely to be working for them. So why is he staked out watching Giles Guedella?"

"We don't know," he said, baldly. "He's a rum cove: read theology at Witwatersrand University. Seems to hate the British for what happened to South Africa and Rhodesia."

"Is the guy we took alive talking?"

"Not really," Darren said. "He's been well trained." The SAS had a lot to answer for. They had spawned similar units across the former British colonies. The units were all trained to similar standards, often by serving or former SAS members. 21 GGK had a well-equipped camp in Malacca where they trained special forces from all branches of the Malaysian military and police. If an SAS trooper could withstand hard interrogation, why not a GGK one? Of course, in determined hands anyone would talk after a while. I just wasn't sure how aggressive the British security services were permitted to be these days.

"PULPAK is a pukka training establishment," I said. "I helped teach a course in urban pacification there when I was in the SDU. I don't remember this Van Ryjn chap, but he may remember me."

"All the more reason not to let his oppo tell him what happened," Dominic said. "Whether or not he talks, we can't let him back into the wild until we've tracked Van

Ryjn down and dealt with whatever threat he poses. We're going to have to lose him in Belmarsh Prison for a couple of months."

"We've had better luck with the Toyota Land Cruiser," Darren said. "Not much for forensics to go over, but we think NR Transport is ultimately owned by a group of right-wing fanatics called 'New Reich'."

"I'm guessing they don't like the Jews, then," I said. "Guedella's grandfather helped rebuild Jerusalem."

"Van Ryjn's theology degree might make him a Christian fundamentalist," Dominic suggested.

"If they intend to assassinate Guedella," I mused, "this may have nothing to do with Project Hatstand – that's what Sir Bernard has codenamed the takeover plan."

"There are a lot of higher profile Jewish targets," Dominic said. "And it doesn't explain why he is interested in you."

"I should come clean," I said, nodding ruefully. "Our paths have crossed recently."

I briefly explained the circumstances of the hit I had carried out on the American embassy official and the fact that he had been guarded by Rip Van Ryjn. Dominic had a look of 'I told you so' on his face, but knew a hit sanctioned by the Brigadier meant he needed to keep that information out of my file.

"He only saw me in disguise," I said. "But that wouldn't necessarily matter if he's as good as his reputation suggests. Just as when I half-recognised him on the top of Haytor Rock because of the way he carried himself, he might have done the same. Or someone else has ordered him to target me independently and this whole thing has got a lot more complicated."

My visit to Dominic had given me much to think about, not least the fact that I needed somewhere to stay. Dominic offered to put me up at his club, but I didn't want to be in his debt. So I took a short walk down to the Chesterfield, off Berkeley Square, in search of a hotel room. McAlistair and I often stayed there when we were in London together. It had the advantage that it was a stone's throw from 'Pamela's' if either of us pulled. Also his wife's company had a corporate rate and I could sign on the account. That way I'd be in McAlistair's debt instead of Dominic's. He was happy to be refunded in cash from a safe deposit box and wouldn't expect me to kill anyone.

I wasn't surprised to discover a message there from him, obviously dictated over the phone to the concierge.

'Jedburgh – they tell me you're in London and I figured you would end up here eventually when the money ran out. If you get this in time I will be over in late April on another book tour. Not quite sure when yet. Julian.'

I smiled. McAlistair had bored me silly about his current book, 'The Ugly Gun' in which the hero was a female contract killer with a disease called Proteus Syndrome that gave her deformities like the Elephant Man. Frankly it sounded far-fetched, but Julian was convinced it would appeal to his extensive female readership. It better had, I thought, because I couldn't see

Terry, the doorman at 'Pamela's', going for it. Or me, frankly, but then I found most of his thrillers far-fetched, even if I read all of them out of morbid curiosity. My biggest criticism was that the good always ended happily and the bad unhappily. In my personal experience the truth was more complex than fiction and the good died young.

When I arrived in a cab at Upper Brook Street to pick up my belongings, I found Missie sitting on my bed, with reddened eyes.

"My father is ridiculous and a bully," she said. "Just when I thought I was starting to understand him, too."

She watched me pack my clothes and toiletries into a duffel and my Gladstone bag.

"I'm coming with you," she said. "To help you move."

"It's not like I have much to carry."

"It's the principle."

"In which case," I said, "there's a suiter in the wardrobe."

As we pulled up at the hotel and before we got out of the cab, she took my arm, looked into my eyes and kissed me tenderly on the mouth. The bellboy took my luggage, which barely filled a trolley, and left us to our own devices.

"I want to thank you," she said as we stood awkwardly in the lobby.

"You don't need to thank me for anything. I should thank you. You've made it fun."

"I spoke to my father. When he told me you were going, he also said that you had suggested I run 'China Crisis'. He told me you'd convinced him I could do it."

"You convinced me you could do it," I said. "You are some lady."

"You realise of course," she said, "that there's more to me than that?"

I looked at her. She was glowing.

"Would you like me to show you?" she asked.

When we went upstairs to my room and I made a move towards her, she stopped me.

"Have you ever had sex with someone where you weren't the one in control?" she asked. I thought of her mother.

"Not until very recently," I said.

"Good, because we are going to do this my way."

"Like you're my Tai Chi instructor?"

"Almost exactly," she said. "This kind of sex is about the mental not just the physical bond."

"I prefer just the physical," I said, desperate to rip her clothes off and see the beautiful soft young flesh underneath.

"But just like in my Tai Chi class, if you do the forms and control your inner being, it will become so much more special. Don't worry about protection. I'm on the pill."

We were standing a couple of feet apart. I was panting like a dog with two cocks and I doubted my ability to control myself, but I also trusted her, so I started to calm myself, despite my desire. She smiled as she realised the power she had over me.

"Now, I want you to look into my eyes and whatever happens I don't want you to break eye contact."

They were like deep liquid pools. I would have happily jumped into them, so it was no hardship. We held each other's gaze and very soon something strange began to happen. Everything around me fell out of focus except her face and I began to match her breathing. I felt the hairs on my skin rise along the back of my arm.

"Take your clothes off, one by one," she said. "Keep pace with me." She was wearing a crisp white shirt and began to unbutton it at a steady pace. I moved my head to follow her fingers down, but she shook her head. I caught a flash of white falling from her shoulders. Then I knew she must be unbuttoning her jeans, as she wriggled downwards and I went with her, dropping my suit trousers at the same time. I realised I could tell from the expression on her face which clothes she was removing. My intuition knew that her soft breasts were uncovered and that her panties were next. I removed my briefs and still I was staring into her eyes and she was smiling broadly now. She parted her lips and a short, trim tongue peeped out from behind her brilliant white teeth and touched the edges of them, just with the tip. I could feel my manhood engorging, edging towards her. Then she was moving her body closer to me. I felt her hard nipples against my chest and she finally broke eye contact, rested her head lightly on my right shoulder and took my cock in her hand.

"The secret to this, Bill," she whispered, resuming her gaze, but now so close I could feel her breath against my cheek, "is to match your internal spiritual balance to your outer physical arousal. We're going to do it together."

She kissed me. I don't know how long she kissed me for but I felt like it should go on forever. Then she placed me cross legged on the floor and lowered herself on to me. I heard a soft moan as she let me enter her and I felt her legs anchor themselves behind my back. She moved slowly up and down on me. Her core was strong and her muscle control was remarkable. Throughout it our gaze never broke contact and our lungs still matched each other, breath for breath. We seemed to do this for hours. I don't think I had ever held out for so long.

I was in an almost hallucinogenic state. I began to see all the hundreds of women I had slept with pass before me, all leading me to this one act of lovemaking. None of them had ever offered me sex like this. Finally, even Missie could not control herself. She began to shiver and shudder and started to count down, each number corresponding to a thrust downwards on to my member as her light touch rested on both my shoulders:

"Ten, nine, eight... let my spirit flow into you ...seven, six, five... I need you to fill me completely ...four, three... we are going to do this together... two, one. Now!" Missie gave an ululating cry of passion, pleasure and exultation, all mixed together. She fell forward on top of me and we came at the same time, like storm-tossed waves crashing together on the beach.

We lay curled together for maybe a quarter of an hour, before I seized her like a lion pouncing on a gazelle, turned her on her front over the edge of the bed and took her strongly and roughly from behind.

"That," I said, "is for making me start to care about you."

19

I was still in bed with Missie the next morning when I heard an insistent trilling from the pocket of my trousers, which were bundled on the floor where I had discarded them the previous night. I realised I had forgotten to return Sir Bernard's Star-TAC. I flipped open the clam shell and answered: "Jedburgh?"

"Bill?" It was Flick Field. "I wasn't sure if this number would still work. I spoke to Upper Brook Street this morning and they said Sir Bernard had let you go."

"He's reconnecting with his Chinese roots," I said. "Apparently I'm a colonial relic and no longer a suitable fashion accessory."

I gave her my pager number for future use, because I wanted to purge myself of obligations to Sir Bernard. Missie could take the Motorola back with her. I wondered if I should get myself my own cellphone. I wasn't sure how long I was going to be in London and it would make life easier.

"So what can I do for you?" I asked. "How's the F&E share price?"

"Picking up a bit," she said. "The market has got wind of a big deal in the offing. I've arranged for Sir Bernard and Missie to appear in the *Sunday Times* 'Relative Values' feature next weekend."

"Missie will enjoy that, I said. I stroked her hair and she moaned contentedly beside me and ran her fingernails across my chest.

"Are you alone?" Flick asked.

"Having coffee with someone," I lied.

"Are you free for lunch? There's something I want to tell you. You'd have to come over to the City."

"Of course."

Missie and I had a couple of hours before I had to meet Flick, so we used it productively. We made love to each other again, more conventionally this time, but just as enjoyably. I finally had a chance to examine her naked body properly. She was the nearest thing to perfection I had seen in a long time.

"Are you OK with me seeing Flick?" I asked her, her knees were around my ears as I had just finished pleasuring her and I was brushing my nose in her lightly trimmed triangle of charcoal-black pubic hair.

"Are you planning to tell her about us?" she asked – 'us', the fatal rock on which all my relationships had foundered.

"I wasn't intending to," I said. "Discretion is my middle name."

"Good," she said. "It's far too early for anyone to know. Plus," she giggled - just as she had the first time we'd met - "you're ancient. If the sex continues to be this good, you'll probably have a heart attack!" My tongue recommenced its work.

I was still thinking of Missie when I pushed open the door of 'El Vino's' wine bar, in Fleet Street, where I had arranged to meet Flick. She was sitting at a table in the back and waved excitedly. She was dressed once again for the City and had a stuffed Filofax in front of her, presumably containing the details of every financial journalist and tack shop in the Home Counties.

"So what's so important?" I asked, once we had chosen comfort food – fish pie and peas - and a bottle of St Véran, my favourite white Burgundy. I was hungry and in need of post-coital sustenance.

"It's funny," she said. "A few years ago, this place would have been packed three deep at the bar with journalists all afternoon. They wouldn't have let you in without a tie and an expense account. God help you if you were a woman. But now that the newspapers have moved out and the investment bankers have moved in, this is probably the safest place in London to share a secret."

"Not posh enough for the new breed of investment banker?" I asked. She had explained to me that the old Daily Express building across the road was now home to the American super-firm of Goldman Sachs. With the growth in financial services, the City had expanded in all directions. Now the firms that had grown up to support the Masters of the Universe – like Flick's investor relations business, City accountants and corporate lawyers – occupied smaller offices in the warren of streets around it. This was still the remains of Dickensian London. We were just South of the Royal Courts of

Justice and next to the Old Bailey. Jack Dawkins would have recognised his old hunting grounds.

"So what is the secret?" I asked, hoping I was about to get some intel on Project Hatstand. Instead she dipped into her handbag and pulled out a small square box which she pushed across the table towards me. I flipped it open. Inside was a marquise-cut diamond ring with sapphires on either side of it. It was a beautiful stone.

"Not cheap," I said. "It's at least a VS1, worth five grand, give or take a couple of hundred quid." I didn't have an eye loupe with me, but I had picked up quite a bit of knowledge over the years while purchasing stones from my friend Jeremiah Rosenstein.

"Bill Jedburgh," Flick said. 'You were a lousy boyfriend then and you haven't got much better in fifteen years. It was a mistake to ask you here." She looked as if she was about to cry. About three minutes too late, I realised what I was looking at.

"It's an engagement ring," I said. "Flick, I'm so sorry, that's wonderful. Does he know yet?" She looked at me angrily, then laughed and cuffed me on the arm when she realised I was joking.

"Seriously," I said, milking it, "who is the lucky fella?" She sighed in exasperation.

"Jeff's agent gave him an evening off to spend with me last night. We had dinner in a little Italian restaurant in Rugeley. I just got back this morning."

"So why isn't it on your finger?"

"That's the problem," she said. Jeff asked me, and of course I said yes, but he doesn't want us to announce anything until the election is over. He thinks people will say he's doing it either to gain votes or that he's over-confident he's going to win."

"But I presume his door knocking must be going well if he asked you to marry him? Politics is a pretty binary occupation. You've either got a job or you're on the dole."

She nodded enthusiastically. "Yes, he's hoping for a landslide" she said. "It's a new seat in a historic mining district, but he says all sorts of people are saying they'll support him. They are all fed up with the Tories."

"That's great Flick," I said. "I'm genuinely happy for you." I wasn't sure what sort of a wife Flick would make, or what the chances were of a marriage surviving the stresses of late night sittings in Parliament – I cast my mind back to Robin Cook and wondered whether Mrs. Cook knew about his secretary – but congratulations were the expected thing. "It's only a week before you can tell the world."

"Jeff needs to tell his father first, of course," she said. "I told mine as soon as I got home. Both our mothers are dead. It's something we have in common. The ring belonged to his mother. I showed it to Dad and he was almost in tears. Jeff's mother lived near us in Devon and she died in a car crash apparently."

"I've met your Father-In-Law to be. I went down to Devon with Missie. Does she know that you are going to be, what would it be? Step-sisters-in-law?" She looked at me with a level of womanly perception which I had scant experience of in my world.

"You like her a lot, don't you?" she said.

"Missie has surprised me in just about every way," I said, honestly. "I think she will make a fantastic success as a business-woman one of these days. Sir Bernard has badly misjudged her."

"Well, if I can help, I will," she said. She looked at me brightly and squeezed my hand. "I do hope you can find someone to make you as happy as I am with Jeff."

"I know you mean well, Flick," I said, "but I am not suited for relationships."

"You weren't the best boyfriend I ever had," she admitted. "But you were probably one of the best in bed."

"I've been practising a lot since then," I said with a cheeky grin. "But that's not a suitable conversation for us to have now you're engaged. Congratulations again."

I walked back to the Chesterfield after lunch. I wasn't in a hurry, and it helped me think. I was a colonial ex-copper revisiting the capital of the vanished Empire whose last remnants I had helped defend. I drank in every historical landmark, possibly for the last time. Who knew what New Labour, with its tin ear for history, might choose to tear down when it got into power.

I passed St Brides Church and Somerset House, walked along the Strand past the Savoy Hotel and the 'Coal Hole'. Crossed over Trafalgar Square, with a nod to Nelson on top of his column, and down Pall Mall with its succession of the London clubs: the Carlton, the RAC and the 'Rag' – the Army & Navy. I turned right into St James past the great wine merchants of Berry Bros and

Justerini & Brooks, before crossing Piccadilly and ending up in Berkeley Square. I took my time along the way, looking at the sights and peering into the shop windows selling everything British gentlemen might need: gold sovereigns, fishing tackle, fine wine, Cuban cigars and handmade footwear. Even expensive lingerie and perfume for their mistresses in St. John's Wood.

Dusk had taken hold. Electric light bathed the streets and the temperature had dropped sharply. When I got to the end of Charles Street, a hundred yards from the Chesterfield, I decided to have a pint in the 'Running Footman'. I liked the anonymity of the English pub. Nobody bothered you. I thought about Rip Van Ryjn and Hu Xianping. I couldn't believe they were working together, but they were both mightily interested in Giles Guedella. It was a three-pint problem.

I swayed into the Chesterfield, exhausted and mildly drunk, around seven in the evening. I was ready for an early night. What I wasn't ready for was a Scandinavian voice:

"Bill Jedburgh, what are you doing here?" Mei Ting was as beautiful as ever. She was dressed in a red silk cocktail dress with black leather patent boots. Her hair was pinned at the back of her head in a traditional Chinese chignon, accentuating her slender neck. As if to prove I wasn't ever intended for monogamy, I felt myself stiffen in arousal.

"I'm staying here," I said. "What's your excuse?"

"I am staying here, too," she replied coolly. "There is considerable interest in Sweden as to what economic policies New Labour will follow, so I am here for the next week."

"And what of Foreign & Ectoxic? I'm sorry," I said, realizing I might have drunk more than was good for me, "Foreign & Exotic?"

She moved closer and tickled me under my chin. She was wearing 'Poison' or 'Opium' or one of those other heavy scents. I felt my senses dulling as alcohol and perfume collided.

"We haven't time to discuss Sir Bernard tonight, I have another engagement. But maybe some other evening we can have dinner?" She didn't wait for my reply but swept out into the night.

20

I slept until lunchtime. It was my second full day of unemployment and my first without company. My body ached from the activity of the previous forty-eight hours, but I now had greater clarity about what I wanted. Events were in play. My pinball had been launched into the machine and it was only a matter of time until the targets started to light up and the bells started ringing.

I grabbed my holdall and walked round to the Lansdowne Club. One benefit of living in the Far East was that I had reciprocal membership of various London clubs. In Singapore the Brigadier had pulled an appropriate amount of strings to have me fast-tracked as a member of the Tanglin Club — which was probably the Lion City's snobbiest club, founded in 1865.

While Dominic turned his nose up at the Lansdowne, which he considered too commercial, it had the benefit of an excellent art deco swimming pool. An hour of sprinting up and down the lanes in a front crawl washed away the remains of sluggishness from my system and I was so carried away by the adrenalin that I followed it up by jogging a couple of circuits around Green Park.

By the time I returned to the hotel it was late afternoon. I contemplated calling Missie, but I wanted to resist further addiction to her company, and her body. Missie was destined for higher things. I was a passing fancy, a battered speed boat briefly coupling with her super-yacht. Soon she would be rich and successful in her own right. I briefly fantasised about us having the life my friend McAlastair had: where his wife made the millions and he wrote his pulpy novels and led a playboy lifestyle with the licence to stray discreetly from time to time. But I knew that would not work for Missie. I was used to discarding women when I had no further use for them. Until now, and I was probably too old to change, women had always been about recreation. The time would come quickly when Missie would discard me. My history, my age and my sexual experience, things she found attractive about me currently, would eventually count against me. I needed to maintain a personal detachment in preparation for that day.

The hotel concierge waved at me as I walked through the lobby.

"Mr. Jedburgh," he said. "Miss Field has been calling for you all afternoon and I have several messages." He handed me a sheaf of them which I read as I took the elevator up to my room. They dated from the early afternoon – the first must have been left shortly after I went over to the Lansdowne: 'Something terrible has happened. Call me, Flick.' In amongst them was a single message from Missie: 'You need to call Flick. I can't believe the news. Missing you, M.'

I dwelt on those last few words while changing into my suit and trying to raise Flick. Her mobile number and the phone at Newbridge House were both permanently engaged, so I decided to head over there in a cab. We were crawling through the rush hour on Piccadilly when I saw a newsvendor selling the Evening Standard. The headline on his board said: 'WESTMINSTER TRAGEDY: LABOUR CANDIDATE DEAD'. I asked the driver to stop and bought a copy. The story was on the front page but didn't have much in the way of detail. What it confirmed was that a body had been found earlier that day in the Palace of Westminster. No formal announcement had been made, but a source close to Tony Blair had indicated it was the Labour candidate for Cannock, Jeffrey Wolf-Madden.

There was a small group of journalists and photographers camped outside Newbridge House. I found the Earl in his study. He looked even paler and more distracted than usual.

"Bill, thank you for coming, my boy," he said. "This is a bad business. Felicity is upstairs in her room. Melissa Li is with her. I'm trying to keep things under control down here. I believe you've met Tony Wolf-Madden, Jeffrey's father?" I recognised the shock of grey hair. He was slumped in an armchair, wearing a dark blue trench coat, the belt tied with a knot. There were paint spatters on his cuff and he had a pale-green woollen scarf wound tightly round his neck. He was clutching a rectangular pint bottle of blended whiskey in his right hand. It looked as if he was drinking straight from it like a hip flask.

"Jedburgh," he mumbled. "You came to the house with Missie. Strong cheek bones. Coiled muscles. You'd be good to paint naked."

"Tony has his London studio near here," Thomas Field explained. "Has done for years, although he mainly paints in Devon now."

"I was up to see the people at the gallery. Got a selling exhibition coming up. Need a new roof on the barn." The artist paused to take a deep swig from his bottle then wiped his mouth on the back of his cuff. "Surprised when Jeff knocked on the door. He was supposed to be doing his politics thing, but he snuck off to tell me about Flick. Damn fool. He'd have been divorced by forty. If he hadn't killed himself."

"Anthony," the Earl had stiffened and there was an intimation of a long history between these two men, and of either distrust or dislike, "I would thank you to remember that Jeff was engaged to my daughter, who would not enter lightly into the sacrament of marriage."

"Nor did we, Tom," he said. "And look how much good it did me: divorced at twenty-three, Audrey dead in a car crash and now in a marriage of sorts with 'Catriona Darling'." He pronounced the last two words in a manner that implied that Catriona Mountfleming's idea of an open marriage, and his own, were quite different.

"We both saw him yesterday," the Earl said. "I was in the House of Lords – we are allowed to use the facilities even though Parliament is prorogued – and he came to see me. He has – had - a researcher's pass so was able to get in as well. We quite often had a drink together in the Stranger's Bar. I enjoyed his company. I gave him my blessing to marry my daughter – not that people seem to need that any more - and that was that. The most important thing was, he agreed to marry in the chapel at Pendragon Hall and was thinking of converting."

Now he mentioned it, I knew the history. The Earldom of Newbridge was an Irish title. It didn't count in London any more. In London he was Lord Pendragon and sat in the House of Lords as such. The Pendragons were an ancient Catholic peerage and I had been dragged sleepily from my bed most Sundays I spent with Flick in Devon to kneel in a draughty pew in the family's baroque chapel. I thought of her as she was then. A dark fury welled up inside me that astonished me. I got a grip before it showed on my face. I'll get the bastard that did this, I thought. She was so happy yesterday.

"I think I need to go and see Flick now, sir," I said.

"Please," he said, looking at me through sad, tired, eyes, "call me Tom. You will come to the funeral, won't you? Tony has agreed we can have it at Pendragon. It will be a private family affair. We have our own burial area and can keep the journalists away."

"Of course," I said. "Let me know if there is anything I can do."

"Just pray for his soul," the Earl said.

"Of course." Prayer had never been my thing. I wasn't going to start now. But vengeance was within my repertoire.

I found Missie and Flick in her boudoir. She was in floral pyjamas, surrounded by paper tissues. Missie was refilling her mug with jasmine tea. The edges of her nose and her eyelids were rimmed in red. She leapt up when I came in and clung to me sobbing. I put my arms around her and let the physical aftershock of her sorrow break itself against my body, until she went limp in my arms.

I placed her gently back in an armchair and kissed Missie on the cheek. We exchanged a glance.

"How has she been?" I asked quietly.

"How do you expect she's been?" she snapped. "You really need to work on your emotional intelligence, Bill. It's as if her entire present and future has been hit by a wrecking ball. She's teetering on the edge."

"Sorry," I said. "We were trained in the police how to inform people that their loved ones were dead, but I was always terrible at it. Other than being told to always say: 'death was instantaneous, and they didn't suffer', I don't remember much."

"Well since in this case he hit the ground from about two hundred feet up, at least one of those statements is true," Missie said, whispering so Flick couldn't hear. "I just hope they both are."

Jeffrey Wolf-Madden had been found dead in Star Chamber Court, inside the Palace of Westminster, having apparently fallen from the rooftop above. The location was apparently notorious because a character in a popular political drama had been thrown off the roof by a Machiavellian – and entirely fictional – Chief Whip some years earlier. The following day's Sun had the headline 'House of Copycats' complete with lurid speculation as to whether Jeff had been thrown off or jumped. Either way, the funeral was not going to be open casket.

"The police told us there is no reason to believe it's not suicide," the Earl told Missie and me when we had calmed down Flick, given her a couple of sleeping pills and put her to bed. "He left a note that simply said: 'There's no other way.' There's still some uncertainty how he was able to get out onto the roof. Something must have mightily disturbed his mind."

That might have satisfied a normal man like the Earl, but I was a professional killer. I had staged enough suicides myself and knew that the best way to prevent a murder being properly investigated was to persuade the police that it was a tragic accident. As a former copper I knew that given half an excuse to classify a death as suicide, any overworked police officer was going to take it. Absent a piece of paper, preferably witnessed by the Attorney General himself, that said 'I, Jeffrey Wolf-Madden, have decided to kill myself in a public and painful way just before winning a seat in the General Election and making an honest woman of my girlfriend', I wasn't prepared to take anything at face value. I could also appreciate that the death raised a lot of questions both for the outgoing and incoming governments, which they would be keen to sweep under the carpet.

"What happens about the election?" Missie asked.

"Canvassing will be suspended and the election postponed," the Earl said. "I understand there is another candidate, a politics lecturer from the University of Birmingham, who is prepared to stand in Jeff's place. He will be introduced at a rally that Tony Blair is addressing in the Midlands next week, before the election. They have asked Flick to attend, but I have forbidden it. She is far too fragile. I remember when her mother died – it was cancer, after you and she had split up Bill – it affected her greatly."

"I'm sorry for both your and Flick's loss, Tom," I said. I was getting the hang of this condolences malarkey now. "The Countess was a good woman."

"Mary heard mass every day," he said. "Went to confession three times a week, even though to my knowledge she never did a bad deed or uttered a wrong word in her life. Unlike me." He looked into the middle distance as if remembering his long life with regret. "We men, Jedburgh, need to live with the reality of this world. It is dark and dirty and fallen. I give thanks daily that my God is one of infinite mercy, because we are in dire need of forgiveness."

"Amen to that," I said, at which he put his hands together as if in prayer. He wasn't wrong about the world being dark and dirty but that's why you had to carry a torch and a broom - or in my case an Austrian handgun with a laser sight, loaded with 9 mm ammunition.

21

We could have borrowed the E-type again, but it didn't seem appropriate. Missie and I took the train from Paddington Station to Devon for the funeral. British Rail was no more, but although 'Great Western Trains' had smart green livery, they were the same grubby old carriages inside, just with re-upholstered seats. We sat side-by-side in a first-class compartment.

Missie was reading a business textbook and listening to music on her Walkman. I was reading the latest Elmore Leonard - *Out of Sight*. I liked the set-up: Older ex-con meets a hot younger US Marshal during a prison break and they end up in the trunk of a getaway car together. That fantasy romance allowed me to pass the time pleasantly until we reached Exeter St. Davids.

We were getting off at Newton Abbot, the next stop, and this bit of the trip had always been my favourite when I visited Flick. The train snaked along the coast, beside red sandstone cliffs that always looked as if they were about to subside into the sea. You were so close to the water you were almost skimming along on top of the blue waves, watched by the tankers and yachts in the far distance, until you turned inwards along the Teign estuary and came past Newton Abbot racecourse.

We took a cab from the railway station, past lampposts festooned with posters urging the inhabitants to vote for all the political parties. The election was only a few days away and Giles Guedella's face beamed out from every other pole. We left the town and headed into the country towards Pendragon Hall. I realised that somewhere within a triangle bounded by Pendragon, Madden Manor and SatBox's factory in Heathfield was the answer to the questions my subconscious had been asking me throughout the journey down: was Jeffrey murdered, what did that have to do with Giles Guedella and where did Rip Van Ryjn and his team of ex-GGK men fit into the picture?

We were stopped by Special Branch men at the gates to Pendragon Hall. I showed them my carry permit and they saluted.

"We've got a couple of VIPs attending the funeral, sir. Just identify yourself to the Chief Inspector on duty when you get out of the car. Sir Bernard arrived about fifteen minutes ago."

Pendragon Hall was a mediaeval manor house with Victorian gothic appendages. A square porch projected from a heavy, square tower at the front of the house above which rose two ancient crenellated towers. The old East Wing ran away to the left and I instinctively looked for the mullioned window that had once been Flick's. Ivy was draped around and across it, just as I remembered. Through bare patches in the ivy I could see the stone shield with the 'dragon rampant sinister devouring a sheep' which was the ancient coat of arms of the Pendragons. To the right was the newer, but still a century old, West Wing with its black granite blocks and the stained glass windows and spire of the family chapel at the far end.

"I should have guessed my father would insist on coming," Missie said. "He knows Giles will be here, and Mummy. He is making mischief again."

"Or perhaps he genuinely wants to pay his condolences? The Earl and Flick both work for him." A snort told me what she thought of that as an idea.

If Sir Bernard was surprised that I had turned up with Missie, he didn't show it. But then he was studiously not showing any emotion. He had shaken Tom Field's hand on entering the chapel and kissed Flick on the cheek, but it was perfunctory. The Chapel was dedicated to St Petroc, a local saint. It was a baroque marble confection that might have stepped from the pages of *Brideshead Revisited*.

For a family funeral there seemed to be a lot of non-family on display. Sir Bernard sat on the right-hand side of the aisle. A few rows in front of him, Giles Guedella – as local MP and a friend of the family – was occupying a pew with the Lord Lieutenant and a couple of dark suited men I guessed were local councillors. In the front pew, awkwardly sat at each end, were two beefy men whom Flick had introduced as John Prescott, the Deputy Leader of the Labour Party and Viscount Cranborne, who was the leader of the House of Lords and presumably, as a hereditary peer, the sworn enemy of the man beside him. Funerals make for strange bedfellows.

Missie and I were on the left of the aisle, the family side, which was entered from the house itself. We had congregated in a side room where the Earl had offered us sherry and then escorted his daughter into the chapel in a bizarre parody of the wedding service, except that, instead of wearing white, Flick was all in black. She was wearing a mantilla over her blonde hair and dark glasses, presumably to hide her tears.

Following them, Missie had the job of steering her stepfather towards the chapel.

"I don't believe any of this papist mumbo jumbo," he muttered. "We turn to dust when we are gone."

"Not so loud, Tony," Missie begged, but he continued to mumble to himself as they set off in front of us. Which left me to escort Catriona Mountfleming, who was as beautiful and elegant as ever. She had hair as dark as any Asian woman's and her perfectly regular features were made characterful by a sensitive mouth and dark, intelligent, eyes. She wore a vintage black dress – I would have guessed Chanel or Jean Muir. She had a single string of natural pearls around her neck and a large diamond brooch above her right breast. She wore the kind of stockings that rustled as she walked. She had deliberately dressed to upstage the entire party. She took my arm and whispered into my ear, in a sultry voice which indicated trouble in store that evening:

"I don't like wearing panties over a suspender belt. They spoil the line of this dress, so I left them off." I gave her a nod and kept the smile off my lips.

The priest was a cheerful North countryman, who although he conducted the funeral mass in English could he heard muttering Latin under his breath. The traditional sentiments of the Earl were made clear in the gales of incense and the plainsong *Missa Pro Defunctis* that a small choir chanted during the service, culminating in a haunting mournful hymn, which Flick told me later was a Russian *kontakion*, that accompanied the dressing of the coffin and its exit from the chapel. Flick has asked me to be a pall bearer, so I joined on at the back and filed out behind the two professional undertakers. The Earl had fiercely insisted on taking the fourth corner, so I contrived to take most of the weight on my side to spare him the burden.

Thankfully the burial ground was no great distance away. I was no great expert on religion, but it ran in my mind that suicides were supposed to be buried in unconsecrated ground. I guessed that was a tradition too far for the Earl.

Afterwards, the guests headed back into the Hall for the wake, but the Earl and I stayed back. He was out of breath and as he recovered it we looked through the metal estate fence at the folly in the distance. It was a round tower that rose some fifty feet into the air. Around it a herd of cows grazed intently, immune to its charm.

"The Seventh Lord built it," he said. "He was in charge of the local excise men. He used to go up to the top at dusk and look for lights on the moor, then send out his troopers to find the smugglers. There are caves and barns up there that were used to hide everything, from brandy, to muskets for rebellion, to wanted men or escapees from Princetown Gaol." I didn't think it wise to add that Flick and I had also gone up to the top at dusk on a number of occasions, to make love not war. I had never seen a light beyond those from the A38 which had spoiled the rural setting of the Hall in the 1970s and destroyed the halt that connected it to the old Teign Valley railway line that now lay abandoned beneath the dual carriageway.

"You know," the Earl said, "there has been a curse on the Pendragons, going back over the centuries."

Well, I supposed if you believed in one sort of mumbo-jumbo, you'd believe in them all. "Flick never said anything."

"It has only ever touched the male descendants, until now," he said. "Have you heard of *droit de seigneur*?"

"The right of the Lord to have any virgin on their wedding night? I thought that was invented for Hammer vampire movies."

"No," he said, "it was a real thing. More honoured in the breach than the observance perhaps. One doubts that the ugly virgins were much troubled by it. But the beautiful ones were occasionally the subject of what we would now, rightly, call rape. My ancestor, Hugh Pendragon, once invoked it. During the act the bridegroom broke in on him, strangled him with his bare hands and left his corpse on top of Haytor to be savaged by the wolves, packs of which roamed Dartmoor at that time, preying on the ponies."

"It sounds like something out of a novel," I said.

"Well, of course, the First Earl went to Stonyhurst with Sir Arthur Conan Doyle. When I first read *The Hound of the Baskervilles*, I did wonder if he had shared the tale when they were students together."

"But surely it is just that, a tale. I used to be a copper and in my opinion man's curse is the inhumanity of his fellow men."

"That may be so, dear boy, but there have been too many unexplained deaths in my family for me to be entirely sure. What is it Faust says? 'no end is limited to damned souls.'"

The whole conversation was too damned gloomy for my soul, so I left him contemplating the folly and his family history and headed back inside in search of a drink. When I got there most of the VIPs and Sir Bernard had departed. The remaining guests were huddled at one end of a mediaeval hall bathed in the lengthening shadows of the Devon evening. It was a long room with a marbled floor and a dais which separated the family dining table from the room where presumably the retainers would have sat. Beyond was a narrow minstrels' gallery. Above dark oak panelling, the Pendragon ancestors looked down on us in sepulchral disapproval, the only splash of colour coming from a portrait of a man in red Cardinal's robes. I was delighted to discover a bottle of single malt scotch on a sideboard. The strong lapsang souchong taste of Lagavulin was more reviving than a cup of tea.

Catriona Mountfleming was deep in conversation with the Lord Lieutenant, who seemed flushed with excitement at having her undivided attention, so I plucked at Missie's hand.

"I need to get out of here," I said. "I've had as much recusant melancholy as I can handle."

"We should say goodbye to Flick," she said, "then get a taxi back to Madden Manor. Mummy and Tony came in the Land Rover and there's no room for us." I hoped

Mummy was driving home, because Tony was slumped at the dining table in an alcoholic stupor.

Flick embraced us both. She looked like she hadn't slept for several days.

"Thank you both for coming," she said, trying to compose herself. She kissed Missie on both cheeks in farewell and then turned to me: "Bill, I have been thinking about this a lot. I can't believe that Jeff killed himself. You were a policeman once. Promise me you'll investigate? There's something awfully wrong about this business. I spoke to Giles after the funeral. He has agreed to help you."

"Of course Flick," I said, and hugged her. "If there was foul play, I will get to the bottom of it."

Supper at Madden Manor that evening was a bizarre affair. Missie and I had changed out of our funeral clothes and were dressed in jumpers and jeans. Catriona insisted in remaining in her finery, because it became very clear she had no intention of putting her panties back on before I had entered her. She placed me beside her, flirted and massaged my leg so blatantly that eventually Missie cracked and shouted in frustration at her.

"Mummy, will you please stop pawing my friend."

She looked at her daughter, seeing her now, as if for the first time, as a sexual rival.

"So you've had him as well?"

"As well?" Missie screeched, turning to me. "Bill, is this true?"

I tried to respond, but was at a loss what to say, which just emphasised Missie's belief that I was guilty as charged.

"He's an adult, darling," Catriona continued maliciously. "He can make his own choices. Maybe you've never had a grown man before?"

Catriona deserved the entire glass of red wine that Missie threw in her face before screaming and running out of the kitchen. I guessed it wasn't the first time that had happened to her. She simply cleaned her face with a napkin, pulled her damp hair back behind her ears and beamed at me with as much sexual allure as she could muster with a drop of red wine still on the end of her pretty nose. I stood up to follow Missie.

"You don't have to leave me, you know," she said, implying Missie was a little girl whose tantrum should be ignored.

"Actually Catriona, I do," I said. Her eyes turned frosty.

This time, rather than stay above the barn, I had taken my bags upstairs and dumped them in Missie's room. I guessed rightly that this was where she had gone. I met her placing my bags outside the bedroom door. She greeted me with a sharp slap on the cheek.

"I deserved that," I said. "I should have told you."

"How could you?" there was a tremor in her voice. "My mother…"

"She's a sexual predator," I said. "I didn't have much choice about it."

"But you didn't stop her either," she said, tears welling in her eyes. "You are sexually incontinent."

"You need to understand, Missie, that when it happened you and I weren't an item. If she had tried it tonight, I would have stopped her."

"Too little, too late," she yelled at me and slammed the door in my face. I was dismissed.

I took my bags to the room across the yard. It felt cold, but not as cold as Missie's rejection. I stood in the darkened room, wondering what to do, when I saw, through the window, a tiny pinpoint of yellow light, glowing steadily in the centre of the black square of the window. Consumed by curiosity, I grabbed my Glock, descended to the ground floor and decided to follow it.

There was an alley consisting of two parallel sets of yew trees that extended along each side of the walk, with a broad grass verge in between. I walked to the end and looked over a wooden gate onto the moor beyond. A track led out in front of it. Missie had explained that it led for miles over the moor to a distant farmhouse, the Manor's nearest neighbour. I tried the gate. There was a padlock on it but when I rattled it, I discovered it had been expertly sawn through so that a simple flick of the wrist was all it took to remove.

The path was solid beneath my Mephistos. It was a dark night. The moon was up, but clouds covered most of the moor in gloom. As my eyes accustomed themselves to the dark, I saw faint spots of luminescence here and there leading onward into the distance. I recognised those. I'd seen them before in the Army. They were waymarkers used to surreptitiously mark a pathway for following troops. I knelt down and examined one. It was luminous paint applied with a tiny precise brush – from a distance it looked like a Christmas tree but on closer inspection was an arrow pointing upwards with a lightning flash on each side. Definitely man-made. Very well then, I thought, the game's afoot. This was the best way to clear my head of thoughts of Catriona and Missie. Sex could give you strength but also made you weak. I was meant to be a hunter, not a gatherer. If there was a wolf out there on the moor – and I guessed it might be a South African one because that was the symbol of 1 Recce Commando – then I was going to find it.

I followed the waymarkers for about a mile until they veered left off the roadway. We were on a narrow path, perhaps used by Dartmoor ponies. The footing was still good, but when I strayed lazily off the beaten track my boots sank quickly into the mud. I understood why the waymarkers were there. This was one of the expanses of bog I had been warned about that could cost the unwary their lives. The waymarkers drew me on and eventually the path started to climb. I could make out raised outcrops of stone silhouetted in the shafts of moonlight which here and there broke through the clouds. We were in amongst the broken boulders of a tor. I focused on keeping my footing, which was a mistake, because the next moment I felt a searing blow on the back of my neck and in the seconds it took to lose consciousness the realisation came to me that maybe I wasn't the hunter in search of a wolf, but a fly which had foolishly become entangled in a spider's web.

22

I awoke to discover myself strapped to a wooden table. There were tight bands of rope across my chest and legs but I could turn my neck. My arms were free from the elbow joints down, but there was nothing within reach for me to grab. For want of anything better to do, I flexed my fingers rapidly to restore their circulation.

I was inside a low-ceilinged outbuilding made of rough-hewn granite. Points of light shone in through the nail-sick slates above me which meant I had been unconscious all night.

There was a low work bench on the right-hand side of the building made out of an old door laid horizontally on rough wooden trestles. It held an assortment of joinery tools, soldering and electrical test equipment - connected up to an old car battery - and a cartridge reloader. I could see jump leads on the bench but tried to stay positive. This looked more like a workshop than a torture chamber.

Sat at the desk was the man with the scar, Rip Van Ryjn, in a one-piece DPM stalking suit. He had chosen, or manufactured, a design that would allow him to blend into the landscape on the moor. His short, platinum white hair bristled on a head which displayed a kaleidoscope of colours. What was left of his undamaged skin was coloured mahogany and leathered through constant exposure to the sun. The skin grafts and scar tissue around his neck wound on the other hand were deathly pale. The scar was even more pronounced when viewed at close quarters. It must have been caused by an incendiary round because burns rippled around the jagged line where the shrapnel had sliced his skin. He was a lucky man. On nine out of ten days he would have been zipped in a body bag by nightfall if a mortar shell had fallen that close to him.

"I let you sleep, Mr. Jedburgh," he said. "You had a busy day yesterday. I watched the funeral." A flash of insight penetrated my throbbing cranium.

"You were in the tower," I said, admiringly.

"At one point, had I brought a rifle, I could have killed both you and the Earl of Newbridge with a single round. I'm as good a sniper as you are, if not better."

"But you prefer to watch," I said, trying to needle him. "Are you just a voyeur or do you work for a living?"

"I have been working harder for my money than you," he said. "My employer doesn't like slackers."

"And who is your employer?"

"A very rich man, who prefers to remain anonymous," he said. "He has an interest in Mr. Guedella and SatBox Communications. I must confess your presence here is simply a bonus, in the light of another project we are working on together."

"Is your employer Chinese?" I asked. He looked at me, then very deliberately spat at the wall behind the desk. A wet plug of chewing tobacco stuck to the granite and then slithered slowly down it.

"I won't work for them," he said. "I would happily send the entire race to Hell." So, he wasn't working for Sir Bernard or Hu Xianping.

"If they are working for the Central Committee, then I completely agree," I said. "But those in other countries are a different matter."

"Like your lords and masters in Singapore?" That brought me up short. If he knew about my links with the Brigadier, and that I could shoot with a rifle, did he know I was the Reliable Man?

"I don't know what you mean," I said, trying not to sound as if I was blustering.

"My employer is rich, well-connected and persistent, Mr. Jedburgh. It took him time and money to confirm that Mr. Kowalcyk's death was ordered by the SID. You supplied the missing piece yourself. When I saw you walk to the pub in Haytor I connected you to our encounter in Wan Chai."

"That's a tenuous link," I said, unwilling to confirm anything I didn't have to.

"You think we don't know you were working for the Singapore Government last year in Atlanta? I have read your police dossier. We've got contacts in the Hong Kong police. Your expertise with a rifle and your knowledge of the island made you an obvious resource for them."

I breathed a silent sigh of relief. Yes, they had connected me to the Brigadier, but not in a way that would be really damaging. I'd worn disguise, so any identification would be based on my size and gait rather than his having clearly seen my face.

"I was working for the Singaporeans in Atlanta," I said carefully. "I don't know anything about Wan Chai or Hong Kong."

He considered my words for a while then said, "I should simply kill you, guilty or not. Brent was a good sort. He liked money, but then we all do. His passports were saving important people from Chinese rule, people of use to my employer. Killing you now would be a pleasure. But we have a better plan for you."

He turned his back and picked up a rifle from the table behind him. It was a Heckler and Koch, the same type I had killed Brent Kowalczyk with. He held it sideways over my chest and then suddenly dropped it. I instinctively reached out and grabbed it before it landed on me. I tried the trigger and the safety catch, but the rifle predictably dry fired. And even if Van Ryjn had been stupid enough to hand me a loaded weapon, I was trussed up so tightly I would have been unable to do anything with it other than throw it at him. Before I could do anything like that, he seized the rifle again. I gave it up willingly, since it was useless to me, only to realise too late that he was wearing fleshtone latex gloves and had a perfect set of my fingerprints on the rifle.

"Do you recognise it?" he asked, with the tone of a man about to make a point.

"It's a PSG1 – we used them in the RHKP."

"You're wrong," Van Ryjn could not disguise his delight. "It is the actual rifle you used when you were in the police." He paced up in down in front of me, deliberately and frustratingly just outside the reach of my hands.

"I told you my employer is rich and I have friends in the RHKP," he pronounced it gutturally – his Afrikaans accent was as strong as if he had just got off the boat from Durban. "The records now show this rifle went missing from the armoury just before you left the force. Which will be very embarrassing for you when it is found at the scene of a violent assassination on the night of the handover complete with your fingerprints and plenty of trace evidence."

I had to hand it to Van Ryjn. He was a cunning bastard. Ice trickled down my spine as I realised what he had in mind. It didn't matter whether he knew I was the Reliable Man or not. He had identified me as a suitable patsy, a believable assassin. Even if I was nowhere near the territory on handover day my prints would be found on a rifle and the killing would be investigated by the no-longer-royal Hong Kong Police, who would be more than happy to ingratiate themselves with Hu Xianping by issuing an international warrant for my arrest and return to Hong Kong. I wouldn't be surprised if they somehow tried to push the blame onto the SID and kill two birds with one stone.

There was only one good thing about this, I figured. It meant Van Ryjn would not want to kill me now. He carefully put the rifle in a gun sleeve and placed it behind him on the bench. Then he bound another rope around me, this time pinioning my hands, which I realised he had left untied simply to obtain my prints.

"I don't think I need to explain to a bright man like you what I plan to do," he said. He was fiddling on his workbench and when he turned round to face me, he was wearing sap gloves. Either that or he was worried about scraping his knuckles when he cut me free.

"Don't worry," he said, ripping open my shirt.

But I was worrying. I knew how much damage the metal sewn into the fingers would do to soft tissue. "You are going to live," he went on. "Just not for too long. I'm guessing that, if the Chinese don't finish you, the old Brigadier who runs the SID will have you killed before you embarrass him by spilling his secrets under interrogation in Beijing."

He stopped talking and started punching me methodically on the stomach. The first few blows winded me, then the pain grew between the blows. He was an efficient and enthusiastic sadist and he took care to leave no part of my upper body and midriff unattended to. I didn't give him the satisfaction of too much noise, but inside I was screaming like a banshee. After five painful minutes he stopped. My kidneys ached and my skin was starting to turn purple.

"Just one last thing," he said, "as one final memento." He had removed the right hand glove and was holding a soldering iron, its tip gleaming red, in his hand.

"I want you to know I am not a complete bastard," he continued holding up a small wooden stick. "I am offering you this as a fellow professional." And with that he thrust the stick between my teeth.

The hot strokes were swift but excruciatingly painful. I bit down on the wood. He had offered it to stop me biting through my tongue rather than out of any genuine sense of compassion.

"What do you think?" he asked. He put a mirror up to my face and angled it so that I could see my right shoulder blade. On it the Christmas tree logo of 1 Recce Commando blazed in an angry red weal. Then he gave me a straight left to the jaw and the Christmas tree lights went out.

When I came to, I was lying spreadeagled on a moorland path. I had a khaki field dressing on my right shoulder and my entire body ached. There was no sign of Rip Van Ryjn or the building in which I had been held captive. He must have carried me far from it to keep its location a secret. The sun was low in the sky but there was enough light to work out that I must be north of Madden Manor – I hoped it was the same path I had started out on the previous night, because I had no option but to set off down it. My throat was baked with a dry insistent thirst, but after staggering a few hundred yards I found a pool of brackish water beside the track. I fell to my knees and lapped up what I could, before resuming my journey. An hour later, when I was almost done for, I reached the gate in the Yew Alley.

23

In my nightmare, I was running for my life down a moorland track being pursued by a shadowy creature. It might have been a dragon, it might have been a wolf, but I knew with certainty that Flick and Missie were dead, savaged by this awful creature. A man with a giant scar on his neck had released it on me. I had watched it seize Flick in its enormous jaws and devour her and then, despite her using every ounce of kung fu skill she possessed, Missie had been its next victim. Now I was running on tiptoe along the Yew Alley towards Madden Manor. If I could reach it, I would be safe. But the faster I ran the more the yew trees stretched out in front of me. The poisonous walls were closing in around me and when I turned, the awful creature was gaining. Fire burst from its open mouth, its eyes glowed and its muzzle was outlined in flickering flame.

I awoke, drenched in sweat, in Missie's bedroom. I was completely naked on top of her bed, having thrown off the covers. Whatever delirious dream of a disordered brain had prompted my nightmare, my fever had now gone. I examined my right shoulder. The field dressing had been replaced with a large green leaf strapped to it with pink tape. I felt it with my left hand. The wound was tender, but otherwise the pain had gone. Beneath the dressing I could smell a pungent embrocation. On the bedside table was a stone jar with a paintbrush protruding. The label on the jar said 'Healing Mixture, Spring 1995'. I felt my chest and realised that whatever was in the jar had been pasted over my body. Bits of herbs and greenery were stuck to my chest-hair.

I got up and looked in the dressing room mirror. My chest was black and blue but whatever was in the healing mixture had done its work and I felt no pain. I looked at my Rolex. It was noon on I knew not what day.

After I had showered and dressed I went in search of Missie. Instead I found Catriona in her parlour with a distinguished looking man with pepper and salt hair and a trimmed beard. He was in his sixties and dressed like a college lecturer in a brown sports jacket, tan cardigan and corduroy trousers. He was wearing bulbous leather shoes that looked like Cornish pasties.

"Bill," said Catriona. "This is Frank Bennett, from *The Guardian*. An old friend from my youth. He came looking for Missie, but she went back to London yesterday evening. He's writing a piece about Foreign & Exotic." The man shook my hand firmly. My shoulder protested a little, but I returned his grip.

"I've been working on an exposé of F&E for some time now," he said, in a precise but slightly ethereal voice. "I was hoping for an interview with his daughter. Sir Bernard refuses to comment on the record. Do you know him?"

"We've met on a few occasions," I said, cautiously.

Bennett explained that he believed that F&E, with the full knowledge of Sir Bernard, had indulged in business practices that ranged from the reckless to the criminal. He spoke of sweatshops in the East Midlands, child labour in China and Indonesia, competitors aggressively discouraged or taken over by legal and illegal means. What Bennett didn't have was anyone from the Company prepared to talk on the record. Without that, or some other smoking gun, his editor was not willing to take on Sir Bernard and risk a libel suit.

"I came down here because I got wind that Foreign & Exotic were planning to bid for Giles Guedella's business," he said. "I thought that information, coupled with the election, would make it topical enough that my editor might run the story anyway. I saw Guedella, but he refused to discuss Sir Bernard, whom he said was a family friend, and insisted that his priority was the election. I think he will lose, based on what my colleagues tell me. Maybe he will talk to me then."

"Frank," Catriona said, putting her sexual charisma into third gear, which was all it took to make Bennett putty in her hands, "I think you'd better go now. I promise I will talk to Missie and ask her to contact you. I've got your business card. Now, Bill had a bad fall up on Fox Tor and needs to rest." She ushered him out of the door and returned carrying a steaming mug of yellow brown liquid. I looked at it enquiringly.

"It's honey brandy with some crushed aspirin in it," she said. "I used it on set every morning to ward off hangovers and keep my voice supple." The warm alcoholic broth slipped down my throat. It was exactly what I needed.

"What was in the stuff on my shoulder?" I asked.

"I don't exactly know," she said. "It's a recipe that Tony had passed down from his mother. I think she was part witch. The Wolf-Maddens have lived here for centuries. Before that the manor was the family home of the Pendragons, until they built Pendragon Hall. Every spring he disappears for half a day and comes back with a plastic bag full of greenery that he dries, grinds with a pestle and mortar and turns into paste. It smells disgusting, but I've never seen it fail."

"What happened last night?" I asked. "The last thing I remember is staggering down the Yew Alley."

"Tony found you outside his studio when he went out to paint," she said. "We carried you up to Missie's room and he dressed your wound and sat with you until the fever broke. He's in his studio now. I'm afraid he may have sketched you while you were naked and unconscious. Artists like Tony and I are no respecters of persons."

"You're both quite incredibly self-absorbed," I took her to task. "You were horrible to Missie. I don't regret the sex we shared, but I care a lot about your daughter. She's pretty special."

"Yes," she said, "I see that now. I apologised to her yesterday morning and we spoke. She waited for you but, when you didn't reappear, she got the train back to London by herself."

"I had an encounter on the moor."

"Tony thought you might have met our wolf - the Beast of Hound Tor."

"Another old wives' tale from his mother?"

"This is a bit more prosaic. The locals say it escaped from a local animal sanctuary. The more of the local beer they drink the more likely they are to spot it on their walks home."

"The animal I encountered was two-legged," I said.

"Those beasts are the worst," she replied.

I found Tony Wolf-Madden in his studio. There was a large canvas on his easel and I could see the outline in sepia watercolour of a naked man on a bed.

"You've recovered," he said. He went over to a side table, poured generous slugs of whisky into two jam jars and handed me one.

"Your body is quite wonderful. A wounded Spartan warrior in repose," he said, swigging from the jar and looking at me dispassionately. "No shortage of battle scars."

I shrugged. "I was a soldier and then a policeman. You get into some scrapes."

"Catriona cares about Missie," he said. "But she has been a selfish beauty since long before I met her."

"Your first wife died in a car crash?"

"Catriona slept with me on the night of the funeral. I had painted her picture not long before and she turned up at the service uninvited. She wore the same black dress to Jeffrey's funeral." He finished his whisky and refilled it. Mine was barely touched.

"Just before she died, Audrey told me that Jeff wasn't my son and that she was planning to leave me," he said. "She wouldn't tell me who the father was." He looked at me as I took in the news. "I didn't kill her," he said, seeing the inquiring look on my face. "I did however strangle her cat."

"And yet you brought Jeff up as your son," I said.

"What else could I do? Catriona wasn't cut out to be a stepmother. She could barely cope with Missie, which suited Sir Bernard just fine. I'm a high functioning alcoholic. I need to be, to paint well. I had just enough left in me after my art to raise a child. Not that I understood him."

"How so?" I asked.

"You never met Jeff, did you?" he said. I shook my head.

"He was always a quiet melancholic child growing up. Idealistic almost, filled with great passions. Socialism was the latest. I think he would have grown out of it just like he grew out of coin collecting. Would you like to see a picture of him? I have one here."

He rummaged through a stack of canvasses and pulled one out, propping it up on the easel on top of my portrait. It was of a meek-mannered teenage boy, with a straight severe face and a firm-set thin-lipped mouth. I had seen the face before, recently. It had been worn by a man in the red robes of a Cardinal, hanging on the wall in the great hall at Pendragon. I looked at Wolf-Madden in amazement.

"You knew, didn't you?" I said. "That Tom Field was Jeffrey's father. Why didn't you say anything?"

He laughed grimly at my discovery and our shared secret. "I suspected," he said. "But I loved Audrey and no good would have come from more scandal. I'm an artist. Catriona and I are not followers of conventional morality. The destinies of the Pendragons and the Wolf-Maddens have been entwined for centuries." He rummaged in his collection of paintings and pulled out another canvas, much larger than that of Jeffrey. An enormous wolf stood over a dead body. It was baying exultantly with blood on its muzzle. Behind it the moor stretched away with the broken stones of a tor in the far distance. It was a raw, powerful, piece of art.

"Did Tom tell you the story of Hugh Pendragon?"

I nodded.

"He probably didn't tell you that the man who strangled him was my ancestor, Roger Madden. The woman he raped lives on in our bloodline. We added the Wolf to our surname in her memory. In those days we lived over the moor in Merripit. Hugh's heir, Sir Thomas Pendragon, gave my family this manor house in expiation of the curse."

Things fell into place. I understood why Flick and Jeff had never been allowed to meet as children. I also understood why the Earl had been so concerned about the curse at his funeral, so obsessed with the sins of his family and so keen to bury Jeffrey in the family plot. But surely a rabid Catholic like the Earl would not have given his blessing to the marriage? He had lied to me, which meant he might have lied about other things too.

"Tony," I said, "before you have any more to drink, could you drive me into Newton Abbot?"

24

Outside Newton Abbot station I was besieged by canvassers. Eager-faced youths thrust New Labour and Lib Dem leaflets at me and I realised it was the day of the General Election. The next train to Paddington was over an hour away and the leaflets reminded me I had unfinished business with Giles Guedella. I strode over to an elderly woman in sensible tweeds with a blue Conservative rosette pinned to her lapel.

"Good afternoon, madam," I said, in a suitably deferential manner. "Can you point me in the direction of the Conservative offices?" She looked at me blankly.

"The Conservative Club?" she asked.

"If that is where I'll find Giles Guedella, then yes."

"Lord knows where Giles is," she said. "Could be anywhere in the constituency on polling day. But the Committee Rooms are up there on the right in Queen Street. You can't miss the balloons."

A ten-minute walk brought me to a shopfront covered with blue balloons and a large poster saying: 'Re-elect Giles Guedella'. Inside there was an atmosphere of controlled chaos.

"It's appalling," a red-faced man in a Barbour jacket was saying. "They're deserting in droves."

I went over to a desk where a harassed man in a tweed jacket sat with a pen ticking off canvass returns against sheets of names taped to a desk.

"Can you help me?" he asked.

"Can I help you?" I said, confused.

"Thanks for the offer," he said. "I'm Craig, Giles' agent. Wait over there, a car will pick you up in a minute." I was lucky. The next car was Giles Guedella's Land Rover.

"Jedburgh," he said. "Come to help? That's excellent man. Roger has to go now to collect his kids. Can you drive?" Before I knew it, I was hurtling down country lanes being given directions by a high-voiced Young Conservative who was squeezed on the bench seat between myself and the candidate. When we stopped Guedella either jumped on the back of the Landie with a loudhailer, encouraging people to vote, or strode into polling stations to thank the officials and find out from the tellers outside how his vote was holding up. Every so often we would get out to knock on doors and check if supporters had voted. Quite a few turned out to have New Labour or Lib Dem posters in their windows.

"Thank God the students are back at university," Guedella said. "This is squeaky bum time."

"Have you lost?" I asked, unable to understand the nuances of our activity.

"Not while we still have fuel in the tank," he said and pointed me towards the next destination. We covered half the county in that fashion and by the time the polls closed my lower back hurt nearly as much as my shoulder blade.

Just after 10 p.m. we pulled up outside the Committee Rooms in Newton Abbot. I'd missed my train, but I was now caught up in the excitement of the democratic process. It was not something we'd ever experienced in Hong Kong, despite Governor Patten's earnest efforts.

I sensed that history was being made here as power shifted from the creaky old right to the flashy new left. We were greeted with news of an exit poll which confirmed not just a Labour victory, but a landslide. The Conservatives were forecast to lose half their MPs and there was no knowing yet if Guedella was amongst them. You had to give the man credit. Staring defeat and humiliation in the face, he stood in the middle of the room and gave an impromptu speech:

"Thank you all for your hard work today," he said. "Whether or not I lose tonight, you are all winners." I caught a glimpse of the charisma Guedella brought to politics. If he departed, the Mother of Parliaments would have lost a favourite son. He came over and shook my hand.

"Thanks Bill," he said. "You didn't need to do that."

"There will be another train to London tomorrow," I said.

"Well, come to the count instead. We'll be going all night and I'll put you on the milk train in the morning. We can feed you too. We're going for a Chinese."

The 'New Era' was a classic British 'Chinese' restaurant – which meant Cantonese, but not as I knew it from Hong Kong. I was confronted by red tablecloths, inlaid wooden marquetry and a list of numbered dishes including the ever popular *gu lou yuk* - sweet and sour pork. We sat at a large round table with a lazy susan piled with dishes spinning round in the middle. There were about a dozen glum people at the table. They divided into chopstick wielders and those who stuck resolutely to a fork and spoon.

I looked around the table: local councillors talking shop about planning applications; Young Conservatives worried about drinking too much Tsing Tao beer in front of their MP; and older military types in blazers who still pined for Margaret Thatcher and the short sharp shock. I had been placed between Guedella – who busied himself talking with the constituency chairman to his left – and a youngish retiree with gently greying hair who had moved to Dawlish after thirty years in Hong Kong. Stephen Hands had helped create the Mass Transit Railway, that since its opening in 1979 had grown rapidly until it now moved a million people across Kowloon, Hong Kong Island and the New Territories every day. Although we knew people in common our paths had never crossed. We both agreed the handover meant that our former home would never be the same again.

"It's funny," he said. "But we never got any thanks for the way we ran Hong Kong. The MTR is a case in point. We invested money and made everyone's lives better. We are not the wicked imperialists the Chinese and the socialists over here make us out to be, are we, Jedburgh?"

"You must find it strange to be back," I said.

"It was my wife really," he said. "If I'd been single, I might have been tempted to move to Singapore like you did. Copied our MTR system they did. I just didn't want to become a drunk old expat in Phuket like a lot of my friends. Would you consider coming back to the UK?"

"No," I said. "This visit has convinced me there's no place for me here. I find the UK's politics, weather and business world a mystery. I understand Thailand and the Philippines much better. But I quite like your MP."

"Well let's hope I am still his MP when the night is over," Giles Guedella said, joining in the conversation. "It's in the lap of the gods now."

"You'll be OK," Hands said, but I could tell from his eyes he didn't really mean it. The whole gathering was subdued as they contemplated the scale of the disaster their party was facing. Around midnight the first of them headed over to the count and eventually there was only Guedella and me left.

He explained that the candidate stayed away until the count was further advanced. Before that was the collection and delivery of the ballot boxes – in a semi-rural constituency like his that could take more than an hour. Then they had to be opened and the ballot papers agreed to the votes recorded as cast at each polling station before the counting proper could begin. During this, the scrutineers from each party could get an idea of the likely outcome. But votes spilling out from a ballot box in an affluent rural or a working-class urban area would look very different, and it was only after several hours, with the ballots starting to pile up, that you could see whether your candidate was in with a chance.

Guedella and I stayed in the 'New Era' drinking Great Wall wine while we waited for his agent to send someone to fetch us. The wine was as toxic as the last time I had drunk it during a visit to Shanghai. Now that the adrenalin of election day had subsided, he looked tired and drawn.

"It's a sad truth," he said, "that all political careers end in failure. Every MP when first elected believes that they could become Prime Minister, or at least a member of the Cabinet. Few do and most are sacked or leave office having achieved a fraction of what they wanted to. Look at Maggie."

"So why bother?" I asked. "You seem like a man of action, not talk, to me." He looked me in the eye and I saw a gleam return to his.

"I suppose because I also dream of becoming PM," he said. "But mainly because when Parliament does its job properly, there is no more intoxicating place to be. The proximity to power, the feeling that you are part of a centuries-old tradition, the ability to help real people and to occasionally make a difference. These things become absorbing."

"More absorbing than running a leading satellite business?"

"Different," he said. "I'm fed up of juggling the two: a demanding scientific team and regular international travel doesn't sit well with constituents wanting you to open a village fete in Trusham on a wet Saturday in June."

"So if you lose, you won't sell to Sir Bernard?" I asked. He looked at me and started to say something, but then thought better of it.

"What do you know?" he asked. "It's supposed to be confidential."

"I heard reference to a Project Hatstand," I said. "Missie confirmed it. I must say," - now seemed as good a time as any to push Dominic Tweddle's agenda - "that I don't like Sir Bernard Li or the company he keeps. Johnny Aston is a friend and he's worried."

"Burcotts will make a good fee advising the board if a bid is launched. That assuages a lot of doubts." Guedella seemed conflicted, I sensed. He didn't want to have this conversation.

"Johnny likes you," I said. "There must be a better way."

"Just stay out of my business," he snapped. For a few seconds his guard dropped. The anger wasn't directed at me, but at whatever bind he found himself in. It disappeared as quickly as it arose, but I was left with a feeling that something other than his own free will was behind the sale.

"Of course," I said. "I'm sorry, I didn't intend to interfere."

"Are you sure about that?" he said. "I have a feeling that you and trouble are on first name terms. I'm not even sure what it is you do? You just seem to float around the place, turning up here and there." There was a suspicious look in his eyes.

We were interrupted by Stephen Hands. Craig, Guedella's agent, thought it was time.

"It's very close," Hands whispered to me as we walked over towards the leisure centre where the count was being held. It was a brick and steel shed that smelled of sweat and cheap anti-perspirant. A large sports hall more used to midweek badminton matches had been transformed into a sea of paper and milling humanity. Long trestle tables were piled with votes. In some places counters sat inertly with piles of votes in front of them, talking amongst themselves. On other tables they worked feverishly placing ballot papers into piles for each candidate and then binding them together with elastic bands like twenty pound notes. It all felt a bit Victorian. Nothing much had changed since Disraeli and Gladstone jousted in Westminster.

People carrying clipboards – wearing rosettes to confirm their affiliation – were watching the process and occasionally arguing with each other and the officials. In the centre of the room at a table was a harassed man who Guedella explained was the acting returning officer. He was the Newton Abbot Town Clerk who ran the logistics of the count on behalf of the actual returning officer – an elected politician who would struggle to add up a round of drinks properly.

On entering the room Guedella was surrounded by his activists. Some were gloomy, others mildly positive. Everyone agreed he was neck and neck with the Lib Dem – a curly-haired politics lecturer who lived in Teignmouth and had assiduously knocked on every door in the constituency over the past five years, since coming second to Guedella in 1992.

I wandered out into the tearoom, where I bought a cup of coffee and a Kit Kat. The television was tuned to the BBC. The results seemed worse for the Conservatives than the exit poll had been. I watched a succession of blue rosettes putting on a brave face when they lost their seats. Computer graphics showed John Major being deluged with bricks to indicate the scale of the landslide – the worst for over a century. Things might only get better – the New Labour slogan – but they would have to get a lot, lot, better before there would be another Tory government. If a foreign correspondent like Martin Bell in a white suit could defeat a Tory – albeit one who allegedly took cash for questions – in their fifth safest seat, who knew if the party even had a future? By three o'clock in the morning Tony Blair already had enough MPs to form a government and the Lib Dems were winning seats as well.

Inside the sports hall, Stephen Hands was leaning against a wall talking to a couple of activists from the other parties.

"We look like we might be heading for a recount," he said. "It's too close to call."

"Not for us," said a man wearing a red Labour rosette who had the weather-beaten face and stocky build of a fisherman. "It's between your man and the Liberal Democrat. I hope that Red Fox keeps the seat to be honest. He's been a good constituency MP even if I do disagree with his politics." That comment offered a glimmer of hope for Guedella. If enough people thought like that it might tip the balance.

There was a commotion at the table in the middle where the acting returning officer was talking to the candidates and their agents. Guedella looked grim. Eventually, the Conservative agent called his activists together:

"We're about four hundred votes ahead," he said. "That's a 0.8% majority and well within the margin of error. At the request of the Lib Dem candidate, the returning officer has agreed to a partial recount. They will be scrapping over every vote."

He explained that there were always dubious ballot papers. People put crosses in the wrong place or against more than one candidate. There were also numerous ways to 'spoil' your ballot. In one case a voter had crossed out the female Labour candidate's name, written in TONY BLAIR and put a cross by it. Spoilt vote.

I had no part to play, so I went for another coffee. On the television, a grinning Tony Blair had arrived at the Royal Festival Hall to a rock star welcome. Would it make any difference with him as Prime Minister? As Dominic had said: whoever you vote for, the government gets in. But it felt like a decisive break from the past.

Back in the hall the candidates were assembled on a makeshift stage and waiting for the returning officer to announce the result. The names of the candidates would be read out in alphabetical order along with the number of votes cast. First, we had the Greens, Labour and then the candidate for 'Rainbow Dream Ticket' – a party apparently founded on the advice of aliens – who got 150 votes. Eventually there were only two candidates left. Guedella got just over 25,000 votes, to strong applause and a few jeers. The emotion in the room was extraordinary. When the returning officer said "...Liberal Democratic Party, twenty four thousand..." the precise number was drowned out by whooping cheers and the stamping of feet. The actual majority, I discovered later, was 281.

"...and I declare the said Giles Fox Guedella, duly elected as the Member of Parliament for the Newton Abbot constituency." The Red Fox had beaten the odds.

25

After the celebratory drinks with his supporters. After the newspaper interviews. After the television reporters, still not sure what the big stories of the night would be. After a final round of handshakes with the returning officer and the local coppers. After all that, Giles Guedella headed home. Which turned out to be a small worker's cottage behind his office in Heathfield. I returned with him and grabbed a few hours of kip in the guest accommodation next door, before we caught the train together to London.

I left Guedella at Paddington Station. He had been thoughtful for most of the journey. Perhaps the heaviness of his party's defeat, despite his own lucky escape, was weighing on him. Maybe it was the decision he had to make about the future of SatBox. He was clearly wary about confiding in me. He did agree to meet me at the House of Commons the following day so that we could look at the site of Jeffrey Wolf-Madden's suspected suicide.

Some of Guedella's good luck had rubbed off on me. They say it comes in threes. I arrived at the Chesterfield in a cab just as McAlistair stepped out from the one in front of me. He was, as usual, travelling heavy. I reckoned at least one of his cases contained a tracking device larger than a microwave, installed by his wife.

"Bill," he growled as we embraced. "Good to see you, mate. I'm rushing to see my publisher. The wankers are moaning about the neo-colonial tone of my novel. Let's meet up for dinner." Then he rushed off.

Second, a note had been left for me at the front desk. "Can I see you tonight? There's a private party at the Kensington Roof Gardens – late till early. Missie may be there. Love, Flick."

Finally, as I stood waiting for the lift, a third slice of serendipity:

"Buaya Brother!" – the upper-class English voice was unmistakable.

"Dago de Souza, you dodgy old shoemaker!" I said. He grabbed me and gave me the full-on double cheek kiss – the genes he inherited from his hot-blooded Spanish father temporarily eclipsing those of the upper-class English debutante whom he had swept off her feet.

"What the hell are you doing in London?" I asked, delighted to see him.

"Flogging Cinderella her latest slipper," he said cryptically.

"Tonight," I said, "we are having dinner with a third brother." He looked at me in astonishment. He didn't know yet that I had persuaded McAlistair to have a crocodile tattoo – the same one that Dago and I shared - inked onto his wrist. The Buaya tattoo was similar to the Lacoste logo but faced the other way, was about two inches long and normally crouched hidden beneath a gentleman's wristwatch.

Which is how the three of us found ourselves in 'Langan's Brasserie' that evening, starting dinner with a shot of tequila, each of us lapping salt from our respective Buaya tattoos. A bit of an indignity for the Herencia de Plata Reposado that Dago had brought with him and for which McAlistair had paid an outrageous corkage, but we planned to finish it at leisure after the meal. We both admired McAlistair's Buaya. Although ours had been done by Wing Cam's devilish tattoo master Mr. Duong in Vietnam, Julian's had been etched in Bangkok, with mine as the model. Slowly we were adding members to our exclusive club. A Scotsman called Rory had applied and we were considering whether his vices met our stringent entry requirements.

Over dinner I brought the lads up to speed on Sir Bernard and Missie. McAlistair had seen her picture in the *Tatler* and showed a gratifying level of envy when I confirmed that we had made the beast. The food and more wine arrived. McAlistair was in charge and so it was the signature calves' liver and bacon paired with a Chapoutier Le Pavillon Hermitage.

"I had lunch with Harry Bolt just before I left," he said, pushing his empty plate aside and reaching again for the wine list that had been expressly left by his elbow. "Harry was just back from checking on his investments in Hong Kong." – paying off the right Chinese middle-men in advance of the handover more like – "The word on the street is that the Chinese want their own trading *Hong* to exploit the export potential of the SAR. They've supposedly done a deal with Sir Bernard. He gets a new banking licence and funds it with the sale of half of F&E

to mainland Chinese investors, who are holding it on behalf of the Central Committee. In exchange, Sir Bernard becomes the next Chief Executive of the SAR once Tung Chi Wah has done a year or two and is ready to retire. Harry says it's practically a done deal, but they won't announce it until sometime in the autumn."

I had been feeling shockingly mellow, but this news hit me in the face like a bucket of ice water. No wonder Hu Xianping had wanted me well away from Sir Bernard. It was like twisting the dial to open a safe mechanism: to and fro in different directions, but with each significant move another tumbler dropped into place.

Tung Chi Wah had run his family's shipping line OOCL - one of the largest in the world when he took over from his father - close to bankruptcy. The Chinese government had bailed him out. That made him an eminently loyal choice as Chief Executive designate, despite his questionable management skills. If he faltered, as he was almost bound to, Sir Bernard would be a dark horse hidden in the pack who could take over and lead from the front. No-one would imagine that the favourite had been nobbled by his own trainer.

If Sir Bernard stepped up in a year, it would conveniently be after he had taken control of SatBox. I wondered how Missie would feel about being at the beck and call of Beijing? It would be the final betrayal from a father who had majored in it throughout her short life.

McAlistair and Dago got on as well as I had expected. When you met Julian there was always a danger of appearing in one of his books. He harvested his experiences to produce pulpy, sardonic thrillers and - because he and his wife were wealthier than Donald Trump - he didn't give a tinker's cuss about what anyone said or thought about him.

Dago, it transpired, was in London to work on footwear for London Fashion Week the following September – designers were always a season or two ahead of the rest of the punters.

"I have some great ideas," he said. "But I need that big breakthrough." He deserved one. His shoes were outrageous, but great. That evening he was wearing a pair of cranberry suede brogues that might have tempted even me.

My name was on the guest list at the 'Kensington Roof Gardens': 'Bill Jedburgh plus ?' got the three of us in. The joint was banging. I had known it as Derry & Toms Roof Gardens – as a teenager I had enjoyed Michael Moorcock's books – before I ever visited it. Unlike Jerry Cornelius in *A Cure for Cancer* I wasn't expecting to be napalmed by NATO helicopters, but given the last few days I wasn't ruling anything out.

The roof gardens dated back to the 1930s when Barkers Department Store bought out Derry & Toms and built them to attract shoppers. Now they belonged to Richard Branson, of Virgin records and airline fame. It was the only place I knew outside of Florida where you could party with pink flamingos. Around the pavilion were three separate gardens of which my favourite was the Spanish, with its Moorish columns and palm trees. Which is where we found Flick Field, on a banquette in the cloister with a bottle of upmarket Cava. There was a stiffish breeze, but it was warm enough to sit outside without shivering and the deep bass from the featured DJ was far enough away not to be unpleasant.

I introduced her to Dago, who fitted right into the surroundings. Their eyes locked and for the first time since I had met her for lunch in El Vinos, she smiled. McAlistair had wandered off somewhere but I assumed he would find his way back.

"Thanks for coming, Bill," she said. "What happened? I spoke to Missie and she said you disappeared." She fixed me with a long look for longer than was comfortable, then asked me: "Can I just check that you never slept with my mother?" I shook my head: Mary Field had only ever had one real boyfriend and that was the Lord Jesus. I had never met a more religious woman in my life. I suspected that the only times she slept with the Earl had resulted in Flick, her two sisters, who had become nuns, and her younger brother Ruari, now a film producer in LA. After which she had bound her legs shut with a rosary.

"I went for a walk to clear my head and had an encounter with the Beast of Hound Tor," I said. She scoffed.

"Had a few too many pints in the 'Cleave' in Lustleigh and couldn't find your way home across the River Bovey more like," she said.

"Anyway, I spent the day canvassing with Giles Guedella instead, who is delighted to have won his seat. I'm meeting him tomorrow to investigate Jeff's death." I looked at the expression on her face and kicked myself.

She was probably thinking that Jeff too would now be an MP had he lived.

"I'm sorry," I said. "Blair's victory must be bitter-sweet for you."

"If you must know," she said. "I wasn't looking forward to the whole MP's wife bit – I know the ways that they stray. Of course, he wanted me to give up my job and work for him. I was torn between losing my own career and keeping an eye on him."

"You must follow your own way," Dago said emotively. "Be true to yourself. By the way, did anyone tell you how beautiful your calves are? You have fine legs and a delicate foot." Flick blushed. I don't think her feet got much of an outing other than in sensible shoes and Hunter wellies.

I left the two of them to get better acquainted and went in search of McAlistair. He could be a bit of a loose cannon after drink had been taken. Beneath his urbane charm lay a frighteningly violent man. His sergeants in the police force had always referred to him as *Din Gau* – meaning Crazy Dog. They had found him a most effective interrogator because his unpredictability cast fear into the hardest Triad Red Pole.

Julian was on the dance floor. He seemed to have attracted his usual bevy of exotic beauties. He was strutting his stuff to the Spice Girls.

"Meet Beatrix Van Hoensbroeck," he said. She was well over six feet tall and very blonde. I figured she was either Dutch or German. "She's involved in relaunching the Almanach de Gotha. Because she's going to be in it," he continued, "twice. She has a Dutch and a German title." I left them to investigate their family trees by themselves.

My Buaya brothers were pairing off. I was still by myself and there was no sign of Missie Li. One person I recognised, standing by the bar, was Mei Ting. She was wearing a long silk midnight blue evening dress with a side-slit up to her thigh. Strobing coloured lights played across her honey-coloured skin and glittered in her eyes. She smiled in delight as I sidled up to her. She linked her arm in mine, directing me into a quiet corner of the garden.

"Have you finished your piece on Tony Blair?" I asked.

"Gordon Brown," she said. "He is the man that will keep Blair in power. Because he wants to be Prime Minister when Blair makes way for him."

"I don't know if anyone ever gives up voluntarily. Do you think Sir Bernard Li will retire voluntarily?"

"Only if he is offered a more glamorous job," she said. She seemed remarkably well-informed.

"You've heard the story then," I said. "Is it true?" She smiled in that particularly feline way of hers which reduced me to the size of a small and helpless rodent in her paws.

"Journalists hear everything," she said. "We like pillow talk. Perhaps I can interest you in some." She moved closer, for the kill. The heavy musk of her scent was on my nostrils. She raked a crimson fingernail down my throat, parted her ruby lips and whispered in my ear. "My sources tell me you should stay away from a man called Hu Xianping. He has been asking questions about you. They say he is a trade counsellor at the Chinese embassy, but I know he is a spy."

"How so?" I asked.

"Some of the diplomats talk in their sleep," she said. "They are afraid of him."

I wanted to know more. But I sensed that if I wanted to learn it, I would need to trade some pillow talk of my own. I was suddenly tired. I wanted to see Missie again, for no other reason than we had unfinished business.

"Maybe we could have dinner soon and discuss it," I said, kicking the can down the road without ruling out in which gutter it might find itself in the future. She looked disappointed but put her hand to my face and stroked it gently.

"Don't wait too long," she said. "I'm going back to Stockholm early next week. You interest me very much, Bill Jedburgh. You are not the boring bodyguard that you pretend to be. There are hidden depths to you."

"If you're lucky," I said, teasing her, "I will reveal all when we meet again."

By the time I returned to the bar in the pavilion, McAlistair was by himself with a bottle of Macallan. Dago and Flick had left together. I signalled for the barman to bring me a glass and joined him.

"Beatrix abandoned me for a Von Thurn und Taxis," he said. "It's like bloody Eurotrash Top Trumps in here."

"They're not like us," I said. "Oh for a night out in Pattaya."

"The Russians are really taking over there," McAlistair said with a snort of irritation. "Can I pay you to go and clean things up like that time with the German gang?"

"That was a bloody disaster," I laughed. Don't remind me. Now I advise you to focus on your work. Don't let some dalliance here or there distract you from the important task of becoming the new Somerset Maugham."

"Which one of your arms would you like me to rip off for that kind of frivolous comment? For that, I'm going to return the favour. You're getting a bit googly eyed over that Missie lassie. You carry on like this we'll expel you from the Buaya Society."

"She's a bit special," I said and felt stupid when I heard the words come out of my mouth.

"Unlike you to fall that hard for a woman."

"Must be getting older."

"She's not for you. Enjoy the ride while it lasts."

McAlistair and I had worked our way through most of the bottle before Missie turned up. She was wearing white Guess jeans and a bright red puffa jacket. She clearly wanted to talk to me alone, so we walked off towards the edge of the roof gardens. Before I could open my mouth, she stopped me:

"Let me say this, please," she said. There was salt water in her eyes. "I don't blame you for what happened. Mummy explained how she took advantage of you. But I think we need to put a stop to our relationship. I loved having you as a friend, but I can't see a future for the two us as lovers."

As soon as she said it, I knew she was right. Missie Li was an extraordinary woman. I had no close female friends. Women had always been for recreation. I loved them and I consumed them, but I didn't interact with them on an emotional or intellectual level. But if I were to choose any woman as a friend, it would be Missie.

"Missie Li," I said, kissing her on the lips for old time's sake. "You are far too sensible for someone so young. Let's work on that platonic friendship thing."

26

Everybody has heard of Guy Fawkes. He's even got his own night on the Fifth of November when they burn him in effigy on a bonfire for failing to destroy the Houses of Parliament. The world's most unsuccessful terrorist and even Catholics launch fireworks to celebrate his capture. Hardly anyone remembers Richard Weobley, who actually did destroy the Palace of Westminster, in 1834, by setting off his own bonfire inside it.

Weobley had been told to burn tally sticks – the pieces of wood that had been used for centuries to keep government accounts on – because they were now obsolete. The furnaces used were under the House of Lords and the resultant fire spread into the chamber and destroyed more or less the entire palace. It was the biggest blaze in the capital between the Great Fire of London and the Blitz.

What replaced it had become the most memorable symbol of London alongside Tower Bridge and Nelson's Column. Big Ben chimed the quarters and – across the airwaves – hours, imitated by timepieces all over the world, even in the LegCo in Hong Kong. It was the Mother of Parliaments, and it was now under the control of Tony Blair and his New Labour buddies.

Giles Guedella was waiting for me at the St Stephen's entrance. The only nod to modern security was a small grey-green Portakabin by the entrance in which sat a walk-through metal detector and a security man. I'd left my Glock in the hotel safe to avoid any misunderstandings, so I passed straight through. Guedella, as an MP, was allowed to walk straight up the steps and was talking to the policeman on duty when I joined him.

"Lot of new names to learn, sir," the policeman was saying. "At least you'll know what you're doing."

"Well yes," he said, "but I'll still have to remember to turn right not left when I enter the chamber. Come on Bill, I'll show you what I mean."

The place still had a school holiday feel to it. As we walked he stopped occasionally to greet the few fellow MPs who had come in early, to either commiserate or congratulate. I noticed he seemed to be equally well-liked by MPs from all parties.

"Most people won't be coming in until next week," he said, "so I think it will be OK to show you the Chamber." We walked along a corridor full of statues into the Central Lobby - a square gothic tower, with four tall stained-glass windows celebrating each of the four countries making up the United Kingdom. This was where any constituent could attempt to 'lobby' his MP. From the Central Lobby you turned right into the Lords or left into the Commons. At the entrance to the Commons was a statue of Winston Churchill, his foot worn away where hundreds of MPs had touched him for luck. The Chamber was smaller than I imagined.

"After the Germans bombed it during the War," explained Guedella, "Churchill insisted they rebuild it just as it was."

Green leather benches ran along each side, rising in tiers. Like so much about Britain it was archaic. The front benches on which the ministers and their 'shadows' from the opposition sat were two swords' lengths apart. There wasn't room for every MP to get a seat. The Speaker – a former chorus girl - sat in a chair at the far end in ceremonial robes, with the Parliamentary Mace in front of her as a symbol of its power.

The Government is on the left of the Chamber," Guedella said pointing. "Their benches are going to be stuffed to overflowing. We will be on the right with a lot more room, sadly."

We retraced our steps, but not before I had stood in front of the despatch box where Tony Blair would shortly give his first address to the House as Prime Minister. I tried to think what I would say in those circumstances. For some reason the line from *Twelfth Night* came to mind: 'Dost thou think, because thou art virtuous, there shall be no more cakes and ale?'. Then I addressed myself to Jeffrey Wolf-Madden's death.

"Where do we start?" I asked.

"A better question," said Giles, "is where we should end. The Palace has two miles of corridors, over a thousand rooms and 11 courtyards. I think we should start from where he jumped." He took me up several flights of stairs and into a small rectangular room with a low ceiling. It had a table at the front with a dozen chairs facing it.

"This," he explained, "is the lobby correspondents' briefing room."

I looked at him blankly.

"The lobby are the newspaper and television correspondents," he explained. "They cover Parliament and are able to talk to us in the Member's Lobby, hence the name. They are briefed by the PM's spokesman, but anonymously – attributed to 'Downing Street Sources'. That used to be Gus O'Donnell on behalf of John Major, but will now be Alastair Campbell, I would imagine."

"And we're here because?"

"Because of this." There was a fire door at the far end of the room and Guedella pushed it open. It gave on to the roof of the building.

He ducked and headed out onto the rooftop and I followed gingerly. It was an amazing view, over the leaded roofs, with the Clock Tower in front of us. I looked round, amazed there were no snipers in evidence. If this was LegCo there would have been a couple of my former colleagues watching the roof for intruders. Here there were only pigeons.

"The Palace is the domain of the Speaker," Guedella explained when I asked him. "Ever since the time of Charles the First, the Police have been kept at arm's length. Frankly, it's an anachronism. I can't see it lasting much longer."

We worked our way around the side of the Star Chamber Courtyard until we were looking back at the St Stephen's Tower we had entered through. Westminster Hall, one of the few buildings to survive the 1834 fire, was on our right. I looked down. No-one could have survived a fall like that. But there wasn't a lot of room for a struggle either. This looked more like Reichenbach Falls. If Jeff had been pushed, he would have more than likely taken his attacker with him.

My shoelaces had come undone and I edged my way back cautiously, not wanting to trip over them and become another dead body in the courtyard. Once we were inside I knelt down to tie them.

"Shall we discuss what we think happened over a drink?" Guedella asked, while I was fiddling with my shoelaces. He led the way down to a small elegant bar called the Pugin Room which was shared by Peers and MPs.

"I know that Flick is concerned about foul play," he said. "But I just don't see it. I spoke to the Serjeant-at-Arms and the suicide note had been left on the desk in the lobby correspondents' room. If the Serjeant hadn't got to it first, it would have been photographed and appeared in all the papers. It was sealed in an envelope addressed to the Speaker, in the same handwriting as the note inside. Tom Field identified it as Jeff's. Whichever way you look at it, it must be suicide."

I wasn't so sure, but then Guedella hadn't spotted what I had as I bent down to tie my shoelace. A glint of silver which I had palmed then slipped unobtrusively into my pocket.

We sipped an indifferent claret in silence for a while. Perhaps we were both reflecting on our memories of Flick. Or maybe Project Hatstand was the elephant in the room. It was time to be more direct with my questions.

"Now you've been re-elected," I asked. "Will you definitely sell SatBox?" He looked at me with furrowed eyebrows and then relaxed, waving away whatever impediment had been between us with an extravagant hand gesture.

"I will tell you what is happening," he said, "but it must remain confidential between us. And if I discover you have used the information to enrich yourself, I will have you hunted down." It was an odd phrase to use, but I was happy to agree.

"I've no desire to make a financial killing," I said. "I have enough income for my modest lifestyle." That was being disingenuous. I loved making money more than the average Brit. Avarice was Hong Kong's legacy to its children.

"That's good," he said. "Project Hatstand will give me enough money to pursue politics without worrying about whether I am a minister or not. Only the very rich in here are truly independent. I told you the truth that I want to be Prime Minister, but only on my terms. I'm not sure if my fellow Conservatives would ever elect me and frankly, we may never have enough seats to form an administration again while I am young enough. The next Conservative PM may be younger than you."

"But why sell to Sir Bernard Li? He is going to do a deal with the Chinese, I'm certain of it. You are giving our best British company and important communications assets to a potential enemy." My news didn't surprise him. It was there in his eyes and in the way he reacted. He knew. He was silent for a while then he said:

"You know, Bill, you and I are on the same side, but this deal is more important to me than you could imagine. The money alone is transformative. Perhaps your experience with Missie has coloured your view of Bernard. I don't want to believe he is a traitor."

"That's just the point," I said. "He won't be a traitor. In May a lot of people in Hong Kong who formerly owed allegiance to the Queen are going to find themselves kowtowing to the new Emperors in Beijing. Even people I would have trusted with my life and liberty might deprive me of it then, if instructed to do so by their new masters. Sir Bernard is a calculating and vicious businessman. You can't trust him to do the right thing just because he is 'one of us', because despite his knighthood and his British passport and his house in Upper Brook Street, he won't be one of us any more."

Guedella, for the first time that day, refused to look me in the eye. He knew I was right, but he was wilfully choosing to ignore it.

"My mind is made up," he said. "I need the money." I could do nothing further. I got up and shook his hand. Part of me respected that. If a man wanted money it was his right to sell what he owned. Unlike Dominic Tweddle and his ilk, I was neither a patriot nor a sentimentalist. I was just a bloke who did dirty work for money. But in this case it had started feeling personal.

"I don't understand why, Giles," I said. "But if that is your decision, I won't mention it or try to change your mind again." What I was going to have to do was find a smarter way to stop the deal.

When I got back outside onto the pavement in Parliament Square, I fished the object I had found upstairs out of my pocket and realised I might have found a solution to my problem. In the palm of my hand was one of a pair of cufflinks. It was solid silver with a coat of arms engraved on it. A cufflink I had last seen Tom Field wearing when he was drinking with Giles Guedella in Islington, the day that I had lunch with Robin Cook and Flick. A coat of arms that depicted a dragon devouring a sheep.

27

I was having breakfast with McAlistair when my new cellphone rang. I had decided to take a few days off and had spent them accompanying Julian on his usual round of shopping, drinking and book-signings. My body still ached from the beating it had taken from Rip Van Rjyn, but regular sessions in the Lansdowne Club pool and the gym at the Chesterfield were having an effect, not to mention visits to a couple of Soho massage parlours, of which McAlistair seemed to have an inexhaustible list in his little black book. We hadn't seen much of Dago, who seemed to be doing his part to distract Flick from the grief of losing Jeff.

I was still mulling over the strands of the problem in front of me. It was probably the most complicated set of circumstances I'd faced since I came up against Maupertuis in Sumatra after refusing to kill Cardinal Tosca. That was a story so baffling I hadn't even told McAlistair.

"Bill," Dominic sounded stressed on the other end of the phone. "Johnny and I need to meet you. It's got to be somewhere discreet. Could you find your way to the 'Kings Head' on Chiswell Street, beside the Barbican, as soon as you can?

"Barbican? Is that near the Tower of London?" I asked. He sometimes forgot I hadn't lived in England for fifteen years.

"By London Wall," he said, "which is north of the Guildhall. You'll find it on the tube map. If you ask a local they might know it as the 'Brewery Tap'."

I emerged at Barbican tube station - the iron logic of the underground having taken me from Green Park via a change at Kings Cross - to find a grey concrete sixties monstrosity of aerial walkways, half-moon skylights and tall balconied towers. In search of the 'Kings Head', I walked through a tunnel choked with diesel fumes and contemplated the mess that the British had made of rebuilding their cities after the Second World War. I assumed the entire area had been destroyed in the Blitz, but knowing the blatant disregard for history that the gods of mammon encouraged, maybe someone had just been bribed to knock down whatever it replaced.

The 'Kings Head' was a classic double fronted English boozer which was surprisingly full for 11 a.m. on a weekday. I bought a pint of Trophy Bitter and found Dominic and Johnny at a table in the back.

"Why do they call it the 'Brewery Tap'?" I asked.

"The old Whitbread brewery is next door," Dominic explained. "It closed in the 1970s, but the Head Office is still here. The banks and lawyers are moving up here now, but this part of the City was always a border area: Cripplegate-without-the-walls. This is where you find printers and small traders, students and the few locals who actually live in the City. After the war there were less than 50 people left living in Cripplegate. Then they built the Barbican and invited in all the yuppies."

"You didn't bring me here for a history lesson," I said. "And I bought my own pint. Shall we get on with it?"

"There's been another offer for SatBox," Johnny said. "I was contacted yesterday by Deutsche Morgan Grenfell. They have a Central European corporation ready to buy it for cash and which has provisionally offered a higher price than F&E. They will provide me with the name of their client and proof of funds in the next couple of days. At that point they will be a bona fide potential offeror and able to ask for any information we have provided to F&E."

"Isn't that a good thing?" I asked. "It blows the Chinese out of the water."

"The problem is," Dominic said, "that Guedella doesn't want to accept the offer. He still wants to sell to F&E."

That stumped me. I won some thinking time by draining my pint – which required the subsequent purchase of a fresh round and a couple of whiskies from the bar.

"Guedella told me he was only interested in the money," I said. "If that's all that motivates him it makes no sense. Could he be on the Chinese payroll?"

"It's possible," Dominic admitted. "But he helped us out in Moscow during the 1980s and we vetted him then. There was absolutely nothing to indicate it. Anyway, if he was a spy, he could simply hand over the details of the encryption system to his handler."

"I agree," I said. "He strikes me as a patriot. But I'm not the best judge of that quality. I think there is another problem."

"What's that?" he asked.

"Rip Van Ryjn's employer. I suspect he's behind the other bid."

"Who the hell is he?" Johnny asked. "He sounds like a Dutch porn star."

"He's the boss of the two Malaysians who staked out Ashurst Manor the other day," said Dominic. "The ones that Bill worked out his aggression on." Johnny winced. The memory was clearly still vivid.

"Van Ryjn said his boss had an interest in SatBox," I said. "It would explain why he was observing Guedella in Devon."

"If he's employing Van Ryjn he could be as bad as the Chinese," Dominic said. "Especially if he's funding the group that Van Ryjn is in bed with – New Reich. Central European would fit the bill – there are a lot of influential neo-Nazis in the former Warsaw Pact countries." Johnny Aston looked worried:

"There's got to be somebody I can sell this bloody thing to that won't give me or HMG nightmares," he said. "I've got to earn my fee somehow."

"I have had the impression for a while," I said, "that there's another reason Guedella wants to sell to Sir Bernard. It's there in front of me, I just can't fit the pieces together."

"That's OK," said Dominic, "we can do what we normally do with you, Bill."

"Which is?" Johnny asked.

"Ask him to become the tethered goat."

Johnny had to head back to the office and Dominic had a meeting at the Bank of England later and was planning to spend an hour in the Kings Head reading the *Financial Times*, so I walked back through the tunnel towards Barbican tube station. I was halfway along it, just by an office block set back from the roadway around which the tunnel seemed to have been built, when I heard an American voice call out my name. In the entrance to a residents parking garage was the man I had seen at Haytor with Giles Guedella. He was still wearing his trench coat, looking like a Jewish Inspector Clouseau. I approached him warily.

"I've seen you before," I said, "with Giles."

"I'm a friend of his," he said. "Abe Berenson. I've got a rare book business in Museum Street. Can we speak?" I wasn't a book collector, and I didn't think Guedella was either. Antique radios, maybe. I owned a couple of historic firearms. But it was an interesting turn of events.

"Sure," I said, assuming it wasn't about books. He led me through the parking garage and up onto the high walk above. We found ourselves in probably the prettiest part of the Barbican, not that this was a high bar. There was an ornamental pond with fountains. Strips of greenery broke up the grey-brown concrete and gave the balconies of the flats ranged around it something to overlook. In the middle was the Guildhall School of Music and here and there on park benches around it were students carrying instrument cases. We found an empty bench and sat down.

"You need to know, Mr. Jedburgh, that we are on the same side," the man started. He had a friendly face, but with an underlying hint of menace. He looked more like a restaurateur than a bookseller, but then you can't judge a spy by his cover. And I'd met enough of them by now to know this man was a spook. I wondered why the CIA were interested in me, but I wasn't going to let him have it all his own way.

"Mr. Berenson," I said, "I'm fed up of people telling me we're on the same side and then either lying to me or trying to kill me. If we're on the same side, you can tell me what's going on."

"All I can tell you for now," he said, "is that it is vital that you stop trying to interfere in SatBox. Giles knows what he is doing."

"Does he?" I asked. "You must know Hu Xianping. Whatever game you think you're playing with Guedella, he's too smart to fall for it."

"If you value your life," he said, standing up. "You won't use that name in public. It could be the death of you."

I don't know whether it was the mention of the word death, the sixth sense you needed to stay alive in my game, or the fact that I moved my gaze slightly to follow Berenson and caught the flash of light reflecting in a telescopic sight. I reacted just in time. The force of my shoulder knocked Berenson off balance and he crashed to the ground with me. As he did so he gave a sharp cry and blood appeared at the waist of his raincoat. The first shot was followed by two further rounds that I heard ricochet off the concrete beside us. There was no sound from the rifle, so the sniper must be firing with a suppressor. I dragged Berenson towards the shelter of a low brick wall beside the water feature.

"How badly are you hurt?" I asked him.

"I think it's just a graze," he said, grimacing. "I don't think it's a gut shot."

I had unholstered my Glock, but I didn't dare lift my head above the parapet. I guessed it was Van Ryjn: he'd boasted to me about his sniper skills in Devon. I knew roughly where the shot had come from, but the complex was a maze of walkways with multiple lines of fire and if Van Ryjn had any sense he would have relocated and given himself a second chance at taking me out when I tried to go after him. Then I thought about it: Van Ryjn needed me alive. It's not always about you. Sometimes it's about the person you're talking to. He had been trying to kill the American, probably to stop him talking to me.

"Stay where you are," I ordered him, somewhat redundantly as he showed no sign of breaking cover. Then I crawled along the wall seeking an alternative vantage point, which I found just around a corner, where there was enough of an overhang from the balconies above to keep me in shadow. I spun over on my back and pulled a Zeiss monocular out of my pocket. Scanning the surroundings I realised he could be anywhere. After five minutes I stood up and instantly zigged then zagged. No shot. I looked over to the low wall where I'd left Berenson, but he was gone. A City of London policeman with the distinctive red and white chequered cap band was now standing there talking to a student with a tuba case. That explained why the shooter had shut up shop.

Berenson was nowhere to be seen, which is precisely where I needed to be before the student pointed me out to the cop. I made my way out of the Barbican by a roundabout route – there had obviously been no money left over for signposts when they built the place – and went back to the Kings Head.

Dominic was still in the bar and had moved on to the *Investors Chronicle*. He looked concerned when I relayed the news of the attempted assassination, which had been accomplished so quietly that even now there were no police sirens piercing the City air.

"I think this guy Berenson must be CIA or some other American alphabet agency," I said. "Could Guedella be working with them? That still doesn't explain why they would be interested in selling SatBox to the Chinese though, does it?"

Dominic smiled one of his enigmatic spook smiles.

"It's even better than that," he said. "Abe Berenson may not know his cover has been blown, but I happen to know he works for Mossad."

28

It was later that evening when I presented myself at the Earl of Newbridge's door in Islington.

"Bill, come in," he said. "I'm afraid Flick is not at home." I had planned it that way. She had gone to the cinema with Dago to watch Val Kilmer in *The Saint*. That, and anything they had planned afterwards, gave me a couple of hours.

"It's actually you I've come to see, sir," I said. "Could I have a quiet word in the library?" As an assassin, I had come to like libraries. All that wood pulp masked the sound of gunshots.

He quietly ushered me in to the room, looking even more distracted than usual. I think he had been waiting for me, or someone like me, to call. I put the silver cufflink on the writing table between us. He poked it with his long forefinger and flipped it over to reveal the Pendragon coat of arms.

"You found it, my boy," he said. "That's excellent. I couldn't work out where I'd dropped it."

"You dropped it when you spoke to Jeff in the lobby briefing room in the House of Commons," I said without emotion. "Just before he either committed suicide or was pushed." Whatever colour was left in the Earl's face drained away and he sat down suddenly in one of the high-backed brown leather library chairs beside the fireplace. There was a decanter on a table nearby. I poured us both a brandy and handed him one. Then I sat in the chair opposite, but not before removing the Glock 17 from its belt-holster and placing it on my lap.

"I want you to know," I said, "that Flick is very dear to me. As boyfriend and girlfriend all those years ago, we were both a disaster, but I still wish her well. Why didn't you tell her that Jeff was her half-brother?"

He squirmed in his chair, then finally said: "I promised Audrey that she and Jeff would never meet and that I would never tell him who his real father was. It was almost the last thing I said to her, before we crashed."

"You were in the car with her," I said. This tale still had the power to surprise.

"I was sulking that she had rejected me," he said. "We had been seeing each other for three years. When we met, Tony was going through a period of manic painting and boozing in London and Mary was on a silent retreat in a convent in West Cork. We were both invited to a friend's house for dinner and one thing led to another."

It wasn't hard for me to visualise, knowing the personalities. The Earl was an unworldly man, but an affectionate one.

"What happened that night?" I asked. His eyes strayed to the Austrian metal on my lap and he got the message that reticence was not an option.

"There's a house in Merripit that's part of the Pendragon estate where we used to meet. Because people would recognise us, we had to find out-of-the-way places to meet. She told me that, although she had once considered leaving Tony, her mind had changed now the baby was born. She wasn't prepared to leave Jeff with a nanny while she saw me. She was going to try and be a better wife to Tony."

"You must have been angry," I said.

"On the contrary," he said. "I had expected it for some time, but it still hurt. Audrey was driving me home across the moor and we were bickering. She turned to say something just as a Dartmoor pony appeared in the middle of the road. Audrey loved animals. If we'd just run into it the car would have been a wreck, but we would probably both have survived. Instead, she swerved and the driver's side of the car hit a stone gatepost and killed her instantly."

"What happened next?" I asked. I had checked the newspaper accounts that afternoon and she had been alone in the car when the Police found her. My initial hypothesis had been that Tony Wolf-Madden had followed Sir Bernard's example and cut the brakes. He seemed like a man who could do more or less anything in a drunken rage.

"I came around a few minutes later," he said. "I realised Audrey was dead and I could do nothing. My presence would have made things worse, so I got out, wiped my fingerprints from the car door and the dashboard and walked the rest of the way home. I burned my clothes in the furnace under the East Wing. Mary never asked what happened to them."

"Then you did your best to forget him and her."

"I never forgot her," he said. "I could never bring myself to confess her either, because that would have required me to repent of our time together. I have been in a state of mortal sin ever since." He looked distraught. "'I cannot wish the fault undone, the issue of it being so proper'."

I recognised the quote from *King Lear*, which was not exactly a manual of good parenting.

"When Flick told you that she was going out with him, you should have said something," I said sternly. He nodded.

"I tried," he said, "many times. I hoped the passion would extinguish itself, but they were so very alike."

"When he came to see you that day," I said, "to ask for Flick's hand in marriage, he got more than he had bargained for." He was on a roll now and embraced the open doors of my confessional.

"Jeff tried to deny it at first, but he came to see it was true. Then he said it didn't matter. That the fact they had grown up apart excused their..." he searched for the word, "...consanguinity."

"You threatened to expose him if he didn't break it off," I said. "When he realised you were serious, you fought." The Earl looked sad, slight and broken in his big chair.

"I have never been a fighter, but he struggled against me. That must have been when I lost the cufflink." He was silent again, lost in his own thoughts. I let him compose himself. Silence was always a more powerful interrogation technique than shouting. Neither of course was as good as an electric shock to the testicles, but it was not that sort of an interview.

"Then you left without seeing him off the premises?" I knew the Earl was not the killer, but I also knew that the position in which he had placed his son would have tested the sanity of a stronger man than Jeffrey Wolf-Madden.

"I'd given him an ultimatum. I thought he needed time to come around, but I believed he would agree. I left him looking at a piece of paper, trying to compose a note for Flick. You have to believe me," he said. "If I had known he would use the paper to write a suicide note on and then throw himself off the roof, I would never have left him."

I believed the old man. If there was a Pendragon curse it came from trying to reconcile the reality of human nature with the dictates of conventional morality. I lived outside it myself. I killed and fornicated, and the consequences rarely troubled me. It was easier for me to see that Tony Wolf-Madden and Catriona Mountfleming, bohemian and self-centred as they were, would have been better role models for both Jeff and the Earl. I picked the gun up off my lap and decided what to do next.

"Did you come here to kill me?" the Earl asked.

"It had occurred to me," I admitted. "But I never really thought you pushed Jeff off the roof. You would probably have died falling with him if you had tried. No, killing you serves no purpose and might even make things worse for Flick."

"Thank you," he said weakly, and finished his brandy. "You had such a grim look on your face that I was convinced you had killed before."

I stood up, re-holstered the Glock and poured him another one.

"But you still need to atone for what you have done. Think of me as a priest who cannot give you absolution but can help you achieve some reconciliation."

"Absolution? Reconciliation? What do you mean?" To the Earl these were precise liturgical terms. I was using them in a different way.

"Flick needs a father," I said. "She need never know what happened between you and Jeff. Guedella is satisfied it was suicide and I will tell Flick the same thing, provided you help me with a small matter."

"Do you need money?" he asked, looking worried. "Is this blackmail? I'm afraid we have very little wealth left and Pendragon Hall is heavily mortgaged."

I shook my head. "I don't need any money," I said, "but I do need to stop F&E taking over SatBox. I am going to make a call in a few minutes and you are going to tell the gentleman on the other end of it everything you know about F&E as Chairman that Sir Bernard Li has paid you to forget: the scandals, the potential investment from the Chinese and the fact that Sir Bernard is being lined up to be the next Chief Executive of Hong Kong."

"Is that true?" The Earl was puzzled. "I know about the Chinese investment proposal but that last piece of information is news to me."

"You know now, and it's important that you tell the man that you heard it from Sir Bernard. A venial sin, to expunge your mortal one. Isn't that what you Papists call it?"

He was quiet for a while, and then nodded.

"I love Flick very much," he said. "I admired Jeff from afar, but Flick, Ruari and the girls are my real children. I will do anything to protect them."

"Thank you," I said, and picked up the phone beside me to dial a number I had obtained that morning from Catriona Mountfleming.

"Frank?" I said when my call was answered. "Bill Jedburgh. I've been speaking to the Earl of Newbridge and he has agreed to answer your questions. I suggest you get in a cab immediately and come to Newbridge House in Islington. And bring your tape recorder."

Two hours and most of a decanter of brandy later, I ushered Frank Bennett out of the house and followed him into the street. The Earl had taken the view that if it were done then 'twere well it were done quickly. He had answered Bennett's questions and given him some answers to questions he had never dreamed of. He had also planted the seed of Sir Bernard's appointment as Hong Kong Chief Executive as I had hoped he would.

"This is explosive," Bennett said. "I reckon when I write this up it will make the front page of *The Guardian*."

"I'm counting on it," I said.

As he headed off in one direction, I saw Dago and Flick turning the corner from the other. They hadn't seen me and so I retreated back into the shadows until they reached the front steps of Newbridge House. They were deep in conversation and Flick had her arm around him.

She was happy again, for a while. With Dago it was unlikely to last, but he would treat her like a princess while it lasted. Every woman deserved to be treated like a princess at least once in her life. Not everyone – and I included myself in this category – was cut out to be a prince. I was the Lord High Executioner, and quite happy in that role, although tonight I had stayed my axe.

29

Mei Ting called me at breakfast-time. I was sitting in my suite at the Chesterfield, in the hotel-provided towelling robe, digging into a grapefruit. The danger of staying in British hotels was that frequent consumption of bacon and eggs thickened the midriff, hence my precautionary attempt to murder a citrus fruit. It was either that or run three times round Hyde Park and I was expecting a busy day on the phone.

"Are you free for dinner this evening?" she asked. Delivered in a voice that resembled satin curtains being drawn together, it was more an instruction than a question. I took it that way and said I was very much at a loose end, McAlistair having flown to Jersey on the next leg of his world tour. We agreed to meet for a drink in the bar that evening and then head out to dinner.

Since Missie and I were now simply friends, I couldn't think of a better way to spend an evening than grappling with the Business Correspondent of the *Svenska Dagsbladet*. Business correspondents were the theme of the day - I had just finished reading the man in *The Guardian* declare the revelations published on the front page of the paper about Sir Bernard Li, to be 'staggering'. The morning news on the BBC had led with the story and I'd watched a Brummie business reporter interrogating a City pundit on the effect this would have on the F&E share price. I wasn't particularly surprised, therefore, that my next phone call was from Johnny Aston.

"Was that your doing, Bill?" he asked. "Next time you plan to crater a share price could you have the good grace to let me sell my personal holding first? You've cost me ten grand this morning."

"If you hadn't lectured me quite so pompously over dinner the other weekend about the dangers of insider dealing," I said smiling to myself, "I might have. But I'll buy you a bottle of Cristal the next time I see you to soften the blow."

The day before I had instructed a broker I used in Liechtenstein, who believed me to be a German dentist called Karl Graunitz, to 'short' – that is sell stock I didn't own – F&E's shares. Ironically it was Johnny who had taught me how to do this when we met in New York the previous year. I would ring my broker later and buy the shares back at the new cheaper price to complete the trade and bank a £50k fee for my hard work in putting Frank Bennett and Tom Field together. Harry Bolt would have been proud of me. It was illegal, but so was being the Reliable Man and that had never stopped me getting a good night's sleep.

"You can bring the pop round to dinner at my place in Wapping on Friday night," Johnny said. "Better make that a couple of bottles. Just got word that Tweddle's finally off to Hong Kong at the weekend, so I'm having a little party of close friends and City types. Porter

Garland is in town from New York on business and I've got a private floor show planned for after dinner."

"Sounds fun and potentially very bad for my liver," I said. "I'm in. But returning to business: have we killed Project Hatstand?"

"Looks like it, old boy," he said. "I had a call from Ishbel at Hoare Govett this morning. Their board is reconsidering its strategy. Which is code for: if the CEO didn't own so many shares he would be toast. Instead he is going to have to eat a lot of humble pie. My guess is Tom Field will have to fall on his sword instead."

"Greater love hath no man than to sacrifice his friend for a life," I said, misquoting St John. Frank had not named his informant in the article, but it wasn't going to take Sir Bernard long to work out that the Earl of Newbridge was the 'source close to the Board' who had comprehensively knifed him.

I was feeling very pleased with myself when I put the phone down, but the next call, from Flick Field, took the smile off my face.

"I've lost the F&E account," she said. I could tell she had been crying. "They're bringing in some big guns from Burson Marsteller to do crisis management and Sir Bernard said it's 'inappropriate' for me to be involved as Dad is Chairman." She burst into tears. "I think he's planning to fire him."

"It will probably be for the best," I said, trying to soothe matters. "Why not have lunch with Dago and then spend the afternoon in bed?"

"You're dreadful Bill," she said. "But he is wonderful. That's exactly what I'll do, if Dago's free. I still feel that

I'm being unfaithful to Jeff. But I realise now how much he was obsessed with the game of politics rather than with me."

"Dago is just as obsessed by shoes," I pointed out.

"He's made me the most beautiful pair," she said, with real emotion in her voice. "Six inch stilettos and they make my feet look beautiful. He's working on a pair of riding boots. We're going eventing together at the weekend."

Maybe their relationship would work. But I was too much of a cynic to believe in happy-ever-after. Happy-for-now was the best most of us ever got. Guedella and I had met with her the previous day and told her that we were satisfied that Jeff had committed suicide.

"I'm so pleased Flick. We will never know what brainstorm caused Jeff to kill himself," I lied, "but some happiness for you is definitely in order."

"Thank you, Bill. It's been lovely to have you back in my life as a friend," she said. "I think these past few weeks have healed something for both of us." Although I hadn't thought about the woman once in the previous fifteen years before we'd reconnected, she was probably right.

In anticipation of an active night, and in the knowledge that with a thoroughbred like Mei Ting I was going to have to bring my 'A' game, I slept most of the afternoon. I was freshly showered, shaved, suited and booted when I walked into the hotel bar that evening. Mei Ting was already sitting at the bar wearing an electric-blue cheongsam mini-dress and drinking a Blue Lagoon to match. Her hair was fastened behind her head and she wore long white horsetail earrings that brushed seductively around her long neck when she turned to face me. Her slim bare legs occupied most of the area between the bar stool and the floor and her high-heel shoes had a partially open front revealing immaculately manicured and painted toenails. If she had lived in old Shanghai in the 1930s – and she had about her a sense of that decadent time and place – she would have given Lin Guisheng, the notorious beauty of the Green Gang, a run for her money.

This was beginning to feel like an enjoyable evening, so I started with a pink gin. It didn't match my suit, but it did match my mood. I would be quite happy lapping something pink for most of the night.

"Sir Bernard Li will not be a happy man this evening," she said.

"Do we have to talk about him?" I asked. "I no longer work for him. Nor his daughter."

"A free man, then?" she said.

"Free, yes, but I am very particular with whom I spend my time." I ran my hand down the outside of her thigh. I was never subtle at the best of times. She caught my wrist in her hand and looked me in the eyes.

"There will be time for that later," she said. "I have booked a private room at Mosimann's. Just for two."

I liked that idea. Anton Mosimann's private dining club in Belgravia was the perfect appetizer to an evening of debauchery. A private room would allow plenty of scope to fool around over dinner. The look on her face told me she was in a similar mood. I ordered another pink gin. We were in an elaborate dance now. We both knew what we wanted. It was like a striptease. You had to play by the rules to get there, but in the end, everything would be on display.

Mei Ting knew how to put on the Ritz. When we emerged from the Chesterfield there was a Rolls-Royce Silver Spur waiting for us. It was also electric blue and matched her dress. By this stage my head was zinging with the alcohol I'd consumed. I wanted her badly. She must have had the same idea because she said to the uniformed driver: "Take the long way via the Mall."

She had chosen a car with plenty of room in the back deliberately. There was a bottle of Taittinger in the cocktail cabinet, so I poured us both a glass as the car pulled into traffic, but she waved hers away.

"Suit yourself," I said, taking a sip, because I had an inkling what she had in mind. I always found Taittinger a touch too acidic for me, but this one cut nicely through the fuzz from the pink gin.

"I want something else to drink first," she said, and got down on her knees. I obliged her by draining my glass and dropping my trousers.

It was one of the most erotic blow jobs of my life. She started slowly around my base and worked steadily upwards. Every so often her horsetail earrings brushed against my balls and her sharp tongue and long fingernails gave me minute flashes of sensation as she worked. She finally took me inside her mouth just as the Rolls was going round the statue of Queen Victoria in front of Buckingham Palace. She gently squeezed her teeth against my glans, and I came with gusto. I looked up at the Empress of India and wondered whether she ever serviced Prince Albert as well as Mei Ting had serviced me.

Afterwards she sat beside me like a princess, delicately patting her lips with a handkerchief and reapplying her makeup flawlessly from a compact she retrieved from the centre compartment. It was clearly a routine she had perfected. I knew we were only a few minutes from Mosimann's and I thought I'd try and get myself decent as well. But try as I might I couldn't get the motor function together to pull my trousers back up. I started to giggle. Sex and alcohol didn't normally have this effect on me, but Mei Ting was some woman. I looked over and my vision started to swim. We were pulling up on the other side of the road from Mosimann's and I needed to get my act together.

I was still flailing around when the door opened and the chauffeur reached in. He pulled my trousers up from my ankles and fastened my belt. Then he grabbed me under the armpits and hoisted me out. By this stage I was almost limp in his arms. The alarm bells that should have been going off since Mei Ting refused the glass of champagne started to ring. The trouble was that I now had so much sedative in me that they sounded like they were three floors above me and somebody had put a tea-cosy over them.

There was a door open opposite the rear passenger door, leading down a flight of steps into a basement bar. I heard myself mumble:

"Mosimann's is over there. Wrong restaurant, darling."

"Oh Bill," she said, "I warned you to stay away from Hu Xianping. I may simply have forgotten to mention to you that I work for him."

She took one of my arms from the chauffeur and helped him usher me into the mouth of 'Hades' - which was the name on the red signboard above the door through which we were descending.

30

Hades was modelled on a Chinese gambling 'hell' of the Victorian era. The only thing missing was the sweet aroma of the opium. Inside, hardened gamblers, eyes rimmed red from cigarette smoke, alcohol and lack of sleep, sat at circular tables covered in red baize. They barely looked up from their cards or Mahjong tiles when we entered. I assumed that drugged victims of Chinese Military Intelligence were a regular part of the evening's entertainment.

I'm not sure how many of those victims ended up flat on the floor, but when I tripped over my shoelaces that's exactly where I ended up. I scrabbled to get up and would have collapsed again had the chauffeur not grabbed me and pulled me to my feet.

My mind was starting to recover – it wasn't the first time I'd been drugged – but my motor function was about as reliable as a dodgem car in Ocean Park. There was a large mirror on the wall in the back – I presumed it was two-way and provided the manager with a view of the gaming floor – and they hustled me through the door beside it. There was an opening at the rear, separated from the office by an opaque plastic curtain wall which parted as they pushed me through it. At which point I fell again.

I could feel blood at the back of my throat, but I had too little sensation to know whether I had broken my nose in the fall. As they pulled me up again I realised there was a small spot of blood on the shoes of the person in front of me. Hu Xianping was dressed head to toe in black, but the sort of black you buy in Savile Row not Beijing. He was tall and dark and looked like Chow-Yun Fat in *'God of Gamblers'*. He had been present on the last occasion that a woman and her goon had taken me somewhere against my will – in New York with Lavender Daai.

He said something in Chinese and in what seemed liked seconds – I think the drug was sending me in and out consciousness - my arms were handcuffed above me, around a metal pipe in the ceiling.

"Wake him," Hu Xianping ordered. At this point captors usually produced a bucket of cold water, but instead someone unstoppered a bottle and waved the vilest smelling salts I have ever encountered under my nose. It was like rinsing your mouth with Drano. The acrid fumes hit my throat and I was wide awake, pupils dilating. For good measure, Hu Xianping decided to slap me across each cheek. He was a man who normally left the violence to others, so I took that as a compliment.

"Good evening, Mr. Jedburgh," he said, his voice full of genuine menace. "Mei Ting told me I would need to appeal to your baser instincts to overpower you."

"I'm also on the phone," I said. "A simple invitation might have worked."

"I think not," he said. "You've shown propensity to cause me trouble." His English was as irritatingly perfect as you'd expect from a man who'd studied at the London School of Economics.

"It's the female company you keep," I said. "Isn't it time you wheeled in a nice male torturer to extract whatever you're after?"

Hu Xianping smiled inscrutably before replying: "Wrong on both counts. I need no information from you, and my torturer is female."

I seemed to attract insanely beautiful devil-women. No sooner was Lavender Daai off the scene than Mei Ting stepped up, or in this case stepped around Hu Xianping.

"I'm surprised," she said. "Everyone tells me that you like strong women, controlling women." She had a riding switch in her hand and without warning lashed out across my face. The end caught me beneath the ear and drew blood. Then she ripped open my shirt, advanced towards me and bit my left nipple. I would have screamed louder if the remains of the drugs hadn't still been in my system.

"Stop." Hu Xianping spoke quietly but she heard and stepped back obediently. He examined my shoulder blade, pointing at the fresh brand of the 1 Recce Christmas Tree.

"What do you know of the *Bahen shashou*?" he asked. "Do you work with him?" Mei Ting squeezed my balls hard for added encouragement.

"No," I said. "But the Scarred Man has made his mark on me. If you release me I'd be happy to put one on him for you."

"You keep bad company, Mr. Jedburgh," he said.

"*Quod erat demonstrandum*," I replied, but it went over his head.

"Is it time?" Mei Ting asked impatiently.

"Once I have explained what is going to happen my sweet," he said, turning to me. "Unfortunately for Mei Ting, who enjoys torturing men to death, I have been forbidden to kill you. The Central Committee is concerned there should be no diplomatic incidents to mar the handover. But you have now upset my plans for a second time and this cannot go unpunished."

"We spent a considerable time debating how to punish you while complying with our orders," Mei Ting was smiling like a buddha, but she had yet to enlighten me. "I believe we have the answer."

As she spoke, Hu Xianping was unzipping her from her dress. From the way he looked at her, I knew they were lovers. Beneath she was naked apart from a tiny pair of blue lace panties that appeared to be purely decorative. Her friend the chauffeur pulled down my trousers and underpants. Despite the pain and the drugs, I started to harden at the sight of her perfect body.

"Excellent" she said. "And to give you a hand, I have brought this." She was holding a small white tube. She put a latex glove on her right hand before applying a generous amount to her index finger.

"You served in Northern Ireland?" she said.

"Not my favourite posting," I replied. "Don't tell me you're the business correspondent of the *Belfast Telegraph* as well?"

"This is something you should be familiar with," she continued, ignoring my wisecracks. "It is nitroglycerine. As well as being an explosive, it is a powerful vasodilator."

"I thought only women used those?" That wisecrack earned me a slap across the right cheek with her left hand, then she smeared the ointment onto my cock with her right. Almost immediately I felt it grow even longer and harder.

"You should learn more about your own body, Bill," she said. "A vasodilator increases the flow of blood to the organ in question. I need you extremely firm."

"We could have stuck to the traditional way," I said. "You were doing so well on the ride over here."

"Fool!" She spat in my face and it dribbled down my chin.

"Are you familiar with the suspensory ligament?" she asked. I shook my head. "It supports the penis," she continued. "Sadly these can occasionally become damaged, generally by blunt force trauma. Worse still is penile fracture. That is truly a medical emergency."

The chauffeur handed her a metal baseball bat. I realised she was intent on making me exceedingly bent, like the Old Man of Kent in the limerick. I began willing my cock to become flaccid but it had a mind of its own. Mei Ting was right, without the nitroglycerine the thought of what was about to happen would have sent me from sixty to nought in a couple of seconds.

Which was why I was delighted when smoke billowed into the room from the gambling den outside. It filled the room with an acrid smell which started me coughing. Hu

Xianping and a couple of his men went to check on the screams and commotion in the other room. No sooner had they left than the lights went out.

Apart from the anatomical difficulty of being stiff as a post, I had been testing out my reactions for some time, preparing to take my chance when it arose. I had also palmed a handcuff key when I fell the first time. Inspired by Houdini I had asked my New York tailor, Mr. Alan, to sew small pockets into my suits to take a variety of picks and keys. It's always good to let a captor believe you're more securely held and incapacitated than you really are.

I lashed out with my bare foot at the space where the baseball bat had been and was gratified to connect with metal and hear it spin off behind Mei Ting and land with a clatter. I heard her curse loudly in Chinese and I aimed at the sound. My foot spun in thin air. It was time to uncuff myself before Mei Ting came back with a knife. She had cat's eyes. I wasn't going to bet against her being able to see in the dark.

In the outer room the screams had abated and the persistent ring of a fire alarm could now be heard. I moved towards the open door made visible by the strobing light from the alarm. Just as I reached it, Mei Ting's chauffeur grabbed my shoulder. My blood was up now, literally and metaphorically. I wrestled free and turned my body in towards him, jabbing the hard bone of my elbow into his solar plexus then spinning round to deliver a sharp right uppercut onto his jaw. He careered off backwards and smashed against a wall.

I didn't have time to get back on balance before I heard a high-pitched scream. Mei Ting had a sharp pointed dagger in her hand which she had pulled from her hair. This, no longer held in place by the weapon, swirled around her like a halo. Her breasts were still exposed and she launched herself towards me. As I crouched into a defensive position, I felt a wind blow past my cheek followed a half-second later by the 'pop-pop' of a suppressed weapon firing behind me. Two spots of red appeared between her breasts and she dropped dead like a stone. The man with the gun moved past me, shifted his gun arm to the left and repeated the double tap on the chauffeur. Other than the two bodies the room was empty. Of Hu Xianping there was not a trace.

"Evening sir," the man said. "I told you the Browning High Power rarely lets you down." It was the bank messenger from Ashenden Delacroix and he had one in his hand.

"Eric Capper, sir," he said. "We weren't properly introduced before. Mr. Tweddle asked me to keep an eye on you and keep you out of trouble. I'm afraid it took me a while to find the right junction box to switch off the lights. Luckily I had a couple of L83A1 smoke bombs in the glove compartment as well."

"Thanks, Eric," I said, retrieving my jacket and trousers from the table behind the dead woman. I was still at half-mast but the nitroglycerine must have been wearing off because I managed to get the zipper done up. "I owe you, and Mr. Tweddle. He had a darn sight more foresight than me tonight."

"Don't blame yourself, sir," the grey-haired veteran said. "I often find the brightest and best have a tendency to think with their dicks. Now, is there anything you need to retrieve? We have to get out of here before the London Fire Brigade arrives."

"No," I said, with a great deal of relief, "that's all the business taken care of."

31

I was still shaken by my manhood's narrow escape from a life in splints, when I caught up with Frank Bennett at the House of Commons the following day. The *Guardian* reporter was cock-a-hoop at the reaction to his scoop and showed me a copy of that morning's *Private Eye*. The satirical magazine claimed it had been highlighting the failings of Sir Bernard Li for years and used the exposé as an excuse to republish its greatest hits. These included a piece implying that his divorce from Catriona Mountfleming had been caused by a royal scandal: *'As Sir Bernard's Bentley drove off to his office at the front of the house, Rodney's Aston Martin'* – all the members of the Royal Family were given nicknames – *'arrived discreetly at the rear.'*

Frank had invited me along to the Press Gallery to hear Foreign Office Questions. The view from the gallery was very different to the one I'd had on my private tour. From behind the Speaker's Chair, looking down from above the chamber from sharply raked benches, I could just make out the top of the immaculately coiffured white hair of Madam Speaker as she called MPs to quiz the Foreign Office team.

I was amazed by how easy it would have been to kill a member of either front bench – although escaping afterwards would have been a greater challenge. The planner in me started calculating: three of the new M84 stun grenades and lots of blue smoke would probably be needed. There were no protective screens to prevent an assassination and at that distance I wouldn't even have needed a firearm – a mini-crossbow or a carefully lobbed bag of anthrax or ricin would have done the trick. It made me wonder whether I should investigate some of the legislatures closer to my home in Singapore. While I tried to exercise my profession with caution, the odd 'statement killing' helped to reinforce the Reliable Man's brand and kept the assignments rolling in. There were plenty of corrupt lawmakers whose demise made their countries an easier place for my clients to do business. I drew the line now at reformers who made things better for their people – although I was unsurprised by how many "champions of the people" turned out to be just as corrupt as the politicians they replaced. The only leader who had lived up to his promises in Asia was Singapore's Lee Kuan Yew. The rest of them couldn't help getting their snouts into the big trough of greenbacks as soon as they wrested power from their predecessor.

We had to endure a series of dull enquiries to junior ministers before finally, just before lunch, the Chamber filled and the Speaker announced loudly: "The Foreign Secretary," and Robin Cook stood up at the despatch box. I looked around. Where there had been acres of green leather on display when questions started – Frank had explained that the aim of most questioners was simply to get their name in Hansard, the official parliamentary record, rather than listen to what others were saying – there was now no green to be seen, especially on the Labour benches. There were even people standing at the front, behind what Frank explained was the 'bar' of the House.

The Foreign Secretary was even smaller in this setting than when we'd met for lunch, but he clearly commanded the House's respect and attention. A hush descended on proceedings.

The first question was from the Liberal Democrat spokesman on Foreign Affairs, who seemed to be named after Ming the Merciless, the villain in Flash Gordon. He asked in a cultured Scots brogue:

"Whether the Foreign Secretary had seen the press reports regarding the potential sale of SatBox Communications. And would he make a statement?"

All eyes in the chamber and above it turned to look at the man with the red ponytail on the opposition benches. Then they looked back to Robin Cook. Giles Guedella was reclining in his seat and I saw his eyes glance up to the public gallery. The man I now knew as Abe Berenson, minus his trench coat, was sitting in the top left-hand corner. I watched Guedella scan round the gallery and followed his gaze past Tom Field in the Peer's section and then finally somehow his eyes found me in the Press Gallery and his look darkened.

Robin Cook had a calm measured speaking voice. He was much less histrionic and declamatory than the average politician, but more authoritative as a result. He stated that he had no idea whether the allegations were true or not, but that the Government had a responsibility to ensure, as part of its new ethical foreign policy, that sensitive items of intellectual property were protected. Accordingly he had asked his colleague, the Secretary of State for Trade and Industry – a sharp faced woman minister on the bench beside him, who was nodding intently like one of those dogs you get in the back of a car – to issue orders preventing the export of such technology while a review was held into the circumstances surrounding any sale.

"Meanwhile," he continued. "As my Right Honourable friend the Prime Minister and I will be in Hong Kong shortly for the return of the territory to China, we intend to instigate high level talks with senior Chinese politicians and officials over this matter." He paused to take a breath and get a measure of the Chamber.

"I must say that if the allegations made in *The Guardian* newspaper are true," he continued, unable to resist making a party political point, "it ill behoves the party opposite to lecture us about patriotism, as they did repeatedly during the last parliament, while one of their own is facing such allegations."

Uproar ensued. There was a mass of jeering and barracking from the other side and Conservative MPs rose en masse from their seats to try and catch the Speaker's eye. The man at the centre of the storm though, Giles Guedella, stayed seated, silent and stony-faced. A few minutes later Robin Cook, when pushed by the Shadow Foreign Secretary, said that he had not intended to imply that any honourable member would behave illegally, especially given that the allegations were aimed at the purchaser of SatBox, not the seller. Like all good prosecutors the Foreign Secretary knew that the press would report his first allegation and not the subsequent retraction.

"Good old Cook," said Frank, when we got back to the Central Lobby after questions ended. "That will give me my frontpage headline for tomorrow. We can keep it running now."

I realised Bennett was no different from the rest of us. He had his agenda, which probably involved a bonus or promotion, or a prize for investigative journalism. Did they have Pulitzer Prizes in England? I had no idea.

"Jedburgh!" It was Guedella, storming across the Lobby towards me, "we need to talk."

"Of course," I said. I owed the man as much. I signalled to Bennett to make himself scarce. I had no desire to read a transcript in *The Guardian* of my conversation with Guedella.

Guedella grabbed hold of my elbow and steered me out of the Lobby, down some stairs and out onto into the cold spring air. Sun slipped through gaps in the clouds and I shaded my eyes to take in the view. The Terrace of the Houses of Parliament was wide and stretched the length of both Lords and Commons. Like the interior, it had a section for each. Beyond the stone parapet was the slate-grey River Thames, foaming in the wind and with the wash of boats and barges passing along it. On the far left were the green arches and cast-iron lamps of Westminster Bridge, with double-decker buses and other traffic near-stationary on top of it.

At this time of year, the Terrace was deserted. It was cold and Guedella shoved his hands deep into his trouser pockets and looked at me searchingly. His eyes still appeared friendly despite his flushed face.

"Was this your doing?" he asked.

"You lied to me," I said. "You wanted to do a deal with the Chinese. I respect people who want to make money, but you could have sold to the other bidder for more. Johnny Aston told me." He was silent, surprised at my knowledge.

"Berenson thinks you're a spy," he said at last. "He just doesn't know on whose team you're playing."

"I'm not clever enough to be a spy," I said. "Simply a fellow-traveller. A blunt instrument directed by others."

"Not that different from me then," he said reflectively.

"Very different," I said. "Mostly, I'm an educated thug. I'll quote you Keats and Milton while I knee you in the balls. You're a much cleverer and more moral man than me, which is why your behaviour confuses me."

"It's above both of our pay grades," he said, which was clearly the important message he wanted me to take away. "But we are really both on the same side."

"But I'm not working for the Israelis," I said. "Berenson is Mossad, isn't he?"

"Abe is a good friend," he said, but I could tell my knowledge had shaken him. "My family have a long history in Palestine and I am a Conservative Friend of Israel."

Personally, I had no issues with Mossad or the Jewish state. I'd never done any work for them, had only come across them infrequently. They were the best state-funded assassins in the world which is why they didn't need my services. Their Kidon units could do anything I did with a hand tied behind their backs. And they had the best kit to boot – like my favourite weapon, the Meraglim Mark III. In my profession they were truly God's chosen people – the ultimate spear of national vengeance.

I said a little harshly: "Your deal is dead now. Tell Berenson he should focus on finding the man who tried to kill him. He works for an outfit called New Reich – I don't think they like the Jewish people very much."

"New Reich?" he said. "I've never heard of them. Sounds Teutonic."

"Ask Berenson, I'm sure he'll know. They were observing you in Devon. The man is South African and he's a seasoned killer. He doesn't like me much either," I added ruefully.

"I'm a businessman and a politician, Bill," Guedella said. "I don't want anyone to get killed. I'll talk to Abe." He started to walk away.

"If you ever become Minister of Defence, I'll remember that statement about not wanting anyone killed," I commented, and followed him back indoors.

32

Johnny Aston, when in London, lived in a converted warehouse on Wapping High Street. Oliver's Wharf had been turned into luxury flats in the 1970s, long before the East End of London had become fashionable with City bankers. When I had left England the exotic produce that had filled the warehouses of Wapping - spices, coffee and cocoa, wine and wool, as well as the eponymous product found at Tobacco Dock - was long gone. What shipping remained had transferred to the container port downriver, the dying embers of an enterprise that had once made London the trading centre of an empire and employed hundreds of thousands of people. Now the once-derelict six thousand acres that made up Docklands had been transformed into riverside homes, an airport, distribution hubs and a financial city-within-a-city, Canary Wharf, that had come to encapsulate the best and worst aspects of Margaret Thatcher's political legacy.

I met Dominic at Ashenden Delacroix's City offices near Monument and we decided to walk over to Johnny's. Our route took us past the Tower of London, squat and brooding alongside the iron gothic of Tower Bridge, then through St Katharine's Dock with its cruisers and houseboats. Eventually we reached the tall warehouses and cobbled streets of Wapping High Street and were buzzed up to Johnny's penthouse flat.

It occupied nearly the whole of the top floor of the building and contained a huge open-plan living area with exposed brickwork. High ceilings reached up into the rafters, the ancient wooden beams supported by cast-iron pillars. Arched gothic windows overlooked the river with the lights of South London twinkling behind on the opposite riverbank.

There were six of us. The gathering was entirely male, apart from the catering staff whom Johnny had employed to cook and serve our dinner. I handed over the bottles of Cristal I had brought, then went over to chat to Porter Garland. The Head of Burcott's New York office was chomping on a Cohiba Robustos with a bottle of Jefferson's 15-year-old Kentucky Bourbon in front of him. His dark hair looked freshly brilliantined.

"Jedburgh, you old dawg," he said. "I gather you're taking Mr. Tweddle under your wing in the Orient. We're going to miss him in Manhattan."

"I'm sure he'll be back," I said. "Once you take a bite out of the Big Apple, it's impossible to get the poison out of your blood."
I poured myself a large slug of amber-yellow Bourbon and took a sip before continuing: "So what brings you and Randy to London? I don't believe it was simply a desire to see Dominic off in style."

"Randy's the real reason we're over here." Porter indicated a small round-faced man talking to Johnny

Aston. Randy Stein had been Porter's junior at Burcotts. I had met them both in New York the year before.

"I don't know whether you knew that prostitution is legal in Nevada outside the Las Vegas city limits?" he asked. I shook my head, unsure where this was going. If he told me it was legal to kill your wife on Tuesdays in Nevada, I'd have believed him. The Wild West was still just that.

"Randy left Burcotts three months ago to become the CEO of a quoted Nevada 'ranch resort' called Beddems," he continued. "Golf, massage and erotic services. They're a client of ours and Randy and I are over here looking at setting up a clubhouse in London – tasteful and strictly legal table dancing and high stakes poker only, of course."

None of this surprised me. I remembered a conversation Randy and I'd had in the VIP room in Stringfellows in New York. He had been mapping out his career path into the adult entertainment business even then.

"I need to introduce you both to my friend, Harry Bolt," I said. "He owns a gentlemen's resort called the 'Bolthole' in Thailand and is opening one soon in the Philippines. Johnny's a member. He may be interested in joining forces. He's a man with all the right contacts and he's got the money to back it up."

Garland smiled. Mixing business and pleasure always made an investment banker happy. Harry's business interests were wide-ranging and numerous, but he had a soft spot for ones that involved drinking, golfing and whoring. I was sure taking a stake in a quoted brothel group would appeal to him. If I approached it the right way Harry would agree to pay me a finder's fee. I started to consider what form that might take, because I'd had some interesting ones from him. My personal favourite was a Ducati Monster which I kept at the 'Bolthole' and which had powered me around Thailand over the past few years.

The sixth member of our select table was Dominic's younger brother, Jimmy. The awkward teen I had known – he was seven years younger than Dominic – had grown into a self-assured property agent who specialised in high end retail. He largely talked about his favourite subject – himself - and the large number of property billionaires and retail entrepreneurs he dealt with. The talk flowed easily amongst us over dinner – rib of beef and all the trimmings, followed by Eton Mess, washed down with 1982 Cos D'Estournel and Chateau d'Yquem. None of us had anything to prove to the others and we shared an approach to life which was devoted to the finer things in life. My recollections of what we discussed are hazy. Johnny began talking about shotguns at one point. My gun collection would have put his to shame but I felt I'd had enough of them for now. I preferred to talk about scuba diving instead. I had spent the last fifteen years reef diving around the Far East and I loved the excitement and occasional danger. Now he was going to be in Hong Kong, I planned to take Dominic scuba diving in the Philippines and introduce him to the delights of that sport and country.

If the meal was excellent then the floor show afterwards was even better. Randy had arranged for a posse (or was that a pussy?) of women – eager auditioners for jobs in his new club – to strut their stuff for us. I was delighted to see that he had included a well-endowed Filipina for me. Given a choice I still preferred Asian to European women, although I had to accept that some of the Russian talent on display that night would give anyone pause for thought.

By the time I left the door of the flat in the early hours of the next morning, pleasantly drunk and with my cock still tingling from its encounter with Rosalie's pert and willing body, I was ready to go home to the Chesterfield and sleep. Instead, I found myself face to face with Rip Van Ryjn. He emerged from the doorway of the 'Town of Ramsgate' pub, next door to Oliver's Wharf and now in darkness, with a gun in his hand. The only advantage of encountering him on a darkened street was that the scar on his neck was in shadow.

"I see your hatred of the Chinese doesn't extend to their weaponry," I said, sobering quickly. The South African had a Type 67 pistol in his hand. It had an integrated suppressor and a nine-round magazine - the People's Liberation Army had used them for decades.

"We're both professionals, Jedburgh," he said. "You pick a tool for the job." I didn't like the sound of that. I knew from personal experience that the Type 67 was not terribly accurate at long range. But from a few yards the effect of its 7.65 mm ammunition was silent and deadly.

"I thought you wanted to keep me alive, temporarily?" I said.

"Relax," he gestured for me to walk in front of him down a narrow passageway to the right of the pub, "we just need a talk, that's all. This is just to take care of anyone who tries to interrupt us."

The passageway widened out beyond the pub. I had to admit it was a secluded location for a chat. Moonlight revealed a flight of steps at the far end, which I presumed led down to the Thames itself. It was high tide and I could hear water lapping against the stonework.

"Do you know your history, Jedburgh?" Van Ryjn asked. "I've been reading the guidebook. Those are Wapping Old Stairs and they lead down to Execution Dock. They hanged Captain Kidd, the pirate, here. Twice, actually: the first time the rope snapped and he fell in the mud. When he was finally dead, they tied him to a stake and let the tide cover him repeatedly until his body was blackened and bloated. I tried the same thing on a Chinese insurgent in Malaya once. The local villagers got the message loud and clear."

"Let's talk," I said and sat down on the short flight of steps that acted as a parapet between the alleyway and the way down to the dock below. I had no wish to hear a litany of atrocities that the *Bahen Shashou* had committed on 'active service'. On the other hand, I needed to play along and watch for an opening. This might be my best opportunity to make the problem of a rifle bearing my fingerprints go away.

"You've done my employer a favour," he said in his clipped guttural accent. "You've removed the Chinese as bidders for SatBox and reduced the price. I saw you with Guedella. You were on the Terrace with him at the House of Commons this afternoon. Despite what you've done, I can tell he likes you."

A cold gust of salt wind blew down the passageway from the Thames and its icy blast chilled my brain as his words sank in. Given Van Ryjn's long range surveillance and sniping skills, Guedella and I would be only a high-powered rifle-shot away from death until I dealt with him. Now was definitely not a bad time to try, I thought. If I could separate him from his weapon, the odds would be close to even. I wished I hadn't drunk quite so heavily, but unlike when I had faced Mei Ting in Hades, I wasn't drugged.

"So what's the deal?" I asked, playing for time and working on my next move.

"Persuade Guedella to sell to my employer. He is offering cash and he has powerful friends in Austria. He will be an acceptable bidder to the British Government."

"And in exchange?" I prompted.

"In exchange," he said, "I told my boss I would find another patsy for the job in Hong Kong. I've found a policeman over there who would be just as convincing a fall guy as you."

"I'd need the rifle with my prints on it, just to make certain you didn't change your mind," I said, pretending to consider the idea. Actually, I was genuinely considering it. I didn't like the idea of a bunch of neo-Nazis getting hold of SatBox's technology, but as long as I warned Larry and the Brigadier not to use it in Singapore, there was much less danger from that outcome. The problem was, I knew Guedella by now. Whatever was going on between him and Abe Berenson meant he would be unlikely to accept the offer.

"That can be arranged," Van Ryjn said. "But only when we are certain the deal is going through." He was too professional to drop his guard, but his body language had relaxed. This was a negotiation now, not a standoff. Which was why neither of us was prepared for what happened next.

We heard the sound of running feet – coming from the Wapping High Street end of the passage – at about the same time. Van Ryjn turned and I saw behind him in the distance a trench coat whose owner I recognised. Berenson raised his right arm and fired. It wasn't an easy shot, because he had a narrow field of fire and I hoped he was trying to miss me. He clipped Van Ryjn's right ear and I saw a spurt of blood and cartilage as the bullet impacted. The South African spun round, disorientated, and I took my chance. I launched a flying kick with my left foot that caught hold of the pistol and propelled it over the low concrete wall beside him and into the Thames behind. The momentum brought my knee round and it hit him in the stomach forcing him back against the low concrete wall on that side of the alleyway. He swore in Afrikaans and pulled a knife. Now we were even, because I had my trusty Mikov switchblade out and was circling round so that he had to go through me to get to Berenson and I was herding him towards the stairs.

"I haven't got a shot, Jedburgh," I heard Berenson shouting in his American brogue behind me.

"You don't need one, Abe," I said, feinting and parrying with Van Ryjn, who had adopted the low stance of a street fighter. It felt good to be in my element again and I had to admit that despite our bruising encounter in Devon, Tony Wolf-Madden's miracle paste had done its work well and my body felt fit for the test. In our last couple of meetings, the South African had had the drop on me. Now he had to face me properly. He was still a deadly opponent, but so was I.

He was a precise and powerful fighter. His Ka-Bar was bigger than my Mikov, but I still managed to nick his arm and by staying out of his reach avoid his thrusts. There was a ragged patch of dark liquid on the right shoulder of his jacket. It looked black in the moonlight, but I knew it was blood from his wounded ear. I wanted to try and kick him off balance, using my steel-tipped shoes, but the Ka-Bar was a sharp weapon and if he found one of my arteries as I lunged I would bleed out in minutes.

In the end it was the fact that he was trapped at the wrong end of the alleyway, with his escape blocked by Berenson, that decided the contest. He stepped backwards and in a swift expert movement threw the knife straight at me. The Ka-Bar is not a great throwing knife but I only just managed to avoid it by forcing myself sideways against the wall on one side of the passage as it sliced through the air and clattered against the brickwork behind me. Taking advantage of the distraction Van Ryjn ran up the stairs and dived off them into the Thames below. I heard a splash, but by the time I had got to my feet and peered over the edge, he was gone.

Berenson came up alongside me. He was carrying a Jericho pistol and a flashlight but had no more luck than me spotting the South African.

"He may have drowned," he said hopefully.

"He is one tough little fucker," I replied. "I wouldn't bet on it." We sat side by side on the steps and watched the water flow past us. Berenson reached inside his trench coat and pulled out a hipflask. He took a swig and handed it to me. It tasted like a single malt and it hit the spot.

"Thank you for turning up," I said. "I don't think he intended to kill me this time, he was saving that for a later date. But with Van Ryjn I wouldn't have bet my pension on it."

"He probably had the same idea I had," he said. "A quiet chat with you. Just got to you first. I spotted him in the doorway, so I thought I'd keep an eye on proceedings. Then I thought: why not take him out? Thanks for making the connection to New Reich, by the way. Giles told me."

"So, he does work for you guys," I said.

"Giles is a patriot," Berenson said. "He advances the interests of the State of Israel only when they are aligned with British interests. What we are involved in has been determined at the very highest levels of our governments. There was a very private understanding between Prime Minister Netanyahu and John Major. I doubt he bothered to tell Tony Blair. I was only going to tell you because you've screwed the whole thing up and I need your help with our Plan B."

"Could we do that after I've had a decent night's sleep?" I asked. "I've had more than enough excitement for one day already."

"Sure," he said. "Why don't Giles and I meet you for dinner tomorrow evening at the Groucho Club?"

33

When I got to Ashenden Delacroix the next morning, I was greeted by Eric Capper as an old friend. I had brought him a bottle of Stolichnaya, which he had told me was his favourite, as a thank-you for keeping my member alive.

"I'll take you straight down to the briefing room. Mr. Tweddle and Mr. Mace are waiting for you." I had called Dominic from the Chesterfield. I was meeting Berenson and Guedella that evening and I had arranged to call on Sir Bernard Li in between.

Dominic was dressed in a pair of jeans and an open-necked Ralph Lauren polo. Mace was wearing a replica Chelsea shirt. I was in my suit.

"It's FA Cup Final day," Dominic said. "Had you forgotten it's a Saturday? Darren and I have got tickets." In all the excitement I had forgotten it was the weekend. Chelsea were playing Middlesbrough at Wembley that afternoon.

"I'll be out of your hair soon," I said. "I just wanted to try my theory out on you first before I see them."

"Fire away," Dominic said. I shut my eyes and tried to marshal all the facts. They had been slipping and sliding around my mind for weeks now, and were finally coming together.

"Guedella is working with Mossad. Berenson claims it has been sanctioned at a very high level, by John Major when he was Prime Minister. Guedella needed the F&E merger to go through. I don't know why yet, but they must have known that Sir Bernard was in bed with the Chinese."

"We'd heard rumours about him," Dominic said, "but nothing concrete. The head of Ashenden Delacroix in Hong Kong is ex-officio Deputy Head of Station, so I'm read in on operations over there, and there's nothing in the files. But if it is above my pay grade I will probably need to go through the Chairman of the Joint Intelligence Committee to find out, so it won't be easy to get verification."

"I reckon the Chinese were getting something they hadn't bargained for in SatBox. Maybe one of the senior people there is under deep cover and this is a way to get them in close. Given it's Mossad they may plan to assassinate someone – hopefully Hu Xianping. I think they might tell me this evening. Which would be helpful."

"I've got more good news," Darren said. "You won't have to watch your back for Van Ryjn from now on. I've just had notification from the Special Branch ports team that he boarded a ferry from Harwich to the Hook of Holland early this morning using a false Dutch passport. Positive confirmation from the CCTV tapes, although the ferry had left before we got it. We've put out a request for him to be detained when he gets to Holland."

"Good luck with that," I said. "He's too wily to be caught, but I'm pleased he's not in the UK. He's a touch too handy with a sniper rifle."

"I'm still going to lend you Eric this evening," Dominic said, "just in case the Chinese aren't done with you yet."

"Thanks," I said. "I'm off to have a chat with Sir Bernard Li next, and that might well stir things up."

I had texted Missie to let her know I was coming to Upper Brook Street and she greeted me at the door with a hug.

"He's been in a really foul mood, Bill," she said. "He feels betrayed by Tom Field. Tom resigned yesterday. I think he would have been fired if he hadn't."

"Now you know what your father has done, how do you feel?" I asked.

"Honestly?" she said. "It explains a lot. I think he has lost sight of what makes him such a creative businessman. He was never a great father, but money and power turned his head. I hope I can be better than that."

"You will be," I said, "and I may have an idea. Have you met Flick's new beau yet?"

"Dago?" she asked. "Not yet, they've been inseparable. I'd have been a gooseberry." I smiled at that very English turn of phrase for a third wheel. She was so flawlessly Eurasian, but you couldn't separate it from an English convent school education.

"Then come to brunch tomorrow at the Chesterfield," I said. "I'll invite Dago. I think it would be good for both of you. See if Lola Beaulieu can come as well. I've finally read her novel."

"I'd love to," she said then gave me a long stern stare and tapped me on the chest. "You're not a bad man. If you're planning on shagging Lola, just remember she's not as worldly as she makes out." She reached up on tiptoes and brushed me lightly on the lips. I closed my eyes and smelt the aroma of her hair and perfume, imagining for a second what might have been. This was a woman who could read my mind.

"Good luck with Daddy," she said.

"You've got a nerve coming here, Jedburgh," Sir Bernard said. In honour of the weekend, he'd abandoned the desk in the office for an Eames chair by the window and was drinking green tea, poured from an ornate teapot. He wore a striped short-sleeved shirt, chinos and docksiders. Yet again I felt overdressed.

His new Chinese bodyguard was standing motionless in the corner of the office with his hands clasped in front of him. He appeared to be a thug straight from a TVB soap opera – crew cut hair, flat peasant face - but I figured that Hu Xianping would have chosen a deceptively intelligent man with a good command of English. I debated asking Sir Bernard to dismiss him, but figured they would have the room bugged as well. In any case there was nothing I needed to say that would compromise him, or me, with Chinese Military Intelligence - at least no more than I already was.

"I'm not your enemy, Sir Bernard," I said. "At least not now the SatBox merger is dead in the water. I've always admired you. You are one of the greatest entrepreneurs in the history of Hong Kong." I adopted the persona of the bluff man of action which fooled most listeners into believing that my outrageous flattery was a deeply held belief. He perked up immediately, as I knew he would.

"Then why are you here?" he asked.

"To tell you that you still have the opportunity to come out of this debacle well," I said. "I understand that Tom Field has resigned."

"You have been irritatingly well-informed throughout," he said. "I still don't know how you encouraged him to speak with *The Guardian*."

"I have no idea whether he was the mole or not," I lied, "he's an honourable man. The good news is that his departure allows you to be bold." I looked him in the eye: "Your daughter won't tell you this, but she is about to graduate with an MBA and a Dean's Prize from the Judge Business School in Cambridge."

The look on his face was priceless. He was genuinely floored, so I pressed home my advantage: "Missie is your daughter. I believe your refusal to engage with her is because you are blinded by seeing her mother in her. That is not the dominant truth. I've spent a lot of time with her and she has shown me who she really is. It is your genes which are dominant, not Catriona's flighty, selfish ones. She's studied business, is incredibly intelligent and has worked hard to understand F&E's operations. She wants to help."

He was silent for several minutes before replying. "Why am I discovering this from you and not her?"

"Because she is more like you than you think," I said. "She wanted to be accepted on her own terms. She is desperate for you to discover her real talents for yourself. If you talk to her now, she will tell you. She has great ideas for F&E. I think she could be an inspired choice as Chief Executive of the Company. Under your guidance as Executive Chairman."

I could see him considering what I had said. The Chinese are often called 'inscrutable' but what you see behind their eyes is rapid mental calculation of profit and loss, reputation, risk and potential personal gain. It is the mental abacus that most Chinese men and women are born with. It is an innate capacity to evaluate and to manipulate.

"What you say makes sense," he said, finally. "On your way out send Missie up to see me. You may go." He fluttered his hand in dismissal. The Lord High Executioner was being dismissed by Pooh-Bah, the Lord High Everything Else.

Back at the Chesterfield I changed into a more comfortable open-necked shirt and jeans and spent the afternoon in the bar watching the FA Cup Final. Watching other people play sports – especially football – had always struck me as a complete waste of time. But I enjoyed the human drama that came with it and it was an excuse to drink and be sociable. Chelsea scored in the first minute and after a nervy game got a second ten minutes from time. I guessed Darren Mace would be happy. I doubted he'd been alive the last time they won anything.

When I got to the Groucho that evening, it was Abe Berenson and Giles Guedella who were wearing suits and I looked underdressed. Sometimes you just couldn't win.

The Groucho was nice and relaxed, as befitted its location in bohemian Soho. Berenson explained that it was predominantly a media hangout that took its name from the famous Groucho Marx quip about not wanting to belong to any club which would have him as a member. We had a booth in the big airy dining room at the back. I recognised a couple of people from television but couldn't have told you any of their names. A few people waved at Guedella while the rest ignored him or glared frostily. The media world was currently very New Labour.

"I hope that Rebekah Brooks can't hear us," Giles said. "We don't want this appearing in *The Sun*." He indicated a redheaded woman having dinner on the other side of the restaurant with a bald-headed bruiser. "She's the Deputy Editor and a close friend of the Blairs. He's in *Eastenders*." He looked at me and added for my benefit: "That's a soap opera about working class people."

"I think we're far enough away," Abe said. "Being involved with me is making you paranoid Giles. The more relaxed and nonchalant we look the less people will think we are sharing secrets."

"I agree," I said, "and if you wear a trench coat no-one's ever going to think you're a spy." He looked at me quizzically.

"It was a present," he said. "From an Englishwoman."

"Makes a change from the clap," I said trying to be funny and Guedella rolled his eyes.

"Put him out of his misery, Abe," he said. "Otherwise he will just insult us all night." I put my hand up to make him stop.

"Before I do, let me try myself," I said. "Because I think I've figured it out."

It had come to me in a blinding flash during the football that afternoon, and Missie was partly responsible. I'd been thinking about how I had engineered her into the Chief Executive role. I didn't have to convince Sir Bernard that Missie would make a better CEO than him. I had to convince him that he would make a better Chairman for Foreign & Exotic than a CEO, and that Missie was better than the other candidates to replace him. By changing my perception of the problem, I got what I wanted without Sir Bernard realising that he had given it to me. Which was when I finally understood what Guedella and Berenson were up to.

"You had me fooled." I said. "Sir Bernard's determination to buy SatBox hid Giles' desperation to sell to the Chinese. Until New Reich came along, I thought it was just that he wanted the money and didn't care what the Chinese did with his technology. Now I realise you were giving them a Trojan Horse. The Chinese thought SatBox would allow them to hack the

West's communications. What they would actually do was connect up a system to let Mossad and GCHQ hack them. If the SatBox products were integrated into the Chinese communications, you would have been able to read every secret signal they sent."

Berenson gave me a slow hand clap: "Bravo," he said. "Which is why your meddling has screwed up one of the cleverest operations we've worked on this decade." His face took on the aspect of a stern Old Testament prophet. "If you hadn't saved my life, Mossad would have punished you for this, but all is not lost. You need to redeem yourself now by helping us deliver Plan B."

34

Berenson took a photograph out of a folder and placed it in front of me. It showed a laboratory desk with a ruler on it. Alongside the ruler was a black cylinder with a number of wires protruding from the end farthest from the camera. It was just under thirty centimetres long and about half that in diameter.

"What is it?" I asked.

"That," Guedella said, "is the Babel Inverter."

"Like the Tower of Babel in the Bible?"

"Exactly the opposite," Berenson said. "Where the Tower of Babel was overrun with multiple languages, this device turns them all into a single stream of code. It is the decoder at the heart of the SatBox system and the piece of equipment that the Chinese most covet."

"One they were prepared to pay £150 million for," Guedella said with pride. "Designed in Heathfield by my team of boffins."

"I'm guessing," I said, "that it doesn't work exactly as they imagine?"

Guedella smiled.

"It will turn espionage on its head," he said, "which is not the inversion they are expecting. With this they expect to read our signals, whereas they will actually read, and believe, only what we want them to."

"If that was all there was," Berenson continued, "it would in itself be a tremendous piece of deception. But the real brilliance is that the Inverter will also suck information out of China's state IT system as soon as it is plugged in. In six hours we will have downloaded most of their secrets and for good measure will have planted a nasty little bug our team in Tel Aviv have designed that will enable us to shut down the national command system with a simple line of code if we ever need to." The grim Old Testament face was back.

"I had no idea the State of Israel hated the Chinese so much," I said. "I thought you were focused on Syria, Egypt and the Lebanon."

"The State of Israel only exists because it has thought about the future for its entire past," he said. "We know there is a global change coming. The Americans are not always going to be willing to support us in the Middle East. The Chinese are embracing capitalism and soon their money will start to flow across the Arab world and into Africa. When that happens they will find willing allies."

I thought for a while. There was one country that Israel feared more than any other. Because in a weird way they shared the same messianic zeal from the other side of the religious divide.

"You're worried about China and Iran getting together," I said.

Berenson nodded.

"I owe you an apology, Giles," I said. "My own dislike of the communists is such that it never occurred to me that you were out to destroy them as well." Guedella looked smug. He'd taken the accusations I'd thrown at him over the previous weeks in his stride. Like a true politician.

"So how can I help?" I asked. "I'm only a pawn on the chessboard in this game."

"This is my idea, Bill," Guedella said. "You said something to me on the Terrace of the House of Commons that resonated. I've discussed it with Abe. We think it might work."

"Go on, I'm intrigued," I said.

"You called yourself a blunt instrument," he said. I nodded in agreement. "Well we want you to use that instrument to break into the SatBox operation in Hong Kong and steal the Babel Inverter."

When they explained what they had in mind, I had to admit it was clever. The Babel Inverter needed to be close to a satellite uplink feed, and currently that node was in Hong Kong. Given the imminent transfer of power to China, the Inverter was going to be moved to a new location in Australia a few days before the handover date. Only a few people knew the secret of the Inverter and one of them was the scientist I had seen talking to Hu Xianping all those weeks ago in Tango Martini in Hong Kong. He had approached the Chinese agent and claimed he was short of cash thanks to an expensive divorce involving the usual Thai hookers. In reality he was SatBox's GCHQ liaison officer. He had deliberately told Hu Xianping that he didn't have access good enough to steal the Inverter's secrets, but Giles thought he could persuade the Chinese that he'd hired a thief to steal the Inverter itself.

"It's the germ of an idea," I said, "but I can see a number of issues. The main one being that it's too simple." Guedella looked disappointed. "I don't like making your man the link. If they do work out what's going on he is as good as dead. On top of that they may decide to kidnap him anyway to help get the Inverter operational and everyone gives up secrets under torture. It would be best if he were dead before that could happen."

Guedella looked horrified: "You can't kill Jeremy. He's got three children and I've met his wife. The idea's obscene, Abe," Guedella said.

"Of course we can't," I said. "Which is why I might have a better idea."

"Tell us more," Berenson prompted, leaning forward in his chair.

"I know Rip Van Ryjn is going to be in Hong Kong for the handover. If he dies and the Babel Inverter turns up in his possession and is passed to Chinese Military Intelligence, it will feel more realistic – Hu Xianping knows that Van Ryjn's boss is interested in the technology – and there will be no-one to interrogate, just a, literal, dead end."

"I like that," Berenson said. "I'm assuming that you would be prepared to stage the break-in?"

"For the right fee," I said. "Sometimes people forget that I'm not working on this for free."

"Would that include both the break-in and dealing with Van Ryjn?" I nodded.

"How much, and how would you like it paid?" he asked. I thought for a while. I couldn't use my usual Reliable Man accounts without risking a connection being made and it would raise too many questions if it went into one of my regular company bank accounts.

"An account with Israeli Weapons Industries in a false name," I said eventually. "I'd like a credit balance of US$100,000 and guaranteed export clearance for my purchases. For which I am prepared to give you an assurance I will never re-import them into Israel." Israeli weapons were very good indeed and my stock of Meraglim Mark IIIs – the single use lightweight plastic firearm that went undetected through X-Ray machines - was running low. I might never get a better chance to purchase some more. On the black market they didn't come cheap.

"The cost is not unreasonable, but that's a pretty heavy credit line for a bodyguard," Berenson said. I think he suspected I wasn't just one of those. That I did a little bit of arms dealing on the side would make more sense to him. "You'd have to pay list price though. That way at least they'd make a profit to offset it."

"Make it US$120,000 then and we are done," I said.

"Not quite," Berenson said. "I have a condition of my own. I know you are close to Dominic Tweddle at SIS. You are going to have to keep this secret from him. He needs to be told that there is no operation, that Guedella was flying his own kite and Mossad is no longer involved. We cannot afford to let anyone else into our secret."

I thought about it, and realised that could work to my advantage. Dominic was my friend, but this operation wouldn't hurt him. Even better, if I played my cards right I might get paid twice for killing Van Ryjn, because I fully expected him to ask for my help taking him down.

I held out my hand. Berenson shook it - Mossad obviously had access to some serious operational slush funds.

"There's one final thing," I said. "I'm right in thinking this is a joint venture between GCHQ and Mossad?" Berenson nodded. "I want my adopted home in Singapore to benefit too. Your contact Larry Lim," I said, addressing Guedella, "is a close associate of Brigadier Wee, who runs the SID. If we succeed, Abe, I'd like your word that you'll share the intelligence with them."

"I can't give that assurance," Berenson said. "I need to refer it to my director. But I will do my best."

I slept well that night. There were still a couple of weeks left before the handover. We had agreed that Guedella would be in Hong Kong about a week before to help me arrange the break-in. Which gave me time to return to Singapore, recharge my batteries and also seek an audience with the Brigadier. That only left one task to perform and I was free to fly eastwards. I was booked the following day on the same Cathay Pacific flight that Dominic Tweddle was flying out on to start his new posting.

Sunday brunch was the first time I had seen Dago de Souza without Flick since I had introduced them to each other in the Kensington Roof Gardens. We commandeered a corner table in the restaurant and shared a cafetiere of black coffee while we waited for Missie and Lola.

"Honestly, Bill," he said. "Flick is amazing. She is going to come and work with me to promote my brands. We are going to head to the West Coast. Her brother Ruari is going to introduce me to some of the actresses he is working with in Hollywood."

"I think you may have a number of offers at this rate," I said and waved as Missie came into the room with Lola Beaulieu in tow. I noted that Lola had dressed with especial care. While Missie was in culottes and a blue-and-white-striped boat neck top, looking Sunday casual, the redhead was wearing full make-up, a short skirt and a figure-hugging sweater. She appeared to have forgotten to put on a bra. I felt an urge to get brunch over with quickly.

"How did the meeting with your father go yesterday?" I asked.

"I don't know what you did, Bill," she said. "But it was amazing. You are looking at the new Managing Director of Foreign & Exotic Retail PLC. Dad wanted to make me Chief Executive, but I said I thought MD worked better while he was Executive Chairman. In a year's time he will become a non-exec and I will be formally named Chief Executive." Yet again, Missie had demonstrated intelligence that belied her young age. She had efficiently flattered her father while giving them both an elegant way to transition.

"That's fantastic news," I said, "and well deserved. I hope you won't mind if I ask you for a favour in return?"

"Of course not," she said. "I owe you more than you could imagine."

"Then listen to my friend Dago tell you about his plans for his shoe business. Perhaps this might be one of the new retail brands you are so keen to back."

Dago needed no encouragement to pitch. He was a born salesman and Missie was a shrewd negotiator. Lola and I were soon surplus to requirement as they discussed the intricacies of brand development and store rollout. I intervened only to suggest that Jimmy Tweddle might be the man to help with that.

In the meantime, Lola was using every flirting signal in the book to seduce me, touching her face and twisting her hair in her fingers and leaning in beside me. She had all the moves, she was just showing her youth by trying them all at once. She didn't need to. I was already sold on the idea.

"I was wondering if you could help me out with the new novel?" she finally asked, popping a plum into her mouth so I could watch her lips suck on it gently. She had lovely hazel-green eyes and they were concentrated entirely on me. As was her right foot, which was caressing my leg with increasing pressure.

"Are you planning to set it in Singapore or Hong Kong?"

"No, there's actually a scene set in this hotel in my new novel," she said, smiling. "But I've never been inside one of the rooms. Would you be able to show me yours for research purposes?" She looked like butter wouldn't melt in her mouth, but I knew what she really wanted to see. We crept away. I wasn't entirely sure Missie and Dago knew we had left.

Lola was the kind of writer who was only really interested in the mattress in a hotel room. I'd read one or two of her novels now. She was always very keen to tell her readers whether mattresses were firm or soft while her heroines were having orgasmic sex on top of them. I figured mine was like Goldilocks' – just right, so I scooped her onto it and helped her out of her sweater. She had small breasts with button nipples and moaned as I took them in my mouth in turn then moved down between her legs and unzipped her skirt. She seemed to have forgotten her panties as well, which made things even easier. She had smooth alabaster skin which accentuated her triangle of red pubic hair and gasped in delight as she responded to my touch. I went to enter her, but she pushed me aside and started to lick me at the base of my cock instead. Then she dived into her handbag and brought out a condom. I couldn't remember the last time I'd used one, but she made putting it on part of the foreplay. Then she lowered herself on to me and we rolled around energetically, with her screaming in excitement, until we both came volubly.

"That was the best shag I've had for years," she said, panting hard, and snuggling in. I had to agree. I was willing to revise my opinion that English women were all fat and ugly. Some of them could be quite delightful.

35

Dominic Tweddle and I sat next to each other in Marco Polo Business Class on the Cathay Pacific flight to Hong Kong. The plane was half empty and we occupied a rear row upstairs well away from prying eyes and ears. He was on his way to start a new chapter in his career in the Far East. It wasn't Berlin during the Cold War, but I suspected for a spy it was the next best thing. I, on the other hand, wasn't sure if I would be able to visit Hong Kong again after the handover. I wasn't welcome in Hu Xianping's office, that was for certain.

"You were right about Van Ryjn," Dominic said, looking up from a sheaf of papers. "Dutch Police arrested the man carrying his false passport when the boat arrived in Holland. Turns out he was a crewmember whose real identity card had been used to leave the ferry fifteen minutes earlier."

"So he's in the wind," I said. "Well at least we know where he will be on June 30th - somewhere near the Convention Centre and Bauhinia Square."

"You're right," he said. "Our intel is now pretty solid that something big's being planned. We are trying to find out more, but New Reich is incredibly secretive. The Security Service has got other far right groups pretty well infiltrated, but New Reich is watertight. It doesn't seem to be a terrorist organisation as such, although they have no compunction about killing or bombing if they have to."

"Van Ryjn kept referring to his 'employer' – almost like it was a criminal enterprise," I said.

"Like Fu Manchu and the Si Fan?" he asked, referring to the worldwide secret society which featured in Sax Rohmer's novels.

I smiled. "As you will discover, there are plenty of real Triads in Hong Kong without inventing new ones. But I think this man and his organisation are European."

"Doesn't matter what nationality his boss is, we need to stop Van Ryjn," Dominic said, "and he may have more of his ex-GGK crowd with him."

"My old colleagues are more than capable," I said, disingenuously. It didn't do to look too eager to make money. But Dom had known me a long time:

"Don't be shy and retiring," he said. "You know we need your help. You know Hong Kong, you understand how assassins think and you will kill Van Ryjn rather than bring him to justice. Because the next day it will be Chinese justice, not ours."

"So, a paid assignment then," I said.

"Since I can't appeal to your sense of patriotism or fair play," he said with a smirk, "it will have to be a paid gig. Even though the man was trying to kill you." Dominic didn't know about the rifle with my prints on it. It would have given him more leverage if he thought I had my own reasons to dispose of Van Ryjn.

"I don't particularly want to open a corporate account with you as the Reliable Man," I said. "Would you mind if I route this through Brigadier Wee? We've arranged to meet next week."

"It's probably simpler," Dominic said. "I should make contact anyway, given this posting. I usually speak to Larry Lim - he seems to be the Brigadier's Chief of Staff now."

"Yes," I said, "his rise has been swift, but well deserved. He's had a good mentor."

Larry Lim was the nearest thing I had in the secret world to a colleague. The first time I'd met him he'd been keen as mustard and raw as a turnip; like a young Chinese *bom baan jai* passing out from training school in Wong Chuk Hang. Now our relationship had evolved. He was married with kids, had started wearing glasses that made him look professorial, and was climbing the greasy pole to the higher ranks of the SID. The Brigadier might go on for another twenty years – even though he was older than most of the Tembusu trees in the Botanic Gardens – or he might die or be promoted to a Ministerial role, leaving the way clear for Larry. I hoped our friendship would survive Larry's elevation, but I had also seen how responsibility changed people.

We came into Kai Tak on the Chequerboard Approach. No matter how many times you did it, your heart was still in your mouth as the plane came in between the buildings of Kowloon and swung sharp right onto the final approach. I'd always hated flying, relying on a stranger in the cockpit. Dominic took it in his stride. It was still new for him. I'd be much happier when Chek

Lap Kok, the new airport they'd been building, came online and the big birds could fly in on autopilot rather than relying on the skill and experience of a pilot. Assuming, that is, I could still visit Hong Kong by the time it opened.

We separated at Immigration. I went through faster with my Hong Kong ID card while Dominic had to queue up. He had a car waiting to take him to the Embassy. I was going to an apartment I'd rented in Cloud View Road, then the following day I had an appointment with Chop Suey to return my Glock, before jumping on an SQ flight back to Singapore.

As usual Kai Tak Arrivals seemed to have half of the city in it waiting for their relatives. I came down the ramp and shouldered my way through the jabbering masses. I had to be a lot more careful now. The Third Bureau were all over Hong Kong and I had just killed Hu Xianping's mistress. I circled twice round the arrivals hall, looking for tails. The man I saw following me was good, but I got a sight of him at the beginning of the second sweep and was sure by the end. I had seen him before. In Sir Bernard Li's office in Upper Brook Street.

I did some rapid mental calculations. I had retrieved my Glock on the way through customs, but I didn't want to use the weapon in Hong Kong. The paperwork would be onerous and I'd be in G4's bad books for evermore. But I was on home ground. No matter how good the man was on the mainland, I could deal with him here.

Kai Tak was connected to the salmon pink Regal Hotel by a walkway over Prince Edward Road. I headed up into Departures and through the car park towards its entrance, putting my luggage on the conveyor and dawdling across until I was certain he was following me. The building, despite only being about fifteen years old, was already worse for wear and displaying the classic Kowloon construction issues caused by graft and shoddy materials.

The fourteenth floor of the Regal Kai Tak was designed to look a bit like a control tower. It housed a rooftop bar, the 'Flying Machine', which gave a birds-eye view of the big jumbo jets landing and taking off on Runway 13/31. When I dated Cathay stewardesses we often met there or in the 'Five Continents' restaurant next door before nipping downstairs to a room rented for the afternoon. The added jeopardy for the girls of possibly running into one of their bosses doing the same thing made them especially frisky.

I retrieved my Mikov switchblade, gave my bags to one of the bellboys to look after and explained that I was visiting a lady friend in a room on the seventh floor using the fire stairs and would be back down to collect them shortly. I gave him a small tip on the basis that a larger tip from the Chinese agent would elicit the information as to where I'd told him I was going. Then I ran up the stairs to the fifth floor and waited just inside the door to the landing with my foot in the jamb to keep it slightly ajar. I transferred the magazine from the Glock to my pocket – I didn't want it going off if we got in a scuffle - and waited. Sure enough a few minutes later came the noise of feet climbing rapidly up the stairs. I waited until he passed me, thinking I was a couple of flights above him, then I moved smartly out from the doorway and brought the weapon down on the back of his neck. He stumbled and turned so I punched him in the throat with a vertical fist for good measure. In *Wing Chun*, the centreline punch called *Jung Kuen* snaps from the elbow and uses the bottom three knuckles, twisting upwards from the wrist to add more power.

When he regained consciousness, I had him sitting on the concrete steps with his hands cable-tied behind his back and the Glock, now with its magazine restored, pointing at his face.

"Why is Hu Xianping having me followed?" I asked. When the man didn't reply, I pistol-whipped him as he tried to struggle to his feet. Then I kneed him in the balls to make him sit down again.

"It was a simple question," I said. "Answer me and I won't kill you." There was defeat in his eyes. He wanted to believe me, so he answered:

"Not Hu Xianping," he said in a mainland accent. "Bernard Li." I noted that like a good communist he refused to give Sir Bernard his honorific.

"That makes no sense," I said. "Sir Bernard has no reason to worry about me."

"He give me $50,000 Hong Kong Dollars to kill you." For a mainlander that was more than a fortune. Sir Bernard could spend that on a nice lunch. If he wanted me dead he could have at least paid decent wages.

"Did he say why?" I asked, continuing to point the barrel of the Glock at him.

"*Mian zi,*" he said. "Sir Bernard does not like to lose face."

That made sense. Loss of face was a terrible thing in Hong Kong. I had made Sir Bernard look bad in the business community and in front of the Chinese. To regain that face he needed to demonstrate he was in control by killing me.

"Get up," I said, flicking open my Mikov knife. The guy got reluctantly to his feet. "You can go," I said. "Turn round so I can take these off." He shuffled around and I slit the cable ties and pulled them away from his wrist with my right hand then in a single movement tipped him over the balustrade with my left. I looked over only long enough to check that the fall had broken his neck and that there was blood pooling under his body. Then I headed towards the fifth-floor elevator bank to descend and retrieve my luggage.

The next day I went to PTS - the Police Training School in Wong Chuk Hang - to return my Glock. As I crossed the parade ground there were platoons of PTU – the Police Tactical Unit - doing anti-riot drills for the television cameras. Senior officers were out in force giving interviews, presumably reassuring the public that everything was under control in the run-up to the handover. The full panoply of vehicles and weaponry which the Police could deploy was on display. I kept my head down and walked on. In the distance I recognised the frightening figure of Willie Fullerton, Chief Drill and Musketry Instructor, and former Scots Guards Regimental Sergeant Major, surveying his domain, a hand on his pace stick.

Chop Suey was standing almost where I had seen him last in front of a desk in the firing range. He was in deep conversation with Callum Forrester, the boss of G4, the VIP protection unit where I'd worked for two years. Callum had been two squads below me at PTS, but since then his career had deservedly taken him rapidly to Gazetted Officer rank. He was still the youngest Superintendent in the Force. He had worked hard, kept his nose clean and avoided the mistake of drinking and partying with men like me.

Both men were wearing well-tailored dark suits and white shirts with the striped police tie. They didn't notice me for a while because they were looking intently at something shiny on the counter that I couldn't quite see.

"Is the Force paying in precious metals now?" I asked eventually, pushing between them.

"It's the new cap badge," Callum said. "They're issuing them now so the uniform branches have them to change into at midnight on July 1st."

The badge was superficially similar to the one I had worn, and exactly the same shape, but the changes brought home to me the enormity of what was happening. The St Edwards Crown at the top – a symbol of the British Monarch since the 13th Century - had been replaced by the stylised Bauhinia flower that the Chinese had decided would be the new emblem of the territory. Where the word "Royal" had once appeared in the motto below, now I saw the Chinese characters for Hong Kong. The view of the 19th Century harbour with the two ships and the opium bales had been replaced by stylized skyscrapers. The colonial past was being efficiently expunged.

"We've only been 'Royal' for thirty years," Callum said wistfully. "And we only got that for handling the pro-Communist riots. It was always going to go."

He was right. The Hong Kong Police had been formed in 1844 from a motley bunch of Indians, Europeans and Chinese. It had been almost as lawless as the people it was asked to police. It was only fifteen years younger than the Metropolitan Police and had been required in its lifetime to deal with a much wider range of tasks than its London counterpart. As well as burglary, murder and highway robbery it had dealt with the aftermath of plague, typhoons, strikes and riots, Vietnamese boat people and the ever-present machinations of the Triads.

For the last ten years or so it had been forced to deal with large-scale firefights on the streets between armed gangs and the police. It was a complex and quasi-masonic organisation. It had always been a melting-pot of nationalities and beliefs. The Scots and the Irish had left their mark on the force and so had the stain of bribery and corruption, mostly eradicated by the time I joined the force. As a police officer in Hong Kong you grew up quickly and had a much more nuanced view of the world as a result. I very much doubted that the Force could maintain this under Chinese supervision, but its impartiality would be vital if the "one country, two systems" mantra was to be preserved.

"How many expats are leaving after handover?" I asked.

"Not as many as you would think," Callum said. "I'm going to stick it out for a while. Least I can do. There will still be criminals to chase down and freedoms to protect. We are legally neutral and the CP," that was Eddie Hui, the current Police Commissioner, "is saying all the right things."

"Won't be long until you're saluting Chop Suey. His face has got the better skin tone," I said and turned to the Chinese Brummie who was scowling at me as always and brought myself to attention.

"Returning my service weapon as instructed, sir," I said and gave him a snappy salute. "Never fired," I added, as he worked the slide to give it the once-over, "but I cleaned it of course." He nodded in satisfaction and locked it in the gun cupboard.

"I'll get that to the armourer in a bit," he said. "How was the client?" he asked. "I heard from my uncle that Sir Bernard replaced you with someone from the mainland. What happened? Did you screw her?"

"A gentleman, never tells," I said smiling, "so it's lucky I'm not a gentleman. Yes, I did, but it was never going to last. That woman is destined for greatness. It was a great gig while it lasted. I owe you one for that, Chop Suey."

"Being married to a rich woman and playing second fiddle isn't your style, Bill," said Callum. "You're not a lazy git like McAlistair. Find yourself a patient and kind-hearted Filipina to settle down with. That's my advice."

I thought of the girl, Numh, who had left me for an Australian miner and was probably now looking out over a barren outback tending to a young baby and waiting for him to come back covered in sweat from the mines so she could serve him dinner before he went drinking with his mates.

"I'd be a terrible father, Callum," I said. "They always want babies. And I wouldn't be around much with my consulting work."

"You might change," he said with a shrug. "Some of us do."

"I don't really want to," I said. "It would have to be some amazing woman to make me do that."

"So what will you be doing for the handover?" he asked. "Watching it on television from the safety of Singapore?"

"Actually I have a contract, close protection for a VIP," I said, using the story that I had agreed with Dominic. "HMG have asked me to do it, so we may well cross paths on the night. I'll have some sort of security clearance, but this time I'm bringing my own weapons so I can keep the paperwork simple."

"Paperwork," Chop Suey said. "That is one thing you can be damn sure won't change after the handover." He handed me the flimsy for the return of the Glock. "Sign here, here and here," he said.

36

My GMT-Master showed exactly midnight, which meant there were 72 hours to go before the Union Flag came down on British Hong Kong. I was hard at work delivering Abe Berenson's Plan B. There was an easy way of obtaining the Babel Inverter, and then the way that I thought Van Ryjn would have done it. Which is why I was hanging upside down from a ventilation duct in SatBox's communications centre, trying to disarm a tumbler mechanism.

I had met up with Giles Guedella the day before. He was part of a parliamentary delegation attending the handover ceremony and I was notionally part of the protection detail assigned to them by the Governor, Chris Patten. Callum Forrester had rolled his eyes when he saw me turn up for the initial safety briefing.

"You weren't kidding then," he said. "Trust you to have wormed your way in with the great and good while you were in London."

"That's the thing about the Mother of Parliaments," I said. "They know a Mother when they see one."

It had been a relatively easy matter to spend time alone with Guedella and obtain the layout of his Hong Kong operation and a list of employees. I had imagined that the

Inverter would be held at the Gaylord Commercial Building in Lockhart Road, but it turned out that they had another installation out by Stanley Fort in Chek Chue. The British Army had built a satellite uplink station there, part of which was leased to SatBox, and SatBox's ground station was based in an old cold war bunker. Stanley Fort – scene of the last stand between the Japanese and the British in 1942 – was being handed over by the REME to the PLA on July 1st without a fight. The Inverter was being moved to Western Australia on June 29th. According to Guedella a second version of the Inverter was already installed and tested down there so the switchover would be seamless.

We had quickly identified a weak link I could exploit: a Malaysian technician with relatively high-level security clearance. He was currently sleeping off a Rohypnol-induced stupor in a love hotel in Wan Chai with two bar-fined hostesses. If he could remember anything afterwards it would be that he had met a fellow Malaysian who had bragged about his service in the Special Forces before buying a few drinks and suggesting they purchased some company.

I'd recced the site that morning. Stanley was always beautiful with its rolling hills and beaches. It was named after the Earl of Derby, who had been Colonial Secretary when the British had acquired Hong Kong in 1842. I very much doubted any town in the SAR would ever be named 'Patten' after the man who was giving it away.

It had been relatively simple to get inside the compound, which I had achieved by driving up to the gates in a SatBox van I had hot-wired that afternoon. As the guard on the gate leaned in through the open passenger window, I hit him in the chest with a Pneu-Dart. The dose of sedative fired from the Crosman air pistol would have put out the lights in a man twice his size.

The technician's security card got me into the compound through a series of gates, but the Babel Inverter was locked inside a safe – or to be precise a tumbler-protected metal cabinet – positioned above a four-foot-high electronic supercomputer inside SatBox's Communications Hub. The Inverter was plugged in to the computer system so if it was removed for more than a couple of minutes the system would shut down, triggering an alarm. Which was the least of my problems because the room would also Halon flush in the event of a fire. As I had learnt during my planning for the heist, Halon caused coughing, dizziness, headache, breathing difficulties, unconsciousness and death.

In between the front door of the bunker and the room containing the Inverter, was a guard station manned by a man with a sidearm. Van Ryjn might well have considered going in by the front door and taking him out with a machine pistol, but Guedella had understandably drawn the line at that level of realism. I wasn't confident about hitting someone with a tranquiliser dart from thirty feet before he put a couple of 9mm rounds in me, so instead I had accessed the Hub's ventilation system from the roof of the bunker about thirty yards from my destination and gone over his head. You could be a fat police inspector, but you couldn't be a fat assassin. You had to be fighting fit and every so often you had to squeeze into confined spaces on your way to a target and avoid making a sound. I always chuckled when I saw the size of ventilation shafts in movies. In real life you needed all the help you could get to squeeze down them, which is why I had brought with me in the van a little wheeled trolley that meant I didn't need to use my arms.

I was currently hanging from a carabiner above the supercomputer and attaching to the tumbler mechanism a safe-opener taken from a satchel that was hanging off my shoulder. This handy device was made for me by a clever man in Singapore, who believed he had made it for Van Ryjn. I intended to leave it behind when I left as another trail of breadcrumbs leading the police to conclude he was the culprit. The only problem was that it used a 'brute force attack', which meant that it dialed all the potential combinations in turn. Depending on complexity, this could take days, which was why the system was usually programmed to try the most common combinations – I was amazed how many of my victims had left them on the factory default settings – first. This one had the real combination, provided by Guedella, hidden early in the algorithm. I estimated in about ten minutes it would pop the lock and the flashing amber light on the machine would turn green. While it was whirring away, I concentrated on my next moves, which required considerable dexterity.

Guedella had explained that the Babel Inverter wasn't in use all the time. Abe Berenson had provided plans for a dummy Inverter which I had had built for me in Singapore by the same man who made the safe-opener. This looked just like the real thing but would output gibberish if it was triggered. With luck that wouldn't be until after it was disconnected the following day, delaying the point at which the theft was discovered. I had to open the cabinet, detach the connections to the real Inverter and switch in the fake, all while hanging from the ceiling. The problem was that I was overheating and the sweat was running down my nose and over my eyes making it hard to focus on the light, which was still flashing amber. To compound my difficulties, I was dressed in a black balaclava with a rip in the side which conveniently showed scar tissue around my neck to fool the CCTV cameras into thinking I was Van Ryjn. I had turned off most of them before entering the building, but I intended to leave an image on one I had 'missed' as I left, having spent the afternoon practising a walk similar to his.

Eventually the light on the safe-opener turned green. I pulled it off the tumbler and was just detaching the Inverter cables when I heard a lock rattle. I froze. According to Guedella the guard didn't make inspection rounds, but when I thought about it, how would he know?

The door opened and an arm holding a flashlight in front of it came into the room. I was dangling upside down from the ceiling. I was going to be a sitting duck when he spotted me and then reached for the gun he was specially authorised to carry. I had a number of items attached by paracord to my belt. One of them looked like a torch. I'd never used it on a human before, but Larry Lim and I had fired a few on the range at the Commando Camp on Loyang Avenue in Singapore. The Model

34000 Air Taser fired two wired darts with a seventy microcoulomb charge up to fifteen feet towards its target using compressed air. The barbs could penetrate two inches of clothing and the electrical pulses would incapacitate the target for up to thirty minutes. The difficulty was that I was going to have to Taser the guard whilst upside down and swinging on a climbing rope. The two barbs spread about a foot apart for every seven feet they travelled, and both needed to land in flesh to complete the circuit and channel an electric pulse into the target's body. I was only going to get one shot. On top of that the Taser only worked about 85 per cent of the time and if the electrical charge triggered the halon gas system we would both be dead.

These were the moments that the hours in the gym and on the range paid off. My stomach muscles needed to be strong and my aim true. I twisted my legs around the rope to try and steady any swing then pulled myself up to ninety degrees and extended both arms out in an 'A' to give me the steadiest platform for the shot I could muster. Thankfully the guard turned in my direction at just the right time, giving me a wider target. I aimed sideways for just below centre mass. One electrode hit him in the upper chest and one in the groin. The electrical charge disrupted his nervous system almost immediately, causing neuromuscular incapacitation – the flashlight clattered to the ground as his fingers became incapable of holding it. He fell to his knees and I dropped the Taser. It would keep pulsing for up to thirty seconds and I used the time to pull myself upright, swing away from the computer and land on the floor, unhooking my carabiner.

The guard's intervention had simplified matters. I wouldn't have to go back out through the vent. I finished fitting the dummy Inverter - I knew they would work things out pretty quickly, but not to make it too obvious I retrieved the safe-opener and put it back in my satchel. Then I went over to the guard. His muscles were still in spasm, but he was breathing, so I stepped over him and headed for the door. Three-quarters of an hour later I was having a drink in Tango Martini with Mark Hudson and eying up a group of skinny Eastern European models at the next table.

37

A few weeks earlier I'd returned to my apartment in Singapore. Singapore was a great base, but sometimes I'd be away for months staying at my beach house outside Pattaya or just travelling on business. Harry Bolt, who lived in the penthouse at the top of my building, sent his maid in regularly to dust and clean.

I'd phoned Harry from Hong Kong and got one of his girlfriends on the line.

"He gone out," Spring said.

"I'm back in town tomorrow," I told her.

"You've been gone long time," she said in that soft sweet voice that I could listen to all day. "307 days. That's a Chen prime." I had no idea what one of those was, but Spring was a maths genius as well as a very beautiful young woman. Harry had spent a fortune on her education and grooming. I was touched she was keeping count, but I figured more likely Harry had it marked down on his calendar.

"I'll be staying for a fortnight," I said, "then back to Hong Kong for the big handover."

"Hong Kong become communist, eh?" the girl said. "Good business for Singapore. And for Harry."

She was Thai but like me Singapore was now her home. She knew which way the wind was blowing and how to turn it into a pecuniary advantage. With the run up to the handover many large corporations had moved their Asian headquarters to Singapore and so property prices were going up as well-paid expats arrived. If the Lion City and entrepreneurs like Harry Bolt played their cards right, they could suck all the wind out of Hong Kong's sails leaving my old home to slowly fade away like those big industrial cities in the rust belt of North America. Part of me was saddened by that notion, another part didn't particularly care. Life moved on. Empires rose and fell. Who still remembered Carthage, razed to the ground by the Ancient Romans? One of the great empires under Hannibal. Now they called it Tunis.

When I landed at Changi and walked into the spacious modern arrival hall, Bolt was waiting for me. Perhaps this is what Chek Lap Kok would look like when it was completed, I thought idly, shucking my duffelbag higher up on my shoulder.

Bolt was by himself. He was bald - had been since his early twenties. He wore a baggy Hugo Boss T-shirt that made no effort to hide the fact that it was a fake and a loose pair of Bermuda shorts. On his wrist he sported a chunky gold Rolex – that one was real. It had been a gift from me two years ago for a favour he'd done me.

"Hello, brother," he said and we slapped each other on the back vigorously.

"I wasn't expecting a pick-up," I said.

"All part of the service." He waved in the direction of the escalators and the car park.

"New car," I said, impressed. He'd stowed my kit in the back of a silver Jaguar XJS.

"Six litre V12. I have to take it into Malaysia to give it a proper run. They don't make these anymore. This was one of the last off the production line. Like it?"

"Leather smells nice."

"Let's go to the Cricket Club and have a few jars. You can tell me what you've been up to."

The Singapore Cricket Club was located at one end of the Padang, a vast field in the Central Business District, with the Cenotaph at its mid-point. At its other end was the Singapore Recreation Club. Both clubs had been there since the mid-19th Century.

We went to sit in the Men's Bar where the dress code accommodated Bolt's casual sense of style. The usual clacking of balls from the pool tables was absent because of the time of the day. It was cool and peaceful. As it had been for a century and a half while gentlemen planters and traders made their deals and discussed their affairs.

We ordered some Tiger beers from the tap and sat in an alcove. I spent nearly an hour updating Bolt on my adventures in London. I spent more time on the forensic detail of the sex than the violence that I'd encountered at the hands of Van Ryjn and the rest of the gang. Bolt enjoyed living vicariously, since his four concubines – Spring, Summer, Autumn and Winter – left him little energy for any extra-curricular activities.

When I had finished, he gave me a detailed analysis and some heartfelt advice. His was a razor-sharp brain and although he dressed and behaved like a Bugis Street tramp he possessed a first in economics from UCL and several hundred million dollars stashed in bank accounts across town.

"Bad news, brother," he said. "This is a nightmare. You are way too high profile. You are now well and truly on Chinese intelligence's radar. You are so fucked, I can't tell you how fucked you are."

"That's encouraging to hear," I said and frowned into my pint of lager.

"You know me, I'm not going to bullshit you. You can get a hooker in Orchard Tower if you want to hear sweetness and light."

"I certainly can," I said.

"You've got to be watching your back all the time," he continued, getting on his high horse, which if it were any higher would be a giraffe. "You are sticking out like a sore prick at a baby's baptism. The best advice I could give you is to disappear for about two years and change your hair style."

"At least I have hair to change," I said snidely.

"Don't take this lightly, brother. You are totally fucked."

"I will fix it," I said, a surly tone sneaking into my voice.

"You'd better fix it," he said, draining his beer and acquiring a froth moustache in the process, "otherwise nobody will want to do business with you again."

"I understand the risks." Harry shook his head at my naivety, wiping his upper lip with the back of his hand.

"The whole point of having a secret identity like the Reliable Man is that it's secret and nobody knows who you are," he said. "Anyone who can play a hand of bridge and remember five cards will be starting to wonder if there is a connection between you and him." He slammed his beer mug down on the timber table top. The man cared for me, that's why he was annoyed.

"How many people now know that you are the Reliable Man? Let's go through this." He held up his hand and counted down the fingers. "Me, McAlistair, the Brigadier, his boy Larry, now your mate Dominic Tweddle, anybody who has access to his files, maybe some Mossad operative..." He stopped there and shook his head in frustration. "You are as fucked as a Patpong dancing girl."

I looked up and saw Larry Lim coming through the door into the bar. There was someone else behind him.

Bolt said, "Do I have to remind you of the old adage: if you want a secret to remain a secret you can tell two people, but you'll have to kill them both once you've told them."

I nodded ruefully and then got to my feet. Larry and Brigadier Wee were standing by our table.

"May we join you?" the Brigadier said. He was wearing his usual dark suit and regimental tie and there was that contortion on his face which, for the old Hokkien bastard, passed as a pleasant smile.

"To be honest, Brigadier," Bolt said, changing the vowel sounds in his voice so that he sounded like the former public schoolboy that he really was, "I've got a few errands to run. Bill and I were just finishing up. Why don't you go ahead and sit down here." He turned to me and added: "I'll drop your bags off at home. Give me a call later."

He made a quick exit. Usually Bolt feared no living man nor any commercial adversary, but he was afraid of the Brigadier because the old soldier wasn't truly human. Brigadier Wee knew more about Bolt's affairs than my friend's own concubines, I would wager. Larry had an oleaginous grin on his face. Once his boss was installed in Bolt's chair, he went off to get us refreshments from the bar counter.

"How have you been, Bill?" Wee asked.

"I've been having a grand time, sir."

"So I've heard. Associating with beautiful women and being nearly killed by at least one of them."

"That's part of my job description."

"What exactly is your job description?" he asked, inclining his head inquisitively.

"I'd rather not say in public," I replied defensively.

"Nobody else here in the bar but us, Bill. Tell me what your job is?" I gave an irritable snort. Why did he always make me feel as if I was standing to attention in uniform in front of my old District Commander?

"I'm a professional assassin," I said sheepishly. "I kill people for money."

"That's right. And you're one of the best. So why do you insist on involving yourself in business you don't understand? Poking your nose into complex affairs of state will just get you killed." He shook his head but there was a paternal glint in his eyes. "My dear fellow, stick to what you do best. Pulling a trigger and getting paid huge amounts of money for it."

"Not huge. A fair wage," I objected.

The Brigadier waved that statement away with a flutter of his hand. Larry came back with two Tiger beers and a gin & tonic for the boss. Then it was their turn to debrief me on my London adventures. They knew most of the facts already, because GCHQ had already been in contact about sharing the fruits of the Babel Inverter.

"Despite my earlier remarks, I'm not dissatisfied with what you've done," Wee said. "But you could have simply kept your head down. And there was no need to kill the Malaysian operative," he chided me.

"Over-reacted a bit there," I admitted.

"You're not a psychopath. You're simply a man who has little sense of remorse when you kill people."

That of course was my gift. Had always been what set me apart from other men who could sight a rifle and send a deadly bullet on its way. I never had nightmares about the people whom I had dispatched from this world. I killed them and forgot about them. My approach to taking a human life was that of a vet putting down a rabid puppy. Sometimes it was distasteful, but it was always necessary.

The Brigadier said: "I'm pleased with how you arranged things with Berenson, the Mossad man. It would be a monumental coup for us to have a pipeline of intelligence data like this."

That was starting to sound like praise. I glanced at Larry who nodded in agreement.

"Sadly, these arrangements never last for long," Wee went on. "We'll get a few months of excellent intel and then they'll cotton on. The problem is always when you start acting on the intel. And you must, if it prevents disastrous consequences."

He addressed himself to his gin & tonic, then added: "You did very well setting that up. We will provide you with all the support here that you require to achieve your objective. Larry, got it?"

His Chief of Staff indicated that he understood.

"I wanted to ask your opinion, sir," I said. His cool unblinking eyes looked at me, trying to divine what I was planning.

"It's about Sir Bernard Li." I said. "Should we be concerned about him becoming Chief Executive of Hong Kong within a year?"

"Terrible idea," Wee said sharply. "The man's a clown: pompous, arrogant and a wind-bag. He has no idea how Beijing will manipulate him because his ego is larger than the Bank of China building."

I couldn't help it. "Surely you're talking about the current British Governor?"

"Yes, very funny, Bill," he said, like a tolerant uncle who has not quite decided to disinherit you but is coming around to the idea.

"You know exactly what danger Sir Bernard poses," he said. "It is important for our region that Hong Kong has a fair shot at 'One Country, Two Systems', not just for the sake of its citizens, but for all of us who want to do business with the mainland through it. Bernard Li would be the short end of the wedge. We all know that Hong Kong will be assimilated in twenty or thirty years. Putting a man like Li in charge could trigger changes far earlier. That would not be in our interests."

I paused for a few beats to avoid sounding too keen, as if perhaps it was just a faint notion, not one of much importance to me.

"Would you like me to remove Sir Bernard from the chessboard then?"

Brigadier Wee fixed me with his stony-dead eyes and said, "Did you think I came here simply to drink a sundowner with you?"

I controlled the urge to giggle like a schoolboy who'd been caught out planning some clever prank. The old bugger was always a few steps ahead of everyone.

"Sir Bernard sent his Chinese bodyguard after me to have me killed as I arrived in Hong Kong."

His eyes blinked twice rapidly. "The dead mainlander in the hotel stairwell? That makes sense."

"Sir Bernard wants me dead, so I now want him dead."

"Do you expect me to pay you for this?" he asked.

"Man's a fool who doesn't get paid for doing his job."

The Brigadier laughed heartily for half a minute. "Fine, we will pay you to kill Bernard Li. But it must look like an accident. There can be no whiff of suspicion that it is an assassination or that it has anything to do with us."

"I'll work something out," I said. "I won't expect my usual fee. I just wanted your authorisation and blessing." I turned to Larry and watched his face as I said it: "I'll kill Sir Bernard for $8.88."

Larry of course asked: "Singapore, US or Hong Kong dollars?"

"Let's make it Hong Kong dollars, shall we?" I suggested. "In honour of the occasion."

That was just over one American dollar. It was all the pompous tycoon was worth.

38

Sir Bernard owned a sixty metre yacht called *Jiyau* made for him by Benetti in Viareggio. It had three levels and could sleep up to twenty-four people. He kept it at the Aberdeen Marina Club, one of the swankiest in the city. Less than fifteen years old, it was the preserve of local tycoons and billionaires like the Kwok, Fok and Tung families.

I knew that Sir Bernard was hosting a private dinner that evening for a select group of guests, because the Singapore High Commissioner was in attendance and Larry Lim had tipped me the wink.

"Just make sure she is off the boat before you try anything," he said to me on the encrypted sat phone. It's the Brigadier's cousin, Evelyn. I believe you've met." We had indeed, in New York the year before. She was as wily as the Brigadier, but considerably more attractive. Then she had just been a Deputy Consul so she was moving up fast through the diplomatic ranks.

Sir Bernard was planning to spend the night on the boat at the end of his party. *Jiyau* meant Freedom in Cantonese and that could be interpreted in different ways. This evening it would be freedom from the White Devil's colonial yoke that would be celebrated. Without doubt much cognac and Moutai liquor would be consumed. Sir Bernard and his Chinese friends from the mainland would be toasting the glorious future of Hong Kong, now it was back in the warm embrace of its long-suffering Motherland.

Catering would be provided by the Shangri La Hotel who managed all of the nine restaurants in the Marina Club. Before dinner, as cocktails were being served and future deals planned, the *Jiyau* would sail around Hong Kong Island once, picking up some Chinese dignitaries from the Harbour Plaza Hotel in Hung Hom before returning to its mooring for dinner.

I knew Aberdeen harbour moderately well. I'd done some advanced scuba diving courses – the ones where, if you got your maths wrong calculating decompression times, you would die – with a legendary instructor from Mandarin Divers whose shop was on the waterfront.

Carrying out an assignment like this would ordinarily have been meat and drink to the Reliable Man, but Hong Kong was locked down tighter than the Governor's teenage daughters in the run up to the handover. I knew from the briefings I had attended that Callum Forrester's usual team of around 150 officers – G4 was both his designation and that of his unit - had been augmented by another 500 extra from other units who had been given a crash-course in close protection to assist during the events. Some of them would be officers I'd served with previously, so I had to be extra vigilant in my planning and execution.

Thankfully none of Callum's VIP protection officers would be on the boat. Only foreign ministers or above got protection from G4 and most of those were at a dinner being hosted by Chris Patten at Governor's House. Forty-five foreign ministers were expected to attend the handover and each one would get a team of five officers assigned to them led by an Inspector. The only exceptions were the Chinese and the Americans, who as usual were laws unto themselves.

None of the Americans were attending, but nobody could tell me which Chinese dignitaries would be on the boat. Callum and Chop Suey had been grumbling to each other about how irritatingly unhelpful the Chinese were at sharing this type of vital information. It made planning more difficult.

Tensions had been high over the last few months between China and Britain because Fat Pang, playing to the gallery in London, had been driving everyone crazy with his futile advocacy of democracy for Hong Kongers. Beijing considered this kind of talk a personal insult from a man who should, as a politician, have known better.

China was also furious about Britain spending so much of the territory's cash on the British firms building Chek Lap Kok airport. Thousands of construction workers had been brought over to work on this massive project, which was to open the following year.

My plan was as simple as I could make it. I wasn't intending to carry a gun. I was planning to swim in, so if I met any opposition I would be relying on hands, feet and my Cressi dive knife. My principal concern was that there would be members of Guard Bureau Division 14 on the boat, protecting the senior mainland men and their investment in Sir Bernard Li. Division 14 was the counterpart of the RHKP's G4. They were well trained, fiercely loyal and – something I feared most – studied unarmed combat in a Shaolin temple for twelve months, as part of their training.

I put the rubber dinghy in the water, tugged the Yamaha outboard into life and made my way across the harbour in search of a hiding place in the shadow of one of the other yachts. Hong Kong is always crowded, everywhere. I had to be careful to avoid being seen by the fishing boats and sampans that plied Aberdeen harbour even at this time of the night. It was nearly one in the morning.

The *Jiyau* was sumptuously appointed and, according to the plans that I'd obtained from Larry, the master suite had a bed three metres by three while its bathroom sported a Jacuzzi large enough to fit five people. A late-night orgy would scupper my plans, but I was relying on the fact that Sir Bernard was not known as a man who enjoyed the company of hostess girls. I knew from Missie that he visited a Vietnamese concubine in Paris from time to time, but he was scrupulous that she should never set foot in London or Hong Kong.

I watched the yacht through my Zeiss binoculars. Through the picture windows I could see guests in black tie moving around, talking and dancing. I recognised a member of the Central Committee. Most of the guests were men but in addition to Evelyn Wee there were a few other ladies: all young, Chinese and achingly pretty. I identified several Chinese bodyguards. Whether they were with one of the tycoons – Li Ka Shing had briefly appeared on the rear deck and was bending Sir Bernard's ear about something – or Division 14 men defending the politicians, was immaterial. They were well-trained and prowled the yacht constantly looking for unwanted intruders, like a pack of angry doberman pinschers.

Eventually guests started to leave. The state rooms and the rear deck emptied. Small groups of men were still clustered in corners discussing matters of state or the latest win at the Jockey Club.

At last the Chinese politician disembarked, clasping Sir Bernard firmly by the hand as he left, and the human dobermans with him. There would be an armoured Mercedes S-Class waiting outside the lobby of the Marina Club. Li Ka Shing departed soon after, enveloped in a cloud of young men and women. Evelyn Wee was one of the final guests to leave, kissing Sir Bernard on both cheeks. I wondered if the Brigadier had taken her into his confidence and this was a Judas kiss. My gaze lingered on her elegant rear, clad in an expensive designer sheath, before it disappeared inside the Marina Club and the dock was quiet.

I waited another fifteen minutes, then pulled the mask up from around my neck, slipped into my Mares fins, and rolled quietly backwards into the darkness behind me. The water was chilly because I was only wearing a three-mil wetsuit. I looked at the luminescent dials of the compass on my right hand and the Suunto dive computer on my left and began kicking like a frog in the direction of the *Jiyau*. For this kind of clandestine swim it was best to use the gentle, quiet fin stroke that was favoured by cave divers.

My 12-litre tank had been painted black so I'd remain a dark shape even on the surface. It took me a while to find *Jiyau*'s anchor line but finally my fingers grasped it. At a depth of two metres below the surface, I shucked out of the buoyancy jacket and air tank then used two carabiners to attach them to the chain. I removed my fins and clipped them to the BCD. Then I took a few deep breaths, held the last one and spat out my regulator. Cautiously I made my way to the surface, blowing tiny bubbles out of the corner of my mouth as I ascended, to make sure I didn't rupture alveoli in my lungs.

All was quiet as my eyes and ears came out of the water. I listened for a moment then reached into the bag that hung from my belt and retrieved two suction cups with handles. I didn't want to come up the anchor line because that was the obvious place to board a ship. I wanted to go over the gunwales eight metres back from the bow, because that's where a cabin door led downstairs into the crew galley.

I had to push the suction cups down firmly in turn on to the aluminium hull, then flick the lever that created the vacuum which ensured they could bear my weight. I fitted one suction cup, then supported myself with one arm as I reached up and fitted the second cup half an arm's length higher. Larry and I had practised this every day for a week, going up and down ropes in the gym without using our legs, until I could handle the lactic acid burn as I laboriously pulled myself up.

Finally I heaved myself over and dropped down to the deck. Breathing hard, I stowed the suction cups in my bag as I listened intently for the sound of footsteps. Then

I ducked through the small oval door behind which a narrow circular staircase led below deck.

My destination was a tiny pantry that sat between the two largest bedrooms. It was accessible from a crew corridor so that any crewmember preparing to serve breakfast or drinks would not inconvenience VIP guests using the main passageway.

My dive computer showed it was 4.30 a.m. The ship was as quiet as a graveyard. The lights were dimmed and the burgundy carpet was plush. It made no sound as I walked over it in my bare feet.

I had a universal key that allowed a ship's steward to enter any cabin in case of emergencies, but there was no need. Sir Bernard was not the kind of man who locked his bedroom door at night. I slipped into the master bedroom and as expected found a single dark shape lying under the white silk sheets.

I was here to kill the man. I hadn't intended to talk with him. What was the point? Only movie villains had long conversations with their victims before they killed them. But there was a tiny flame of anger flickering inside me.

He had tried to have me killed, after all that I'd done for his family. I'd opened his eyes to how capable his daughter really was. If I'd foiled his plans to acquire SatBox by getting the Earl to come clean, then that was just part of the cut and thrust of geo-politics. Damn the man. I was really pissed off that he'd sent a second-class operator to have me killed or embarrassing him in public.

I shook Sir Bernard awake and put a hand over his mouth. His eyes slowly focused and in the dim light that filtered between the curtains he began to recognise me.

I rested the tip of my Cressi Dive knife on his lowest rib and whispered: "Make a sound and I will drive this knife into you."

He squirmed with fear and nodded his understanding.

"Your daughter is very capable. She will do you proud," I said. He nodded again in agreement.

"Is it true that you are hoping to be Chief Executive after Tung Chi Wah resigns?" He nodded again.

"Did you send your mainland bodyguard to try and kill me a few weeks ago?" He tried to shake his head from side to side but the fear and comprehension in his eyes told me it was true.

Quickly, before he realised what I was doing, I dropped the knife and rolled him sideways. I placed my knees on his back and my arm around his neck. Then I grasped the bottom of his chin and pulled it sharply right then left, snapping his neck. This was an old Ju Jutsu technique. It wasn't taught until you reached 4th Dan Black Belt. He was dead within a matter of seconds.

I went over to the starboard window, drew back the curtains gently and flicked open the levers that locked it. This wasn't a porthole. It was a window large enough to fit a man through. I hoisted Sir Bernard's body up onto my shoulders in a fireman's lift, carried him to the window and rolled him over the sill. There was a two-metre drop to the water. I lowered him as far as I could then let him fall. The splash sounded loud, but the ambient noise that was ever present in a city of six million people would muffle the sound dockside.

After a swift final glance around the cabin – leaving the bedroom door ajar and arranging the bed sheets to appear as if he'd got out of bed to go for a walk or use the head – I rolled my body out of the window. I held on with one hand as I pushed it shut as well as I could. Then I allowed myself to follow him, dropping into the dark waters.

Retrieving my gear from the anchor line I set my compass and scuba dived back to where I'd left the rubber dinghy, at a depth of five metres.

I calculated the prevailing currents would take Sir Bernard's body out to sea, then they'd bring him back in again and he might turn up in Repulse Bay or on Deepwater Bay beach in a week's time, provided the sharks didn't get him first.

Sometimes people fell overboard from their luxury yachts after they'd been eating and drinking heavily. Especially influential and well-known tycoons.

39

It was always going to end on the Peak. It should have been obvious right from the start. This was the last day of British sovereignty over the territory of Hong Kong. Where else but the Peak? From there you could see the entire jewel of a city spread out in front of you as it plied its trade, the little cars and buses careering around tight corners and the boats in the harbour hurrying from one dock to the next.

I'd spent the early morning closeted with Dominic Tweddle and Callum Forrester. Callum's security clearance seemed to be even higher than Dom's. But then he did have almost seven hundred officers under his command, whereas Dominic and I just had to work out who Rip Van Ryjn was going to kill and where he would do it.

"It's got to be Chris Patten," Dominic declared. "He is the man whose death would disrupt everything."

Callum Forrester disagreed: "I've spent the last five years working with his special security detail to plan for today. There is no way anyone could get anywhere near the Governor."

"You can always get near to someone if you don't care about getting away afterwards," I said. "But we know that Van Ryjn wants to live, so I agree with Callum."

"What about a symbolic target?" Dominic asked. "Maggie is here with Geoffrey Howe and Michael Heseltine."

"I think our man is more interested in moving financial markets than making a symbolic gesture," I said. "He's more likely to take a shot at Tony Blair."

We stopped to think about that. Taking out the great white hope of the British public would be a powerful statement.

"My answer is the same as for Chris Patten," Callum said eventually. "We've been planning to prevent that for a very long time. The Prime Minister and Jiang Zemin are the most important state actors in the entire operation."

I left the two of them arguing and went to get a feel for what was happening on the streets. Slung over my shoulder was a small sports bag containing the Babel Inverter, which I was hoping would not be mistaken for a bomb if I was searched by an over-officious policeman. Luckily, I had an access-all-areas pass courtesy of G4 and in any case some of the inspectors and sergeants on duty recognised me and I got cheery waves rather than a full body search.

My photocopied timetable of the day told me that at this time of day I was going to find the Governor at St John's Cathedral. On my way there I bumped into Scrimple.

Scrimple had crossed my path several times over the years. He had hung on in the Force by his fingernails ever since he stepped off the Cathay Pacific plane from London. He was overweight and short-sighted. Trouble chased him as if he were a fox on heat. He'd been involved in a shoot-out with a notorious Triad boss while he was in CID. He'd then been banished to the Police Tactical Unit before ending up in CID again, this time in the New Territories because Kowloon Region didn't want him back. With all the uncertainty around 1997 the Force could ill afford to lose even one *bombaan*. He might never be destined to become a Chief Inspector, but he could fill a chair and sign the paperwork.

"Jedburgh," he said, flustered as ever as his glasses steamed up from the heat that poured from his sweaty body. He wore a loose baggy shirt in canary yellow and running shoes on his feet. "What the hell are you doing here? Can't keep away?" Clipped to his shirt pocket was his warrant card showing a much younger, slimmer man with more hair.

"Short term contract with G4, mate. All hands on deck, so they drafted me back in," I said, tapping my nose. "Can't say any more. But I'm being well paid for the time. Can you get me in?" I showed him my credentials which were a temporary plastic warrant card and a letter explaining my role as a bona fide 'security contractor'.

Scrimple nodded and gave the paperwork a quick glance. He was part of a CID Action Squad that were patrolling the area in plain clothes but not trying hard to disguise the fact that they were coppers. The outline of Scrimple's Colt Detective could be seen over his right kidney as he bent over and moved a barrier aside for us to slip past.

"Come this way," he said ushering me, with as much self-important ceremony as he could muster, into the back of the Cathedral and up into the organ loft. There was a lot of singing and smells and bells in evidence. Patten was right at the front with Prince Charles. I took my monocular out to keep an eye on them but got slightly diverted examining the shapely forms of the teenage Patten sisters. They were known as the 'Three Graces' and I would happily have let any of them grace my bed.

By the time service had ended, Scrimple and I were standing outside again watching the congregation as it filed out. Patten hugged the celebrant emotionally while the slightly bemused Chinese choristers looked on. I glanced over towards the bottom of the Peak Tram just up the hill from the Cathedral. There was a scrum of Chinese security men turning away people from the entrance. I had seen one of the bodyguards on the *Jiyau* the previous evening. They were waiting for somebody senior to ride up to the Peak to enjoy the view.

"Scrimple," I said, grabbing his shoulder, "any idea what's going on over there?" He peered through his spectacles.

"Haven't the foggiest," he said. "The Chinese never tell us anything." He pulled out his light blue notebook and consulted a page but that didn't enlighten us.

Then it came to me. "I'm an idiot," I said. Typical Brits that we were, Dominic and I had been obsessed with protecting our own VIPs without comprehending that the best way to disrupt the handover was to target the Chinese. They had hundreds of PLA units massed on the border – some allegedly in counterfeit RHKP uniforms – and a bunch of trigger-happy middle-ranking officers just itching to rain down hell on the *gwai lo* and their Cantonese running dogs. If a member of the Chinese Politburo was assassinated, they would have the excuse they were looking for. And if my prints were found on the rifle that had killed him I would have a life expectancy as long as that of the *Tan Hua*, the cactus that flowers once a year at night and is gone before morning.

"Scrimple," I said, thinking on my feet, "I need a police motorcycle. There's something going down on the Peak."

Whatever people said about Scrimple's talents as a policeman, when he had the bit between his teeth he was like a man possessed. Within five minutes he was back with a motorcycle and rider. I promptly took possession of the bike and turned to Scrimple:

"Scrimple, you and I are going to rescue the handover," I said. "Jump on the back."

"What the hell are you talking about?" he asked querulously.

"Assassination attempt on the Peak, Chinese senior politician," I gave him the short version.

"How do you know?" he said, frowning and wondering how seriously to take this.

"Information received," I said. "Acting on information, Detective-Inspector Scrimple proceeded to the scene of the crime. You know how it goes." Police officers always proceeded, they never walked, ran or leapt onto Traffic motorbikes.

Scrimple explained to the bewildered constable that this was an order and there was no time to lose. I cajoled the young Chinese lad into handing over his helmet, talking at him rapidly in Cantonese. He wasn't happy but he didn't dare oppose the might of two white *bombaans* on this last day where being a colonial copper still meant something.

"Shouldn't I have a helmet?" Scrimple asked.

"Fuck that, no time," I yelled and gunned the motor. We took off up the hill as he grabbed hold of my belt with one hand and held onto his gun with the other.

It was an old Honda CB750P but was perfectly suited to racing uphill as fast as possible avoiding the traffic and road blocks. I switched on the blue lights but didn't bother with the siren. I had no idea when the tram would start its journey with the VIP on board, but I did know it wouldn't take very long to get to the top when it did. We charged up Magazine Gap Road. I was going like a bat out of hell, but I had to because getting to the Peak Tower by road was four or five times the distance taken by the tram. The Peak had been the height of Hong Kong living, reserved for Englishmen and their families. Only the richest *Taipans* and most important colonial officials were permitted a house on the Peak in the old days. The fact it was hard to get to by rickshaw just reinforced its status.

As I threw the bike from side to side and the engine snarled, another part of my mind was trying to work out where I would be if I were the assassin rather than Van Ryjn.

The last time I'd been up there the new Peak Tower was still being built. It had only opened in May after four years of construction. It was a huge modernistic building with an enormous floating viewing deck that had been likened by locals to a boat or a wok. To me it looked a little like the Red Dragon tile in Mah Jong, which made the symbolism even more ominous.

I dropped Scrimple by the Peak Station. It had started to rain. It was a noisy, heavy downpour that somehow felt ominous for the future of the territory.

"Whatever you do," I said. "You have to stop the Chinese VIPs getting off that tram. If you can't get through any other way just repeat these words to anyone who will listen: *Bahen shashou* – the Scarred Man – and tell them Hu Xianping will understand."

"Hu Xianping. Scarred Man. *Bahen shashou*," he repeated and scuttled off. I just hoped that the Guard Bureau listened to him and didn't plug him full of lead.

"Eeeny meeny miny moe," I muttered to myself and took my best shot. When I got to the Lion Pavilion on Findlay Road, I realised I had guessed right, because there was a dead policeman tucked behind the circular entrance. The pavilion was closed to visitors. It gave a panoramic view of the city and harbour just like the Peak Tower, but it also overlooked the tram's journey up the mountain. Van Ryjn was staring over the concrete balcony on the upper level holding the rifle. He was out in the open and the rain was starting to come down in sheets so that his short-cropped hair glistened with water and droplets collected on the shoulders of his tropical shirt. He had his eye to the telescopic sight of the PSG1 and was tracking the journey of the tram as it ran parallel to Barker Road. I guessed he would take a clear shot if he got one, but the VIP would be on the right side of the train admiring the view, not the left one nearest to Van Ryjn. He would expect to take the shot when his target was on the viewing platform at the top of the Peak Tower. Any earlier shooting opportunity would be an unexpected windfall.

Van Ryjn was so intent on following the progress of the tram that he didn't hear me through the rain until I had launched myself at him. I assumed he'd have other weapons, but I needed to separate him from his rifle first. My knee connected with the barrel and knocked it upwards, loosening his grip. I grabbed it in both hands and threw it over the edge of the balcony so that it fell into the trees below. Then I punched him on the jaw. It was like hitting a bag of coconuts.

Van Ryjn staggered backwards, then shrugged off the punch and swore in Afrikaans. It sounded like a baboon clearing its throat of catarrh. I thought he was going to say something clever, but he just growled and pulled a knife on me. There was going to be no soliloquising, just a good old-fashioned fight to the death. The rain had now turned the deck into a boating lake and our clothes were sodden. He didn't go in for any form of kung fu. He had been a rough-houser all his life and that was what he knew. He had a blade in his hand and was going to try and slit my throat or twist it in my guts.

Which was why I pulled the Glock 17 from behind my back and shot him twice between the eyes. As I saw it, the only definition of a fair fight was one in which the other guy died.

I didn't have long. I tipped him over the edge of the platform so that he would land in about the same location as the PSG1, then headed down the stairs. Once in the undergrowth below the pavilion, I retrieved the rifle, cleaned my prints from it using the alcohol wipes that I'd been carrying with me for that purpose and dragged it and the body into the deepest foliage I could find, taking care to mark its location. Then I took the sports bag containing the Babel Inverter and put it around his neck.

I steered the Honda slowly back towards the Peak Tower. Scrimple was in front of the entrance to the Tram looking exultant. He had co-opted a number of other policemen who were holding back the public. A group of Chinese officials, their umbrellas up to avoid the rain, were glowering at him.

"Crisis averted. Tell them they can go up now," I said to Scrimple as if I were his Superintendent. I barked a few commands in Cantonese at the other uniforms as if I was a boss from another Division. He gave the mainland tourists an imperious wave as if he was directing traffic and they shuffled aboard a lift to the viewing deck.

"They didn't like it at first," he said to me when they had ascended. "But when I delivered the message the team leader got on the radio and then ordered everybody to wait for further instructions." He hooked his thumb in the direction from which I'd come. "Did you find what you were looking for? Or was it just bollocks?"

"I found it alright. Just as I'd suspected. All sorted out now."

He stared at me for a long moment hoping that I'd explain more which I didn't.

"Shall I write it up?" he asked.

"No need. I'll debrief Callum Forrester, the G4, directly. Just leave it with me for now."

He nodded. "What about the motorbike?"

"I'll return that now. Hop on the back."

"You know what?" he said, with a pained expression on his face. "I think I'll take the tram back down. You scared the fuck out of me on the way up. You'll end up killing somebody one of these days."

"Scrimple," I said, glimpsing for the first time a lion hidden behind his sheeplike exterior, "You are a top man. This was a fucking big deal you helped me with. Anytime you need a favour, you come to me. I owe you one." He smiled at that.

"Another thing," I ordered. "Tell all of these *foh-geis* that there's a dead constable by the Lion Pavilion. Once his body is retrieved it is vital that nobody goes anywhere near the area until I can get G4 up there in the morning. Tell them to set up a perimeter fifty yards around it."

"What was it all about?"

"You'll find out. I've got to get back and report in." I kicked the Honda into life. The seat was soaking wet but I was already drenched to the skin so it didn't matter.

The adrenaline from finding and killing Van Rijn was still coursing around my veins, keeping me warm.

It was raining steadily and the view had clouded over. Our final gift to them: true British weather for the new Chinese owners.

"By the way," I asked Scrimple, "who was on the tram?"

"Some politician called Qian Qichen," he said. "Never heard of him."

"Scrimple," I said, "do you ever read anything besides the sports pages in the *South China Morning Post*? Qian Qichen has been the Chinese Foreign Minister for over a decade."

40

A few hours later, in the Convention Centre, I turned a corner and ran straight into Hu Xianping. The man was even better dressed than usual, presumably in anticipation of meeting his masters Jiang Zemin and Li Peng. Hu was surrounded by a group of reporters from the New China News Agency. The sort that were handier with a gun than a typewriter. He extended a manicured index finger in my direction. The corners of his mouth turned up a little, which I suspected was a smile, and he crooked his finger indicating for me to approach. I took in the other men around him. I figured a shoot-out in broad daylight was not Hu's style.

"Jedburgh," he said. "As I learned when I did my language course in Cambridge, you are like a bad penny. You are always turning up."

"We simply enjoy the same type of parties," I replied.

"Your English humour will not be missed after the handover," he said, shaking his head sadly. "How do you feel today? Your country is kowtowing to mine and returning what we lost so many years ago."

"What do you want me to say?" I replied. "Britain is too poor, too lazy, and too weak to hold on to any of its colonies any more. That's why it was the right thing to return this one." Hong Kong had always belonged to China, whatever the English believed.

Hu gazed at me for a few quick seconds.

"Is that what you truly believe?"

"I believe that this is the beginning of an Asian century. China will dominate the world within fifty years."

"You are a much smarter man than my analysts give you credit for, or appears in our files," he said, a broader smile creeping across his face. "You are not this stupid, private security, bodyguard, fellow that you pretend to be. There is something hidden about you that makes me uncomfortable."

"Is that why you wanted to have me killed in New York and castrated in London?" I asked

"Bill, that was just business," he said. He was being more friendly than I had anticipated and it was confusing me.

"We are on different sides of the battle," he continued. "We fight for opposing armies. Don't pretend," and at this point he leaned forward and gave me a friendly poke in the chest, "that you are not fighting for someone. I suspect you are like an old Swiss mercenary. If you are paid well, you are loyal to your general, even if I am still a little uncertain who that general is. Today we are facing each other across the battlefield. Tomorrow we might be comrades. This is how it happens with mercenaries," he said cryptically.

"I will always be a masterless *zhan shi*," I said non-committally. "A hedge knight: I go where I'm needed."

"And today, for the first time, you were of service to my country," Hu continued. I finally understood that my actions on the Peak had softened his view of me.

"I had reason to hate the Scarred Man as much as you did," I said. "Believe it or not, the smooth running of this handover means as much to my country as it does to yours. Some of my friends have been working on this transition for many years."

He looked at me with the same deadly eyes that I remembered from the 'Hades Club'.

"Forrester," he said. "A good man. He can hold his drink. We had many late evenings in Beijing when he was our guest."

"A credit to the RHKP. And he will do as good a job for you after midnight. The Force's loyalty is to the people of Hong Kong. It doesn't matter what flag flies over Government House."

"There will not be much need for foreigners here in the future," Hu said. "You will be welcome to come and go and spend your money, but your time to command is over here. It belongs from midnight to those prepared to sing the national anthem in Mandarin."

"Well," I said, "judging by the singing yesterday, you won't be short of participants." I had been surprised to hear the March of the Volunteers blaring out when I'd gone to see Callum and Chop Suey in their underground lair in May House. I popped my head around the door to find several of the Chinese inspectors pumping iron while trying to learn the words. Good for you, I'd thought. It's your anthem now. I was fairly sure that the remaining *gwai lo* officers would not be singing along, however keen they were to do their job well.

"I have not forgiven you entirely for the death of Mei Ting," Hu said. "But I have been instructed that as long as you commit no offences in Hong Kong you are to be…" he was obviously searching for the right translation "…tolerated here after the handover."

"I'm very grateful, sir," I said obsequiously, bowing as low as I could. "I will not abuse your Country's tolerance of me." He looked at me trying to detect sarcasm, but for once it was me being inscrutable. He shook his head and checked his watch.

"I'm needed elsewhere now. I respect you as an opponent. Don't think you will always be this lucky Jedburgh." He gave a sharp nod of dismissal, then turned and walked away. I stared after him for a while and wondered when we'd meet again.

"The grim expression on your face is something to behold," said Giles Guedella with amusement, when I finally located the British delegation. "Let me get you a drink. Then I want to introduce you to somebody."

He put a large Scotch in my hand and took me over to a group where Lady Thatcher was holding court. She was explaining to a young diplomat how if she had known how John Major would betray her legacy, she would never have appointed him Foreign Secretary.

"Margaret?" Guedella said. She looked up and inclined her head to one side as she looked at us with her piercing gaze. "I'd like to introduce you to Bill Jedburgh. He has been doing some good work for us."

"Well at least he doesn't affect a ponytail," she said. "Which is a mercy. If you want to get onto the front bench, Giles, you will have to get rid of that monstrosity." Guedella coloured, but you could see he was besotted by his former leader.

"We've met before Ma'am," I said. "I was with 14th Intelligence Unit in Belfast for a while. You came to see us on one of your visits."

"Ah," she said, "that sort of work. We lost many brave boys there. You know it is never easy, never easy," she repeated it with even greater emphasis, "to take difficult decisions in the shadows." Then she turned and resumed her lecture on the subject of political loyalty.

"You've had an interesting life," Giles said. "If you ever need a job in the UK, SatBox could use a man with your skills."

"That's kind of you," I said, "but I'm happy being a freelance consultant. You can hire me by the day, the week or the month. I'll give you my number. What will you do next?"

"It's not announced yet," he said, "but William Hague has asked me to be number two to John Redwood as a shadow spokesman for trade and industry."

"Two names that mean nothing to me," I said. "I presume Hague is the new Conservative Party leader?"

"Yes," he said wistfully. "He's ten years younger than me. I'm already a has-been in political terms."

"Winston Churchill was sixty-five when he first became Prime Minister. My dad used to tell me that. He got the top job at an age when most men were retiring."

"You're not genuinely comparing me to Churchill, are you?" he asked.

"No, just trying to cheer you up," I said and poured myself another Scotch.

He eyed me speculatively then asked: "Have you heard the news about Sir Bernard Li?"

"I've been too busy saving the life of the Chinese Foreign Minister to read the newspaper," I said, trying not to appear too nonchalant. "What's the story?"

"There's a rumour he got very drunk at a dinner on his yacht and fell overboard after everyone else had left," Guedella said, lowering his voice as he imparted this piece of shocking gossip.

"If his Chinese guests were forcing him to match them toast for toast with Moutai," I said, putting a serious frown on my face, "then getting legless is not unexpected. Those Northerners from Beijing can hold their drink much better than the southern Cantonese. Did they fish him out of the drink?"

Guedella shook his head. "No, they haven't found him yet. He's vanished. Most likely dead."

I waited for a few beats then said: "Couldn't have happened to a nicer man. I'm pleased F&E has Missie to keep the business going. I wouldn't be surprised if Tom Field makes a return to the Board. Are you still looking for a takeover bid?"

"Perhaps," he said. "The Israelis have expressed an interest, but frankly I'd like a proper English business to take it over. I've had enough of foreigners for a while."

The clock kept counting down towards midnight. The painted harlot was close to embracing her new master. A few hours later I was standing on the right-hand side of the auditorium watching the handover ceremony with Dominic Tweddle. I had avoided getting soaked during the farewell ceremonies at HMS Tamar by the simple expedient of not going. There was a strong smell of damp clothing emanating from the British delegation. They should have brought their Barbour jackets.

"I ran into Hu Xianping earlier this evening," I said. "He thanked us for doing him a favour."

"You did well," he said. "Why hasn't Van Ryjn's body turned up?"

"Stashed so that it doesn't disrupt the ceremonies," I said. "It will turn up tomorrow and be someone else's problem." I had made sure that Chop Suey knew exactly where to find it and that he could ingratiate himself nicely with his new masters if he made sure that the Babel Inverter in Van Ryjn's sports bag made its way to the New China News Agency rather than into a Hong Kong Police evidence locker. He might well be a Superintendent by this time next week and his uncle would have several new mainland noodle franchises.

"Talking of people not turning up," Dominic said, "Sir Bernard Li has gone missing."

"Guedella told me. Maybe he's taken a break?" I ventured. "Now Missie is running the show I expect he can rest easy."

"Don't try and be clever, Bill," Dominic said. "His dead body is going to turn up somewhere isn't it? And I know you will have had something to do with it."

"I'm told he couldn't hold his Chinese liquor." I gave him an innocent smile and he let the matter rest.

The buglers had just started trumpeting and Chris Patten was leading out the Prince of Wales, Tony Blair and Robin Cook. The ginger gnome looked particularly pleased with himself. Up behind him in the celebrity seats, I saw Mrs. Thatcher and Geoffrey Howe looking glum. Perhaps somewhere in their minds there was a tiny hint of regret that handing back this glittering gem might have been the wrong thing to do. After all, Mrs. T had gone to war for 23 sheep and a few farmers in the Falklands. Why couldn't she have faced down the might of China? Or negotiated a clever deal where Hong Kong became like Singapore: independent, fearless and brave.

What a bloody shame.

But why should I even care?

Of course, I cared. This City had formed me. I was an abandoned child of the painted harlot. Not that she cared a jot.

The ceremonial juggernaut rumbled on, consigning six and half million Hong Kongers to the hegemony of a totalitarian communist regime. I felt so bloody sorry for all of the fine people I'd worked and lived with. How could this possibly not go wrong eventually?

Something stung my eye and I wiped it away. It must have been a speck of dust that made my eye water.

Chris Patten looked rueful, Prince Charles looked pissed off and Jiang Zemin looked like the cat that had got the cream. But the bit that made my heart swell with pride was when three Hong Kong policemen pulled down the colonial flag at the same time as another three policemen raised the new red and white flag of the SAR. My old colleagues were the thin green line – or in this case, since they were wearing their ceremonial uniforms, a thin white line – that stood between China, the people of Hong Kong and their traditional freedoms. Nothing like this had ever happened before in modern history and only when that history was written would we know if the old lady up in the stalls had made the right decision. There might yet be blood in the streets before the Century was over.

Much later again, I found myself on a balcony in the Convention Centre with Callum Forrester and Dominic Tweddle, watching the Royal Yacht Britannia and its escorts leaving Hong Kong Harbour. It brought home the diminution of British power. The UK could barely rustle up a dirty grey frigate to escort the heir to the throne home. With one stroke she had made China's economy bigger than her own and removed over ninety per cent of the population of her dependent territories. The British Empire had dwindled to a baker's dozen of random islands, containing more animals and birds than people.

"What will you do now?" I asked Callum. "Sleep for a week?"

"Not a chance," he said. "I've got almost forty VIPs to get off safely over the next week, then a World Bank and IMF meeting in September to prepare for."

"Rather you than me," I said. "I think I'm going to lie on my beach in Thailand for a couple of weeks. What do you say, Dom, fancy learning how to water ski?"

"Is that a euphemism for an athletic sex act?" he asked. "Chance would be a fine thing. Tomorrow's just another day at the bank. Money waits for no man. It wants to be chased all the time. Especially in this bloody town, from what everyone tells me."

"That reminds me," I said. "I'm going to send you an invoice. I've got bills to settle and mouths to feed. Be sure you pay it within thirty days. Otherwise, I might have to firebomb your new flat on Caine Road."

I had earned a break. When you included getting paid by both the Israelis and the British and the money I had made on shorting F&E stock, I had earned around half a million dollars for three months' work, not counting my fee from the Brigadier for killing Kowalczyk, the man who had started this entire adventure in the first place. I reflected on the fact that while I was still merely a well-educated thug, I was now a wealthier and better-connected thug. I'd met some interesting people, slept with some beautiful women, drunk some excellent wine and cleared away some nasty individuals. I resolved to have sex with a battery of nameless women in Bangkok and to steer clear of geo-political intrigue for the foreseeable future.

After some rest and recuperation in Thailand, I had been invited back to London for the opening of Dago and Missie's new shoe emporium during Fashion Week in September. Then I was going to meet Abe Berenson in Israel and go diving in Eilat, before selecting my new weapons from IWI. Only then was I going to return to Singapore and go anywhere near Brigadier Wee and his gang.

The Reliable Man will return in:

RELIABLE IN MANILA

Afterword

Apologies are due to two former MPs, whose constituencies have been misappropriated for the purposes of this novel. Tony Wright, the Labour MP for Cannock and Burntwood was elected to represent the new seat of Cannock Chase in 1997 with over 50 per cent of the vote. Newton Abbot constituency did not come into existence until 2010, but Patrick Nicholls, the sitting Conservative MP, won the Teignbridge constituency (which it replaced) in 1997, with a majority of 281 votes.

The former employees of Candy Tiles in Heathfield and the inhabitants of Pitt House, Chudleigh will note that those buildings have been replaced, by the SatBox Communications factory and Pendragon Hall respectively, for the purposes of this novel. There is no such place as Merripit in Devon, but there is in *The Hound of the Baskervilles*, by Sir Arthur Conan Doyle. Fans of that novel may recognise that Pendragon bears more than a passing resemblance to Baskerville Hall.

Israeli Weapons Industries does not acknowledge the existence of the Meraglim Mark III or IV.

Printed in Great Britain
by Amazon